SEEING DANGER

SINCLAIR & RAVEN SERIES

WENDY VELLA

Seeing Danger is published by Wendy Vella

Copyright © 2016 Wendy Vella

ISBN: 978-0-9941388-0-4

Sign up for my newsletter at www.wendyvella.com

WENDY'S BOOKS

The Lady Seals Her Fate

The Lady's Dangerous Love

The Lady's Forbidden Love

Regency Rakes Series

Duchess By Chance

Rescued By A Viscount

Tempting Miss Allender

The Lords Of Night Street Series

Lord Gallant

Lord Valiant

Lord Valorous

Lord Noble

Stand-Alone Titles

The Reluctant Countess

Christmas Wishes

Mistletoe And The Marquess

Rescued By A Rake

This book is for the readers.
Thanks to each and every one of you.

I can no other answer make, but, thanks, and thanks.
William Shakespeare

PROLOGUE

*I*t is said that when lowly Baron Sinclair saved the powerful Duke of Raven from certain death in 1335 by single-handedly killing the three men who attacked his carriage, King Edward III was grateful. Raven was a wise and sage counsel he had no wish to lose, therefore, he rewarded Sinclair with the land that sat at the base of Raven Mountain. Having shown himself capable of the duty, Baron Sinclair was now, in the eye of the King, to be the official protector of the Ravens.

Over the years the tale has changed and grown as many do. There were rumors of strange occurrences when a Sinclair saved a Raven in the years that followed. Unexplained occurrences that caused many to wonder what it was that the Sinclairs were hiding, but one thing that never changed was their unwavering duty in the task King Edward III had bestowed upon them.

To honor and protect the Raven family was the Sinclair family creed.

CHAPTER 1

"*S*eems a carriage has hit a cart, my lord, filled with—ah—"

"Filled with what, Bids?" Devonshire, Sinclair, prompted his driver through the opening above his head.

"It's a sort of—um—mess, my lord."

"A sort of mess?" Dev smiled at his driver's obvious reluctance to use the word shit in his presence. He listened as Bids cleared his throat several times, followed by a lengthy silence before finally he spoke.

"I believe, my lord, it is some form of animal excrement."

Leaning back, Dev propped his feet on the opposite seat.

"And can you determine the source of the excrement?" he queried, enjoying the conversation hugely.

"'Tis—the smell, my lord."

"Can we go around the mess, Bids?"

"I fear not, Lord Sinclair. We shall have to wait it out."

"Very well, I shall walk the remainder of the journey home, Bids." Dev closed the hatch. Collecting his hat, he opened the door and stepped from the carriage.

"B-but, Lord Sinclair, 'tis near on dark."

"I shall be all right, Bids. We are only twenty minutes from home. I shall probably reach there before you." Slapping his hat on his head, Dev raised a hand to the still stuttering Bids and struck out along the street.

Unlike others, Dev could see at night. Like his siblings with their strong senses, his ability to see far outreached anyone else's. Leaving the excrement behind, Dev took his first deep breath of thick London air.

Twilight was Dev's favorite time of day. Far quieter than any other hour, the buildings lost their weariness, dirt faded, and the streets appeared swept clean. Almost as if the city exhaled after the rigors it had endured, and was girding its loins for the evening to come.

His family would be waiting for him to share their evening meal, and the thought had him lengthening his stride. The day had been a long one and he was ravenous. If he wanted seconds, he would need to get there quickly, preferably before the meal started. With six siblings, five of whom would share his meal, he needed to eat quickly.

Crossing the road, Dev ducked down a lane that would cut at least five minutes off his journey.

"No! Let him go at once!"

Looking to the end of the lane, Dev saw a man and woman running. Behind them was a gaggle of children, and they all appeared to be chasing another person who had a child over his shoulder. The child was yelling to be released, which suggested he was being taken against his will.

"Release him, you cad!" the woman shrieked.

"Damn," Dev muttered. It seemed his meal was about to be delayed, and there would be no second helpings for him.

Hurrying after the little group, something urged him to run faster. He felt a desperate need to reach the boy. Turning right at the end of the lane, he found them just ahead of him.

The woman led the chase, and she was gaining on the man and boy.

"Stop at once!" she cried as the man reached a carriage.

Dev passed the group of children just as the carriage door was thrown open. The man then tried to throw the boy inside, but the woman was on him. She grabbed the boy's leg and held tight. The carriage started moving, and the man roared at her to let go, but she would not relent, running to keep up. Dev then watched in horror as the man, who was hanging half out of the carriage, lifted a hand and swung it at the woman, connecting with her face.

Dev lunged for her, wrapping his arms around her body, pulling her free. The boy came with her and then they were all falling. He rolled, and landed with them on his chest. The breath slammed from his body as he took her weight and that of the boy.

"A-are you all right?" Dev rasped as he struggled to draw air back into his lungs.

"Dear Lord!" The man who had been running behind her reached them. He quickly lifted the boy and then the lady off Dev.

"Are you well, Miss?"

Dev sucked in a deep breath as he moved his body to check for injuries before he regained his feet. He would have a few bruises, but nothing lasting.

"W-we got him, W-Wilson."

Her words were breathless, yet he heard the elation in each one.

"My heart near stopped, Miss, seeing you hanging from the carriage."

"B-but I had to stop them taking him."

"Madam, my name is Lord Sinclair. Will you allow me to help you?"

Her gasp was loud on the night air as she turned her back

on him. Dev then watched her hands reach for the hood of her cloak, pulling it up so she could shield her face.

"I-I need no help, thank you. And thank you for coming to my aid."

She walked away from him to where the four children stood silently.

"They'll keep trying, Lilly." A little boy stepped forward. "They already got five of us."

She dropped to her knees right there in the street, without a care for the dirt and filth. The man she had called Wilson moved to stand at her back.

"There will be no more, Toby. I promise you. We foiled this attempt, and we will foil others."

"But how can we stop them, Lilly?"

"We'll find a way," she vowed. "Now you take everyone to Temple Street, especially Leo. Make sure he is not injured after what he endured tonight. Tell Mrs. Davey that you are to stay there until morning. I shall call by tomorrow, and we shall talk more then."

Dev couldn't fit a name to that soft, cultured voice, and yet a sense of awareness inside him told him they'd met before. He reached her side as she rose.

"Thank you, Lilly." The boy she had just saved also stepped forward.

"Are you all right, Leo?"

He nodded, and she squeezed his shoulder.

"Go now," she said to the children, and seconds later they had fled, disappearing down the road and into the shadows.

"Can I assist you back to your carriage, madam?"

"No, I have help, thank you."

"Why are you out here at this hour? Who was that man who attempted to abduct that child?"

He had so many questions, but the most important was to

find out this woman's identity. Her voice and actions suggested she was from his world, yet surely that was not the case. No woman of his acquaintance would have taken the risks she had tonight. Except his sisters, of course; they would have done the exact same thing.

She was doing everything she could to avoid looking at him, but Dev was not having that. He stepped into her path as she started walking, forcing her to stop.

"Will you give me your name?"

"Please excuse me, I must leave."

"I think not."

Dev grabbed her arm once more.

"Release her!"

"Easy, Wilson," she soothed the man with her.

"Tell me your name."

Shaking his hand from her arm, she stepped back and lifted her face.

"You!" Dev staggered backward. "What the hell are you doing out here at this time of night?"

Lilliana Braithwaite's face did not carry its usual silly expression. Dev saw emotion now, both fear and anger.

"I have no time for this now. No time for you."

Dismissing him, she walked away. Dev shook his head to clear it. That didn't work, so he did so again. When he looked for her, she had vanished.

"Damn." He followed. No woman, even her, should be out in this neighborhood with a single servant to protect her. He walked back down the street, but could see no sign of Miss Braithwaite. Closing his eyes, he changed his vision.

Dev and his siblings had strong senses. His was the gift of sight. With his normal vision he could see long distances, and with his other vision, he could see the colors that belonged to a person, no matter where they hid. Of course, he did not know what color Miss Braithwaite was, but he didn't think too many people would be hiding in this lane at this hour. He just prayed he did not come upon a pair of lovers.

His eyes searched first left and then right. He didn't think Miss Braithwaite and the man could have gone far.

"Why am I bothering?" he muttered. It wasn't as if he even liked the woman, and she had certainly given him no indication she liked him either. He should simply go home and get that second helping. But something was stopping him. Something tugged at him to find her. Sighing, he kept searching.

He saw blue, and then—*it can't be!* Stopping, he inhaled deeply. Christ, the shorter of the two people hidden in the narrow opening between two buildings was his exact shade of green. Shocked to his toes, he tried to take it in.

Every person had a color. Blue, pink, orange, or brown, no matter the color they all had one in varying shades, and yet until this very moment, no one had ever been his exact color match.

Closing his eyes, he reopened them in his normal vision. Was it her? *Surely not*, he prayed silently. The woman was extremely foolish, and then there was the business of her hideous taste in clothing.

Dev walked slowly down the street, finally reaching the spot where she and Wilson, were hiding.

"You can come out now, because I am not going anywhere until you do."

He heard a soft curse, and then she and the man appeared.

Lilliana Braithwaite came out first. She had lowered her hood now that the game was up, and for some reason left off her glasses. For the first time he saw her beauty.

Usually her hair was severely drawn back and covered in

lace, feathers, or some type of flora or fauna, but tonight it had no adornment, was just pulled back in a simple bun.

He'd never really noticed the color before, but realized now that it was golden blonde. Without her glasses, he saw soft feathered brows arched over a spectacular pair of lavender eyes that were framed by curling lashes.

Christ, she was actually beautiful.

Dev looked to her chin and saw the blood there, and felt his head swim. Inhaling, he pushed aside the sudden need to sit. He did not like blood, but it usually only had this effect on him when his siblings bled.

"Y-you are hurt," he managed.

"'Tis nothing." She wiped her chin with the back of her glove. "Now go home, Lord Sinclair, as I will give you no information about what transpired this night."

She brushed past him with the man on her heels. Even her voice sounded different. The high-pitched grating tone had gone. Relieved that his breathing returned to normal now he could not see the blood, he followed.

"Why were you running after that man? And why did you, foolishly I must add, grab that boy while the carriage was moving?" Dev asked.

"Don't tax yourself, my lord. I assure you there is no need, as you will only harm yourself. Forget the events of this night and go home."

She was dismissing him again. He couldn't believe it. The empty-headed Miss Braithwaite was dismissing him as if nothing had happened, and he had not just seen what had taken place.

She tried to outpace him, which was ridiculous given he was a head taller and his legs took one step to her two.

"You don't seriously expect me to do that, do you?"

"Yes." She waved a hand at him as if he had asked her to

dance. "You don't like me and I don't like you. Therefore, I see no need for you to involve yourself further in this matter."

"Tell me about what just happened."

"No, and here is my carriage, so I shall say good evening, Lord Sinclair."

"What the hell is going on?" He grabbed her arm. "You are...." He struggled to find the right words. "Different."

She turned to face him then, and suddenly there she was, the empty-headed Miss Braithwaite that he had always known. She gave him that blank look that he had seen a dozen times in as many ballrooms over the past two seasons. The one that suggested she could not hold a serious thought if her life depended on it.

"Why, whatever do you mean, Lord Sinclair? I assure you I have not changed. Indeed, just this morning I selected a simply stunning new dress to be made for the Merryvale ball. La, it will certainly set every man upon his heels."

"What?"

"The Merryvale ball. Surely you are to attend? La, it will be quite something." She gave that little trill of laughter that grated on his nerves.

"Miss Braithwaite, what the hell were you doing out here, chasing that man?" Dev attempted to get the answers he wanted.

"Lord Sinclair!" She stepped back, clasping her chest in horror. "How could you speak to me, a lady, in such insulting tones? Why, I feel quite faint."

To strengthen her words, she stumbled to the carriage door, which was now open, and into it. Before he could stop her, the door had shut.

"Good evening to you, my lord." Wilson then said.

He vaulted up beside the driver and then the carriage was

moving, leaving Dev to watch it disappear into the London night.

"What the hell just happened?" Dev said to no one, as he too started moving. He had a terrible feeling that whatever it was, it was about to shake the foundations of his existence, and for the life of him he could not fathom why.

CHAPTER 2

*T*wo nights later, Dev was no clearer on what he had seen that evening, or why Miss Braithwaite had been there, doing what she had. He was now about to do what he had promised himself he would not: ask his siblings what they knew.

"Do you know much about Miss Braithwaite, Essie?"

"The same Miss Braithwaite you told us not to bother with, Dev, as a conversation with her is as riveting as watching grass grow?"

Had he said that? Lord, he was an idiot sometimes.

"The very same." His tone was emotionless as he flicked a nonexistent fleck of lint from the sleeve of his evening jacket. Schooling his features, he tried to appear uninterested, as if he were simply passing the time with idle conversation.

Dev had thought of nothing else since the incident with Lilliana Braithwaite. His mind was whirling with thoughts and possibilities, chief among which was that he had sorely misjudged her, and that the persona she displayed in society was not in actual fact who she really was.

Why he thought that based on such a brief meeting, he

was not entirely sure. But he could not seem to remove from his mind the image of her face when she had looked at him in that unguarded moment. He'd seen emotion, and that had shaken him.

Why would a woman he believed to be an empty-headed fool be in that street chasing after that man, who Dev believed was abducting that child? The fact that she had given no regard to her personal well-being and launched herself at the carriage told him the matter was a dire one indeed, and rescuing that boy meant a great deal to Miss Braithwaite.

"But, Dev, you expressly forbade Eden and me from talking to her, and as you know we always obey you."

"I'm sure I never mentioned the word forbid, Essie," Dev said. He hated it when his autocratic behavior came back and bit him in the backside.

"No, you did, I heard it," Cam said.

Dev sighed loudly, then dropped his calm façade and cast his siblings a look, the quelling sort that told them he was in no mood for their taunts. They of course merely smiled at him.

He was escorting his brother and sister to the Alverston ball. Of the seven Sinclair siblings, all except Eden had dark hair and green eyes. Essie, his sister, sat across from him. She had recovered from her broken heart; well, at least she told her family she had. But one year on, and Dev believed she still harbored the scars deep inside. She looked pretty in pale blue silk with ivory trim.

Cambridge, his younger brother, was tall with broad shoulders. He had not yet reached Dev's size, but one day he would. In buff breeches, red and black silk waistcoat, ridiculously high shirt points, and a black evening jacket, he looked as any young rogue should. His eyes were finally cleared of the demons that had until recently haunted him. It had been a hard few months for the Sinclair family. Essie had fallen in love only to have her heart crushed, and Cam had suffered the aftereffects of their father's perfidy.

"To answer your question, Dev, yes. Eden and I do know Miss Braithwaite. Anyone you expressly forbid us to talk to is well worth our time."

Dev eyed his sister's cheeky smile with some relief. Perhaps that bastard had not broken her spirit as he had feared. Now he just had to work out a way to get her to tell him what he wanted to know without arousing too much curiosity.

"Why the interest in Miss Braithwaite? I thought you disliked her intensely. You even told me not to bother asking her to dance, as she would bore me to tears in seconds, and that my title was not lofty enough to interest her. There is also the small matter of her dress sense, which I assure you is enough to repel any man."

"Yes." Dev shuddered. "Those colors she wears hurt my eyes. However, I'm sure I did not say those things, Cambridge." Dev pinched the bridge of his nose. He was a pompous twit. "Besides, you don't have a title."

"I fear you did, brother. Of course I ignored you and danced with her anyway," Cam added. "And yes, she did rattle on, but once I got past the fact she wore that hideous puce dress, I did not find it taxing, as she laughed at several of my jokes. And on the matter of my title, some men don't need them. I can scintillate a lady with mere looks and words."

Essie crowed with laughter as Dev rolled his eyes.

"Indeed, Cam," Essie added. "As you say, she does have a silly way to her, but I have found that eases with familiarity. She is harmless."

"Eases?" Dev questioned.

"I believe it means to give respite, brother."

14

"I know what it means, Cam," Dev snapped.

"Why the interest in Miss Braithwaite?" Essie asked him.

"Keep what I tell you to yourselves," Dev said, and then he related what he had seen out on that London street.

"Good God," Cam said. "And you say she was running after the carriage, and you believe she saved that boy?"

"She was, and did. Since then I have wondered if there is a chance that I may have been harsh in my original summation of Miss Braithwaite's character. Until I gather all the facts, I cannot be certain."

The only sound in the carriage for several seconds was the rumble of the wheels and clip-clop of hooves.

"Do you have any smelling salts, Ess? I'm sure Dev just said he was wrong."

"Very amusing." Dev glared at his brother. "What else do you know about her?"

"Well, Eden and I, like Miss Braithwaite and her aunt, all knit for the children who are less fortunate than ourselves."

Cam looked at Dev, who in turn shrugged.

"How come we don't know about this?" Dev asked, watching his sister's chin elevate.

"You are both busy, and this is a small thing we wish to do. We have so much and they so little."

"But there is more, isn't there, sister?" Dev said. He knew when his sister was holding back.

"I am unsure of all the details, but I have a suspicion that Miss Braithwaite is more involved than she appears. One day I had the carriage stop at this little house in Temple Street to drop off some things we had for the children, and I saw her entering the building."

"Well that suggests nothing other than she was there dropping off things as you were," Cam said.

"Indeed. However, Eden was with me, and she overheard

Miss Braithwaite say she would be in the parlor looking over the accounts."

"Now that changes things," Cam added.

"Who approached you about the knitting?" Dev questioned his sister.

"We were visiting the Countess of Gripley, and she told us about this charity she knits for. Eden, Aunt, and I were interested in helping too. Miss Braithwaite was there also, and it was she who said she knew the person to contact, and sent round a note with the details the following day."

"Is knitting all you do, Essie?"

"I have visited orphanages, and sometimes while I am there I will help if a child is sick."

"You've visited orphanages?" Dev felt ill at the prospect of his sister in such areas.

"You cannot stop me, Dev. I won't let you, and anyway, I am in no danger. I take a footman and a maid if Eden cannot come with me."

The Sinclair brothers shook their heads as if to clear them.

"Am I such an ogre that you think I would stop you doing these things then, Essie?"

Dev was subjected to what he termed the Sinclair look, a thorough searching study from one of his siblings. He had received it more times than he could count, yet it still made him want to wriggle on the carriage seat.

"No. I know you would never stop me doing something like this, Dev." Essie expelled a deep breath. "I just decided not to tell you, as you are very protective of us all."

"All right, we will leave the matter of you frequenting some of the less desirable London streets for now, and return to Miss Braithwaite. Have you discussed the subject of the children with her again?"

"Briefly, but she wished only to discuss scarves and hats.

She is not the easiest person to strike up a conversation with, as you know."

"She simpers a great deal, and then there is the inane giggling." Cam sighed.

The first and only conversation Dev had shared with Miss Braithwaite had been at a ball two years ago. She had been dressed in a hideous ill-fitting gown of mustard, with her hair pulled back so tight it made her eyes squint. Poked in the top of it had been a mustard feather that nearly took out his eye when she nodded. Her glasses had borne a smudge on one lens, and while Dev was not a perfectionist by any standards, he had some... standards. And the woman quite literally hurt his eyes to look at.

There was also the little matter of his body tingling when he had drawn near to her. Disturbing, because he had never felt it before, and equally as disturbing was the fact that he was experiencing it with Miss Braithwaite.

He had made the effort to approach, as he had sisters and would hate for them to be snubbed in any way, but it had been the first and only time. Miss Braithwaite had spent the entire dance discussing the Grey Shrike, a bird that apparently she had spent a large amount of time studying. She had bored him silly with its migration patterns, the size of its feet, and the color of its feathers. By dance end, Dev was more than happy to return her to her aunt and flee. He pushed from his memory his reaction to her, and never approached her again.

Now, however, knowing what he did about her, he knew the source of his reaction. Christ, he could still not believe she had his colors!

Had it all been an act? He wasn't sure why she would put on such an act night after night. It made no sense.

"Essie?"

"Yes, Dev?"

"I want you to find out whatever you can about her."

"Who?" She gave him a sweet smile.

"You know who, so don't play the innocent."

"What do I get?"

A Sinclair never did something for a sibling without recompense. If they did, the requests would never cease.

"I know!" She clapped her gloved hands together. "You will dance with the Riddly twins!"

Dev groaned. "Have mercy, Ess. They are sweet, but you know if I do that, their mother will have me wed to one of them before dawn."

His sister merely smiled once more, and he knew she would not budge.

"Very well, but I expect you to do your bit."

"Done!"

"Well now, I shall enjoy this evening immensely, and watch both of you with interest." Cam rose as the carriage stopped.

After greeting the host and hostess and exchanging pleasantries, Dev and his siblings followed the other guests into the ballroom. Everything glittered and sparkled, including the guests, and he stood for a moment inhaling and exhaling slowly as his senses adjusted to the color.

He felt a blinding flash of pain behind his eyes that instantly eased as he adjusted to the brightness and to the myriad of colors. Releasing another breath, he stood between his siblings, one pressed to either side of him, in case it became too much for him to bear and he landed flat on his face.

"I am well."

They started walking again, nodding as people greeted

them. Soon Essie left to talk with some friends. He and Cam continued to circle the room.

Over the heads of several guests, he found Lilliana Braithwaite seated with a group of ladies along the wall. Once again she wore glasses and was dressed in a hideous shade of purple. Not the color of grapes or lavender bushes; no, this was closer to a moldy fig. Her hair was once again scraped back from her face and piled high and decorated with—

"Christ, is that a tree in Miss Braithwaite's hair?" Cam whispered.

"It appears so."

"I wonder why her aunt lets her dress in such a manner?"

"Perhaps she has little say in the matter," Dev said.

"Perhaps."

"I saw her without her glasses," Dev added. "Her face was also not composed with that vacant look she has perfected. She was beautiful."

"Really?"

Dev nodded.

"What happened between you has really unsettled you, hasn't it?"

"Yes, because I thought I knew who she was, but now I'm not so sure. Seeing her out there, doing what she was, risking her safety for that boy…." Dev shook his head. "I can find no reason for it."

"And you like everything to have a reason. Everything in its place, no unanswered questions?"

He did; it was how he lived his life, and he did not like the unexpected.

"What do you know of her family?"

"Not much." Cam shrugged. "Father and mother have passed, and the aunt lives with Miss Braithwaite and her brother. We both know him; Nicholas. He has the same vices I once had."

"The same Nicholas you lost money to," Dev said, remembering the night he had found his brother deep in debt in the bowels of some hellhole.

"Yes, not a very pleasant type, but as I was halfway down a bottle of whiskey at the time, I can't remember a great deal."

"Excuse me, brother."

"Where are you going?" Cam asked.

"To find out who the hell the true Miss Braithwaite is."

CHAPTER 3

$\mathcal{L}$illy's eyes tracked Lord Sinclair as he drew closer. Surely he was not coming to see her? Two days had passed since that night he had caught her as she lunged at Leo to save him, and she'd believed he had taken her advice and forgotten the entire incident. The look on his face suggested she was wrong.

Her heart beat a little faster as she watched him cut a path through the other guests. He was taller than most of the other people in the room, so she could see him clearly, and although she couldn't read his expression from this distance she was fairly certain he was looking at her.

Of course he was not seeking her out, she told herself. She had turned him away successfully, just as she had the others. And yet, what had happened between them may have piqued his interest. She prayed it hadn't, as she had no time to deal with him now.

The problem was that since that night when he had risked himself to save her, when she would have surely fallen hard and possibly injured herself and Leo, she had not been able to stop thinking of him. His actions had been selfless, and she was unsure many would have taken the steps he had to keep her safe.

Take her brother, for example; he would never have risked his health to save her. And yet Lord Sinclair had, which told her she may have misjudged him, and that in fact, he was a great deal nicer than she had originally believed. Not that it mattered. Lilly let no one close; she held them all at bay with silly looks, boring stories, and terrible choices in clothing. But still, it would be nice to know if he was... nice.

She shot him another look. He certainly seemed to be heading her way. Lilly pressed a hand to her chest. Surely not? Surely he would not question her here over what had transpired the other night?

He had piercing green eyes, which she had only really looked into once before and vowed never to do so again, because she was sure he had read her innermost secrets and seen right down to her soul. Thick black hair and dark brows and lashes complemented a face that sometimes appeared chiseled in granite, and then he would smile—rarely, but usually when his siblings were near—and the effect was breathtaking.

His chest was wide, his shoulders broad, and Lilly had no idea who his tailor was, but she hoped he was paid handsomely for the effort of clothing the man's huge body.

Men did not often unsettle Lilly; in fact, for the most she found them simpleminded idiots, just as they found her. However, one look into his green eyes and she had actually lost the ability to think. It had never happened to her before, that sudden intense attraction that had fleeced her brain of every thought and stuck her tongue to the roof of her mouth. Lilly had never been attracted to another man like she was to Lord Sinclair. When he had offered his arm she had felt the heat of his body through her gloved fingers almost as if the man were a smoldering ember. Luckily she had fallen back on the act she had perfected of the empty-headed Miss Braithwaite.

"Is that Lord Sinclair coming this way, Miss Braithwaite?" Miss Tabitha Pillsworth whispered to her.

"Absolutely not," Lilly said, turning away so she wouldn't gaze at him as she often did when no one paid attention. Her glasses proved a wonderful shield and, as most evenings she sat in some corner, she could observe without reserve.

"I think he is, and he looks extremely determined. Dear Lord, that is a ferocious scowl, is it not?"

"As you can see, Miss Pillsworth, I am at present looking at you. Therefore I cannot see what look Lord Sinclair has upon his face."

"I wonder how he does that?" Her companion sighed.

"Does what?" Lilly said, then bit her tongue; she did not want to know what he was doing.

"Part the crowd without a word."

"He is probably wearing too much scent!"

"Oh that was naughty, Miss Braithwaite!" Miss Pillsworth giggled and then gulped and grew quiet, and Lilly knew why. Without turning around, she just knew that he was standing behind her. She could feel him.

"Miss Braithwaite, Miss Pillsworth, I hope you are having a pleasant evening thus far."

She had to look up at him now; it would be extremely rude if she did not. Yet didn't he already think her rude?

"Lord Sinclair," Lilly said, gripping the edges of her seat.

"May I enquire if you have this dance free, Miss Braithwaite?"

Lilly looked down at her dance card, thereby avoiding his eyes. Damn man, he was far too disturbing this close, and while Lilly studied her card, she knew there was not one name on there.

"I fear not, Lord Sinclair." Lilly fell back on what she did best. She gave him an insipid smile.

"Now that is a shame, considering we have so much to discuss."

That look in his eyes told Lilly the man was not about to walk away from her until he got what he came for.

"Are you wishing to hear more of the Grey Shrike, my lord?"

"No, you were quite thorough in your description, thank you." His voice held humor.

"Perhaps another night then, Lord Sinclair."

Before she could retreat, he had grabbed her card and studied it. Horrified, she knew he saw it was empty.

"Lord Hingle has been struck down with a rare form of lackwit; it is a disease that will lay him low for some time, I fear."

Lilly heard Miss Pillsworth giggle.

"That is extremely rude, my lord. Lord Hingle is a friend of mine, and on his behalf I must protest."

In fact she loathed the man, but he did not need to know that. The slow smile forming on Lord Sinclair's face was not making her heart thud faster, Lilly told herself.

"Please accept my apologies if I have insulted you in any way, Miss Braithwaite."

He wasn't sorry at all, the scoundrel. His green eyes had a wicked glint. She squinted. Men did not like women who squinted, she had ascertained, as it meant she could not see them clearly.

"Oh, Miss Braithwaite thinks Lord Hingle a lackwit also, Lord Sinclair."

"Yes, thank you, Miss Pillsworth." Lilly gave the woman a sharp look, which did nothing to subdue her. They had spent many hours sitting on the edges of ballrooms, and Lilly had let her facade drop occasionally and shared a quip or two about some of the men of society. Now she wished she had held her tongue.

"I shall dance with the silly man should he arrive, Miss Braithwaite, while you dance with Lord Sinclair."

"Excellent." He held out his arm. "What a true friend you are, Miss Pillsworth."

Lilly looked around her but rescue came from no quarter, and as there was no one to come to her aid anyway, there was little she could do but rise and place the tips of her gloved fingers on his forearm.

Neither spoke as they made their way onto the floor. They attracted plenty of glances, because it was no secret she was rarely asked to dance and he was highly sought-after.

Lilly was relieved as a quadrille started when they reached the floor. Not as bad as a waltz, but still he would remain close to her for most of it.

"Are you enjoying the season thus far, Miss Braithwaite?"

"Oh indeed," she simpered. The breath seized in her throat as his large fingers clasped around hers. Even through their gloves she could do nothing to stop the shiver of awareness. She released it with a whoosh as he released her to take Lady Rumble's hand. The woman threw him a smoldering look.

Lilly had never understood women doing such things. But then she'd never understood the need to flirt either. Of course, that was because she had no wish to ever marry. Lilly couldn't marry; she had too many reasons not to, second of which was her children. No husband would allow his wife to do as she did.

She straightened her spine as Lord Sinclair returned to her side. Luckily he did not touch her.

"Do you not like the quadrille, Miss Braithwaite?"

His green eyes smiled, and Lilly hated the feeling of a hundred butterflies fluttering about in her stomach.

"Oh yes, indeed, Lord Sinclair, it is a most beauteous dance. Why do you ask?"

"You're frowning."

Drat. Lilly immediately relaxed her face.

"I like to frown, I-I it gives the face a chance to relax." Mother of God, had she just said those words? *Think before you speak, Lilliana*, she chided herself, *this man is no fool. Try not to appear overly stupid.*

"There is certainly a place for a frown, but one would not think that place was on the dance floor when one is meant to be enjoying oneself."

"Oh yes, indeed," she said for the third time. "La, I do believe this is my favorite dance. Do you know of its origins, Lord Sinclair?"

Lilly had a head full of silly facts. She had researched long and hard on just such things, because she had every intention of dissuading every man who might show an interest in her.

"Ah, no. However, I wish to discuss something else with you, Miss Braithwaite."

"I knew you enjoyed our discussion on the gray shrike, my lord. Let me now tell you of the yellow wagtail."

"What occurred the other night, Miss Braithwaite? Why were you out there, running down that street after that man and boy? What were you saving him from?"

Lilly missed a step, but as he was holding her, he took her weight, and they continued on as if nothing had happened.

"I, ah, have no idea what it is you refer to, Lord Sinclair."

"Miss Braithwaite, please do not try to fob me off. I was there, I saw you, and I caught you and the boy as you fell. That bruise on your chin was the result. So don't play me for a fool, as it will not wash."

"I have no wish to discuss it," she trilled. "It was a silly, reckless moment. It has now passed, and will never happen again."

"Try that again."

He said the words as he left her side, and she had only a few seconds to find an answer. Her thoughts whirled but she could come up with nothing that would appease him and leave him none the wiser as to her actions, so she fell back on the ridiculous.

"I have recently started studying mice, Lord Sinclair. And a rare form of field mouse is found on that street at this time every year. It comes only in the summer, and I was there searching for it when I saw that man grab that boy." Lilly was rather proud of her reply. It sounded like something the silly Miss Braithwaite would do. "I could not, in all conscience, let that man harm the child, and so I set off in pursuit, and that is when you found me. Your actions surely saved my life," Lilly added dramatically. "I shall forever be indebted to you."

"Impressive though that reply was, you don't seriously expect me to believe it, do you?"

"Why, are you suggesting I am telling an untruth, my lord? Shame on you." Lilly gasped, then clutched her bosom for effect.

He took her hands as they walked in a small circle.

"I am unsure if you are an excellent actress, and if so, why? Or you are genuinely...."

"Simple-minded? Oh I assure you I am. 'Tis a constant concern for my family."

He laughed, a deep booming sound that drew far too many eyes. Lilly did not like being the center of attention.

"Now then," he said when they returned to their previous position. "How about we try that again? Why were you in that lane at such an hour, chasing that man, with a handful of children with whom you were obviously familiar?"

"I-I—please forget the entire incident, Lord Sinclair." Lilly gave up trying to concoct a more elaborate story. This man would not be fooled, or deterred, it seemed.

"I don't think that will be possible, Miss Braithwaite."

"Why? My actions do not concern you."

"And yet I was there, as were you. The woman I saw that night, for a brief moment, vastly differed from the one I believed I knew. My curiosity is roused."

Oh no, no, no. This was not good at all. Lilly could not afford to have someone like Lord Sinclair poking his nose into her affairs. Her family had no idea what she did, and she liked it that way. Miss Braithwaite was important to no one. Therefore no one cared about her actions... until now.

"No, you were right in your earlier assessment of my character. I am extremely silly. Why, just yesterday I told Lord Howe that very thing, and he agreed with me."

"And yet, that leads me no closer to what I want to know."

"I am distressed by your line of questioning, Lord Sinclair." Lilly forced herself to trill the words in her usual high-pitched tone. "I have no wish to further our acquaintance, or indeed dance with you again."

She felt his eyes on her, and then he had left her side once more, and Lilly wanted to flee. Pick up her skirts and run as fast as she could, and not stop.

"Had you said those words to me last week, I would have believed them, Miss Braithwaite. Yet now, tonight, I am having trouble doing so. You see, the woman I watched kneel in that filthy London street to talk with children I suspect live their lives upon them, was not extremely silly. So you see my dilemma, Miss Braithwaite," he said in a calm voice that made Lilly want to shriek at him. "You have become something of a conundrum to me."

"I don't want to be your conundrum," Lilly said quickly. "I am no one worth your time, and I wish for things to go back as they were. You ignoring me, and me ignoring you, Lord Sinclair."

Please.

"I think not, but as you will not enlighten me, perhaps your family can."

No, dear God, no.

"Do not question them!" Lilly looked to where her aunt stood. Dear Lord, she would lock Lilly's bedroom door and never let her leave if she knew what she got up to. Dear, sweet Aunt Vi. She would be horrified to realize her niece was out on that street with only a footman for protection.

"I will not, of course, if you do not wish it. However, I would like answers to my questions."

"You will not get them." Her voice was tight with worry, but she cared not. She must somehow dissuade this man from further questioning. If that did not work, then she would make sure to evade him. She could fake an illness—that would give her some time, then perhaps an injury to a leg....

"I shall look forward to conversing with you once more, Miss Braithwaite."

Lilly did not speak again as the dance thankfully ended, and let him lead her back to where her aunt stood with her brother. The entire journey was spent trying to come up with a way to stall him from further questioning her. The only idea she could come up with as they reached her aunt was to run and hide until the evening was over.

Dev released Miss Braithwaite as they reached her aunt's side. He acknowledged Lady James and ignored Lord Braithwaite, her brother. The man had had a hand in attempting to sink Cam further into the depths of depravity when first the Sinclair family arrived in London, and Dev did not forget such things, especially when they involved people he loved.

"Lady James." He bowed before the elderly woman.

"Lord Sinclair, how lovely to see you, and dancing with my darling niece."

Dev studied the older woman. Her dress was in the latest style and the color a deep burgundy. Why then did she allow her niece to dress like a dowdy, color-blind field mouse?

"I believe the Duke and Duchess are from London at this time, Lord Sinclair."

"Indeed they are, Lady James. My sister is at Raven Castle, but due to return shortly. My aunt and uncle are keeping them company."

"How lovely." Her smile was sweet. He knew the woman had many friends and was popular, also unlike her niece.

The puzzle that was Miss Braithwaite grew by the minute.

"If you will allow me the supper dance, Miss Braithwaite?"

"Oh no, my lord. It would not do to—"

"My niece will be delighted to dance with you again, Lord Sinclair."

He bowed then, deciding that now was as good a time as any to leave, because Lady James may be happy he was singling her niece out, but her niece and nephew were not.

"Good evening, Sinclair."

He did not look at Nicholas Braithwaite as he spoke. Turning on his heel, Dev walked away.

The woman had piqued his interest, and when that happened there was little to be done but follow that interest until he had answers to all the questions currently swirling inside his head.

Dev thought about her as he danced with others. He thought about her as he talked with friends and acquaintances. He then returned to partner her for the supper dance. However, it seemed she had fled.

CHAPTER 4

 ev walked around the room, until he was sure he had covered every inch, and still he could not find her. Tempted as he was to change his vision, he was not foolish enough to risk it, and would only resort to that in a dire situation.

Finding Essie, he tapped her shoulder, and his sister detached herself from a group of women.

"Essie, have you seen Miss Braithwaite?"

"Why?"

"We were engaged for the supper waltz."

Essie frowned.

"But haven't you already danced with her?"

"Yes," Dev said, not liking where this was going and wishing he had kept his mouth closed and continued searching on his own.

"Then why are you dancing with her again?"

"People can dance more than once, surely?"

"Not you and her."

No one could annoy him quite like a sibling.

"I am attempting to be nice, is there a problem with that?" Frustrated, he ended the sentence on a growl.

"What did you say to her?"

"What?"

Essie placed her fingers on his arm, then nodded, which Dev guessed meant she wanted to walk. Not an easy task, surrounded by hundreds of people.

"You must have said something to her, if she has disappeared."

"I asked if she would dance the supper dance with me, and her aunt accepted, and now I cannot find her."

"Why would she have fled when she knew you were to dance with her, if you said nothing to upset her?"

"All right, I may have asked her about the other night, which was perfectly acceptable considering the circumstances," he defended himself.

"I thought I was going to find out more about her, and then you would talk with her?"

"I don't remember us discussing that."

"It was what I gathered from our discussion. But as you have now frightened her off, then you shall have to find her and apologize. "

She spoke out the side of her mouth.

"I'm your brother. Shouldn't you be on my side?" he groused.

"I can't help you with her if you don't tell me what happened," Essie said in her calm, rational voice.

"How do you know I need help?"

"You're strung tighter than a piano wire."

"Lord, I wish I had kept my mouth shut," he groaned.

He watched the sweetest of the Sinclair siblings narrow her eyes in a calculating manner.

"If you will alert me when Sir Richard Kimpton is heading in my direction, I shall tell you where I last saw her."

"I thought we were not using our senses in public?" This time Dev looked smug.

"That's the deal, brother. I cannot abide that windbag Kimpton, and his breath is quite foul."

"Shall I warn him off you, sister?" Dev looked around the room and found Kimpton several feet away, fast approaching.

"No indeed, I can do that. But it would be easier if I had warning and could duck out of sight."

"Deal."

"Miss Braithwaite left the room through that door," she pointed over Dev's shoulder, "ten minutes ago."

"Kimpton is approaching fast on your left."

"Love you, brother."

"And you, sister."

They parted. Dev headed for the door and slipped through. Switching his vision now that he was away from several hundred brightly clad people, he began walking the halls.

He saw colors behind doors, some extremely close to each other, which suggested more than just chatting was taking place. Continuing on, he found a set of stairs and descended; at the bottom he found another door, and this one led to a conservatory.

The smell of flowers and trees, both citrus and garden variety, hit him. Cam would love this place. He found Lilliana Braithwaite at the rear, tucked behind a large statue of a Roman gentleman wearing a brief loincloth.

"Hide-and-seek is a particular favorite of my family. Perhaps you would care to join us one day for a game?" Dev said, blocking her escape route.

"Lord Sinclair!"

"The very person."

"What are you doing here?"

She was attempting to appear calm and find that blank look and insipid smile she usually had on her face when he saw her. However, this time, he could see nerves were making that difficult.

"I was looking for my dance partner, Miss Braithwaite."

"Oh well, yes, of course. Good Lord, is it that time already? I had simply hoped for a short respite from the ball-room, and had not realized the hour had advanced so."

As far as lies went it was a good one, yet a lie nonetheless. Dev was slowly coming to the conclusion that the woman was very good at hiding behind what she wanted people to believe she was, when in fact she was far different.

"Do you wear those to see near or far?"

His question about her spectacles threw her off her stride further.

"I—ah... both."

Dev bent closer and looked through them. He saw the glass was plain, just like his bedroom window. The glasses were part of her disguise.

"They do not appear overly strong."

"Th-they are strong enough."

She snatched them from her face and cleaned them furiously with her gloved fingers.

"Oh dear."

"What?" She looked up at him quickly, and he was able to see her eyes clearly once more. Dev felt something settle heavily in his chest as he studied her delicate features.

"Your eyes are an unusual color."

"I-I am happy with them."

"Yes, they are lovely." She really was beautiful, right down to the sweet bow of her upper lip. How the hell had she fooled them all for so long?

"If you will not dance with me, will you come out from

34

behind that statue and tell me what it was that I stumbled across two nights ago?"

"No. However, I would be happy to give you a tour of the conservatory. There is a splendid display of orchids, some quite rare. There is one that is over—"

"I will not be deterred, Miss Braithwaite, so you had best come clean."

"I have no wish to talk of that matter, as I told you earlier, Lord Sinclair."

"Then it appears we are at an impasse. I wish to know and you will not tell me. You wish me gone from here; I wish to stay."

"I overheard your sisters once telling someone that you were a good and fair man."

"That was nice of them."

"They said no woman would ever have anything to fear from you."

"I am trying very hard to imagine what conversation prompted those particular compliments from my sisters. I can only suspect that such nice words were from Essex, and surely I had done something wonderful to get into her good graces."

Her lips pursed, and he saw that she was getting angry but fighting hard to stay in character.

"The point I am trying to make, Lord Sinclair, is that I have no wish to tell you what you want to know, and if you are the gentleman your sisters believe, then you should not force me."

She was clever; he'd give her that.

"Were my sisters the ones walking about London streets at such an hour, chasing men with dubious intentions and rescuing a child I suspect lives on those streets, I assure you I would be questioning them the same way."

She wasn't scared of him, Dev realized, only of what he may learn.

"I am nothing to you."

"Not quite true, but I take your point. However, after saving you from certain

death—"

"Neither Leo nor I would have died from falling on the road," she scoffed.

"You are certainly as ungrateful as my sisters."

He saw the small twitch of her lips, and with it came a flash of two dimples he had not known she had. It was yet another glimpse into the woman society knew nothing of.

"Should someone chance upon us, Lord Sinclair, the results would not please either of us; therefore I would ask you to let me pass."

He knew her words for the truth and yet he could not draw away. Lifting a hand, he traced the bruise marring the pale skin of her jaw. She felt warm to touch and the effect on his body was instant. Every nerve end stood, every pulse thrummed.

"Can we be friends, Miss Braithwaite?"

"No."

The word made her pout. Just a taste, a small brush of his mouth against hers, and this madness inside him would ease.

"No." She shook her head as he lowered his. "I don't—"

He swallowed the rest of her words. Dev was gentle, placing small kisses on her lips, each one opening them bit by bit, until she gave him what he wanted. She had the most kissable lips, full against his and shaped to perfection, and in seconds all thought of this being a brief interlude fled from his head.

Had someone doused him in fire he would not have moved. The immediate and powerful reaction he suddenly felt shocked him to his toes. It was as if she touched him everywhere, yet in truth the only skin he could access was her face and lips. It was enough to tell him that when he got this woman undressed and beneath him, theirs would be a fierce passion.

Lilly had never been properly kissed before. There were several pathetic attempts by men who had drunk too much or declared they were enamored by her, which was of course untrue. She'd soon taught them the error of their ways, but this.... Dear God, this was a slow seduction of the senses.

His mouth, which she had previously believed hard, was soft and wicked as it kissed and nibbled hers. She could do nothing to stop the shameful flood of heat that filled her body. It was as if she had relinquished control of herself to him, as if her body were now his to command.

Of their own volition, her arms moved up his body and her fingers dug into the hard muscles on his shoulders. For a brief moment, she almost wished she did not wear gloves, so she could explore the soft hair at his nape.

"Open for me, Lilliana."

The deep rasp of his words brushed her lips, and she found herself doing as he asked. Felt herself arch into his body, press her breasts against his chest as she sought more from him. More contact, more kisses.

One of his hands cupped her head and angled it so the kiss deepened; the other he kept around her waist, holding her close.

"Lilliana."

"Yes," she whispered against his lips, uncertain what he asked for or what she needed.

His mouth moved to her jaw, kissing the length to her ear, and then he pressed his lips to that place just beneath, where her neck started, and the fire inside her grew. Such a small place, and yet when touched in the right way, by the right man, it was alarmingly sensitive. Lilly managed to swallow her cry of regret when he lifted his head.

She drew in an unsteady breath as he stepped back and away from her.

"Please forgive me. I-I had no right to do that, Miss Braithwaite."

His breathing was as heavy as hers, and she saw that he was as disturbed by the kiss as she.

"I-I don't know what to say to you," she whispered truthfully. "This, it should not have happened, and I'm not sure why it did."

Lilly braced herself as he closed the distance between them once more.

"You are a beautiful woman." He cupped her cheek.

Lilly shook her head. "No, I am not. I'm ugly. Just ask any man in that ballroom."

"But you are not ugly, are you, Lilliana? In fact you are beautiful, and yet you take great pains that no one sees that beauty."

No, no, no. How did he know she took great pains to hide from society?

"I have no idea to what you allude, Lord Sinclair. This entire situation has gotten completely out of hand, and it must stop. What happened the other night was the catalyst, and let me say once more that I have no wish to speak of it further, and this"—Lilly waved her hand between them—"is momentary madness, which will pass."

Before he could speak, she placed a hand on his chest and pushed. He moved, but only, she suspected, because he wished to. Then she was walking from the room. Lilly wanted to run, but made herself walk.

Reaching the door to the ballroom minutes later, she slipped inside, now composed. Well, outwardly at least.

"Miss Braithwaite, how wonderful, I have been looking everywhere for you. Come, we will go to supper together as we have both missed the supper dance, and quite frankly there is not one person I wish to converse with who will aid my digestion."

Of course the last person she wanted to sit with was one of his sisters, and yet she could find no way to escape Essex Sinclair.

"Thank you, that would be lovely."

"We shall find somewhere quiet. I have some questions about the knitting I am doing, as I believe you also knit for the children. Different styles that I think will help the children through the winter months."

Lilly drew in a deep breath as Essex started chattering about the children. She nodded and smiled when appropriate, and tried to ignore the tingling in her breasts and heat that flushed her body. Essex had no idea that minutes ago Lilly had been locked in a heated embrace in the arms of her eldest brother. In fact, she doubted anyone would believe it, even if she climbed onto the supper table and yelled the words to every guest. She was struggling with it herself.

It had been madness; nothing else could explain that frenzied need inside her to be consumed by the man. She'd never felt such raw emotion before. Lilly had never thought of herself as passionate-natured, but right at that moment, there on the cold stone floor, she would have allowed that man any liberties he wished with her person.

"Hello, Cam."

"Essex, Miss Braithwaite."

Lilly nodded to the Sinclair male as they took seats close to where he sat with a young lady.

"I shall get us some food, if you will sit here, Miss Braithwaite."

"Oh, I can get mine."

"Yes, I know, but then someone may take our seats," Essex said before walking off.

The family, Lilly thought, were all quite authoritative in their own way.

Had she responded with such abandon simply because he was handsome, and no handsome man had ever paid her any attention? Not that she wanted attention. But yes, surely that was it, Lilly reasoned, relieved to have worked through why she had behaved in such a way. Feeling better, she even smiled as Essex Sinclair arrived back at her side with a plate of food.

"I was wondering if perhaps I could drop some more things around to Temple Street one day, Miss Braithwaite?"

Suddenly the food tasted like ashes in her mouth.

She looked at Essex Sinclair. The green eyes were not as vibrant as her brother's, and the hair not quite as dark, but there was little doubting the blood tie.

"I—ah, Temple Street?"

"I saw you entering there when last I had some things to deliver. I took them myself as I was heading that way. I thought that perhaps you were in some way involved? Perhaps your family owns the house?"

"Oh, yes of course."

"Forgive me. You seem uncomfortable with my questions."

Stay calm, Lilly. Because one person knows you visit Temple Street, does not mean anyone else does.

"I am involved, yes, but prefer to keep my involvement a secret."

Why was her life suddenly so complicated? First this business with Lord Sinclair, and then with his sister. She had managed to keep her secrets close until these people entered her life.

"Oh, of course, and your secret is safe with me, I assure

you. Indeed, I have several secrets I have no wish for anyone to hear."

Lilly couldn't imagine what this woman could possibly have to hide.

"Excellent. I would be most grateful if you would do so."

"I assume the house is for the children in some capacity?"

"Yes, we treat any sick children there and offer beds and food for those in need."

"How wonderful." Essex looked genuinely interested. "Is there a possibility that I may call around there sometime, and drop off the things I have for the children? I would also like to offer my help if a child is sick or injured. I have quite a bit of knowledge in that direction."

Lilly wondered if this was what it was like being stomped over by a herd of cats. These Sinclairs did not seem to understand the word no, and gently but forcefully persisted until they got the answers they sought. However, she was surprised that a woman of noble birth knew about healing, and while she had no wish for Essex Sinclair to know too much about her life, she was not one to look away from such an opportunity. The children were often sick enough to warrant calling for a doctor, and yet most doctors had no wish to treat children like the ones who frequented Temple Street.

"Yes, well, if you wish."

"Excellent. I shall await word from you as to what day suits you best."

Biting into a savory, Lilly contemplated how she was to bring her life back under control and eradicate Lord Sinclair from it. Many hours later, when she was lying in her bed, she was no closer to finding the answer.

CHAPTER 5

$\mathcal{D}$ ev could hear the laughter as he walked down the long hallway of his uncle's home three mornings after the night he had kissed Lilliana Braithwaite. The nursery was on the top floor and rightly so, considering the noise coming from inside it. Reaching the doorway, he leaned on the frame and looked inside.

"If seventeen frogs hopped seventeen miles and they covered five miles per hour, then how long would it take them to reach Ambrosia Pond? Which I happen to know is the biggest pond in Europe."

His younger siblings were seated around a table; Somerset perched with one leg beneath her. Warwickshire sprawled, looking like Cambridge, long legs taking up the majority of room under the table. Dorset, who rarely sat still, bounced in her chair. Each was silent as they thought through what their tutor, Mr. Linues, had asked them.

Dev had always believed his sisters should be schooled as thoroughly as his brother, and until they had arrived in London and accepted their aunt and uncle's support, he and his elder siblings had undertaken that task. He also knew his views were very different from the rest of society's. His uncle surprisingly had followed them and employed Mr. Linues, a young man with a solemn demeanor behind which sat a wry sense of humor.

"How many frogs are there, and is the road often used?"

"There will be no delaying tactics to put your sisters off, thank you, Master Warwick."

Dev laughed silently. His younger siblings, like their elder brothers and sisters, had lively intelligence. It was only recently he, Cam, Essie, and Eden had found out that they also shared their heightened senses. It had been a blow, as they'd believed them untouched; now, however, they had to teach them how to live with the gifts they had.

Nodding to Mr. Linues, Dev quietly withdrew and went to hunt out his sister. He and Cam lived next door in the other house their uncle owned on the street. They spent most of their time here, especially now their aunt and uncle were away traveling the countryside. It was a beautiful home filled with rich colors and lush furnishings, but more importantly it had plenty of food, and growing up this had not always been the case.

"Breakfast has just been served, my lord."

"Pennyroll." Dev nodded to his uncle's butler as he appeared before him. "Do you know the location of Miss Sinclair?"

"She is in the breakfast parlor, my lord."

Excellent; he could eat and talk to his sister at the same time. He hadn't slept well again, his dreams plagued with visions of Lilly in his arms, her lips pressed to his. Lilliana naked beneath him as he made slow sensual love to her. Lilliana sitting draped across his thighs while he kissed her breasts.

"I shall have another place set for you at once, my lord."

Nodding, Dev kept walking. Bloody woman. He'd been

better off thinking her a simpleton; at least then he had known peace. Since finding out she was not who he had originally thought, she had taken up residence in his head. Then there was the matter of that night he had found her on the street.

He thought he had everything straight in his head about that, but then, he wished she would confirm it.

"Surely the hour is too early for such a scowl, brother?"

"Morning, Essie." Dev walked around the table to kiss his sister and then picked up the plate the maid had just placed on the table. Heading to the sideboard, he began to lift covers. Once his plate was full, he seated himself across from his sister.

Essie was the gentlest of the Sinclairs and the most comfortable to be with, in Dev's opinion. He'd amended that to usually, after their conversation three nights ago. She rarely raised her voice and could actually sit still and silent for longer than two minutes at a time. They ate in companionable silence until Dev had cleaned his plate and rose to refill it. He then watched his sister savor a mouthful of food before swallowing.

Her heightened sense was taste. She could tell any ingredient with just a mouthful. She could also taste fear, anger, and other emotions, especially if they were being experienced by one of her siblings.

"What plans do you have for the day, Essie?"

She looked better with each week that passed since that bastard had broken her heart. The dark purple bruises beneath her eyes had faded and the strain in her pretty face had eased. The sadness was still there, Dev could see it in her eyes, but her color was stronger, healthier. He checked his siblings over at least once a month, had done so since he was old enough to understand his gift. He knew what color they should be and knew if they were sick or troubled. Essie was a bright pink, but for a while, some of her color had lost its strength.

"I'm going out, Dev."

"An enjoyable entertainment, depending on where it is you go to."

He watched Essie as she put jam on a piece of toast, pushing it to the corners slowly, avoiding his eyes.

"Oh, I thought to purchase some new gloves."

She was still not looking at him, and he knew her well enough to know she was not telling him the truth. He just needed to push a little harder. Like Cam, Essie could not lie worth a damn.

"Gloves, now that is an exciting prospect. Is that all you plan to purchase?"

"P-perhaps a bonnet."

"For which occasion?"

Her knife landed on her plate with a clatter as finally she looked up at him.

"I cannot tell you where I'm going, so don't ask."

"Are you in danger?"

"No, of course not!"

Relieved, he continued, "Are you meeting someone I have no wish for you to meet?"

"Um... well, as to that, I am not entirely sure."

"Even more intriguing."

"Could we discuss the weather instead?"

She gave him a pleading look that failed to move him.

"Just tell me, Essie, you know I'll get the information eventually." Which he would. She could never keep anything from him.

"No." She shook her head. "I cannot, as I have promised."

"Then I shall simply forbid you from leaving the house, or follow you, and you know with my sight I will find you."

"You cannot forbid me from leaving the house," she

scoffed. "I will simply ignore you and leave anyway. Besides, you do not usually need to know what I do during the day."

"Not entirely true," Dev said. Since she'd had her heart broken, he'd been much more diligent.

She picked up her toast and proceeded to break it into bits on her plate.

"It is not that I do not want to tell you, but that I have promised not to speak of it to anyone."

"Because it will put someone at risk?"

She nodded, and a small kernel of thought entered his head.

"Risk of exposure to society or another kind of risk?"

"The first."

"So it is a person of noble birth that you are protecting?"

"I have no wish to discuss it further."

"However, you will."

Her sigh was loud.

"It is a good deed this person is doing, and I simply wish to help her. I assure you there is nothing nefarious at foot here, Dev."

"You don't have a nefarious bone in your body; however, there are plenty of people who do. Now, as, if my hunch is accurate, this outing concerns Miss Braithwaite, then let me assure you I would not feel comfortable if you are visiting somewhere that houses her children," he lied.

He had no problem with his sister seeing Lilliana; the problem lay in the fact that he wanted to see her too.

His sister chewed her lip.

"Let's hear it."

"I am going to drop some things to her, and as I know of her house, I am taking them there."

"Her house?"

"Well, she did not directly tell me of her involvement, other than acknowledging that she visits there, but I believe there is more to it than that. She certainly seemed knowledgeable about it when we spoke on the matter."

"And where is this house, and what will you and Miss Braithwaite be doing there?"

He was subjected to a very frank appraisal from his sister, her green eyes telling him his casual question was anything but. However, she chose not to needle him, a heroic gesture for a Sinclair.

"It is in Temple Street, the house I told you I saw her at. It is a place for sick or injured children who have nowhere else to go. I told her I knew of it and she was not pleased. But after I explained I wished to help in any capacity, she organized for me to visit today."

"Essie, I—"

"I am not proposing to leap recklessly into danger, Dev. I asked Miss Braithwaite, or rather Lilliana, as she told me to call her, if I could help with caring for the sick children. Dev, I want to do this. I miss healing like I did at home."

"You know it's only because I worry about you that I am concerned."

Again he was subjected to a steady look. He wondered when she had perfected that, as it hadn't had quite that degree of penetration before. Perhaps after that bastard broke her heart? Did having your heart broken mean you found determination in the face of so much pain? The idea of her suffering made him feel sick.

Her sigh was loud and long and it made him smile.

"I know it is and I love you the more for it, brother. Yet I need to do things, Dev, and I truly care for these children, as it seems does Lilliana. I have our little ones, yet they do not need me all the time, and when Aunt and Uncle get back they will want to spend time with them also."

"Are you lonely without Eden?"

She thought about that one for a while. He watched as she

lifted her cup and drank slowly. She was so slight he could wrap his fingers around her wrist and they would overlap.

"Sometimes, and yet I visit with Emily often."

"Really, do you not find that hard?"

It was James's half brother Tolly who'd broken Essie's heart. As James was married to their sister Eden, it tended to complicate matters, or so he had thought. Tolly had wooed Essie but his intent had been to get at his half brother, a feat he had nearly accomplished. After Tolly died, James and Eden had taken his sister, Emily, in to live with them.

"I like Emily, and am glad she has a family now. She loves Samantha dearly, too."

Dev smiled as he thought about Lady Samantha Raven. Although their mothers were different, the Duke and his sister were raised by their father. He had mistreated them both terribly. She had been timid, but now, he was pleased to say, she was anything but.

"It is hard for Emily, as not only is she illegitimate but also born into poverty, and explaining this to Samantha is not easy."

"James is convinced that he wants Emily to enter society, yet I wonder how hard that will be for her."

"The bastard child of a duke," Essie said. "Very hard, I should think, even with all of us and James's title behind her."

"Greetings, fellow Sinclairs," Cam said, entering the room. "Is it not a day of incredible beauty? Let me at the food!"

"Why, suddenly, do I have indigestion?"

"Harsh, brother, and unnecessary," Cam said, giving his sister a kiss before walking to the sideboard and sniffing loudly.

While to most this would be bad manners, the Sinclairs were used to it from their brother, as his heightened sense was smell.

"You do realize that your shirt points will blind you should you impale yourself upon them."

"I'll have you know," Cam said around a mouth full of ham, "that I am considered quite an arbiter of fashion."

"By who?" Dev said as Essie giggled.

"Many. In fact, Lord Cooper asked if he could have the name of my tailor just last night."

"No doubt so he could avoid him at all costs."

"Jealousy is an ugly trait." Cam sat with a plate over-flowing with food. "What are you two discussing?"

"This and that," Dev said.

"My favorite topic of conversation."

"We were discussing what I am doing today and then moved on to Emily," Essie added.

"Now there's a thought to spoil a perfectly good day," Cam groused.

"She is a lovely young lady, Cam, and it wouldn't hurt you to be nicer to her."

"She is about as interesting as a dishrag, Ess, and looks little better. The woman looks at me as if I am about to ravish her whenever I draw near. Seriously, you can tell her that her virtue is safe with me."

"That is nasty, Cambridge, and not worthy of you!" Essie snapped.

Dev kept out of the discussion brewing. Essie was more than capable of handling Cam, and in fact it was nice to see her spirit.

"I don't like her. How she can be James's sister is beyond me."

"What's not to like?" Dev had to ask. "Emily is polite and well-spoken; in fact there are few women who are easier to converse with."

Color filled Cam's cheeks as he shifted in his seat. Dev

and Essie kept their eyes trained on him, enjoying his obvious discomfort.

"She called me a man of little sense and no morals."

"And the problem with that statement is?" Dev drawled.

"Go to hell."

"What did you do to her, Cam?" Essie asked, ignoring her brother's blasphemy.

He looked at his food then at his cup of tea then back down at his food before answering. "Why do I have to have done anything? The woman's a termagant."

If you wanted to survive as a Sinclair, you learned your siblings' weaknesses and exploited them when the moment presented itself. Cam's biggest weakness was that he hated silence. Therefore, Essie and Dev stayed silent and continued eating.

"I won't tell you."

Dev swallowed his smile and winked at his sister. They would not have to wait long.

"I told her that she would never find herself a husband looking the way she does!"

Now that, Dev hadn't expected. "Cam, you are an idiot!"

"It came out wrong," he said, looking sheepish.

"One wonders how that could come out right," Dev said, lowering his fork. "Remember, brother, make sure your brain is engaged before your mouth."

"It was early," Cam said, waving around his fork. "I hadn't eaten anything for hours."

"Now that I seriously doubt," Essie said, getting to her feet.

"The woman has a way of getting under my skin. It's all that meek-mannered stuff; it grates on me."

Dev, who had also risen, looked down at his brother long enough that the younger Sinclair lowered his eyes.

"Miss Tolly has had a life even you could never understand, Cambridge. She has been subjected to poverty and starvation and most probably ridicule. Her nature is, I am sure, a direct result of that."

Cam squirmed in his seat as Dev continued.

"She is now related to us by the union of our sister to her brother. Therefore she is family and under our protection. I will say nothing further, only that were one of our sisters treated to such shabby manners you would likely seek retribution."

Cam sighed then looked at his brother. "You do that better than any person I know."

"Do what?"

"Serve up a scolding without raising your voice. I am now duly shamed and will seek to apologize with haste."

"Excellent. Now, Essie and I are going out. The children are with their tutor until lunchtime. If you want to join them, I'm sure they will welcome your presence."

Cam thought about Dev's words then nodded. "I wonder if they've had story time yet."

Essie laughed as she followed Dev from the room.

"I don't believe I invited you to accompany me to visit with Miss Braithwaite, Dev. Perhaps you dancing with her and that other incident that happened the other night will go some way toward changing your dislike of each other. However, I don't think she'd want you knowing about the house in Temple Street."

Following his sister silently down the stairs to the front entrance, he thought about his words.

"It is my duty to ensure your safety, sister, and to do that I need to see where it is you go. Starting with Temple Street."

Essie scoffed, then snorted as she put on her jacket, hat, and gloves.

"Do you honestly believe I will fall for that line? You are

51

interested in Miss Braithwaite, no matter how much you deny it."

Taking his time, he too put on his hat and gloves before answering.

"I have no idea what you are referring to. There is also the small matter of her choice of clothing. I could never befriend a woman who wears mustard and brown together." Dev faked a shudder.

Essie looked at him for several seconds and then, smiling, she patted his hand and walked out the front door. Dev followed, not liking the look on her face one bit.

CHAPTER 6

*L*illy woke slowly and lay in the dark for long minutes, remembering her dreams. The children had been screaming and running, trying to evade a man whose face she could not identify. Desperate to reach them, she had run too, but could never quite catch up to them. Then he had been there, Lord Sinclair. Like some dark avenging angel, he had protected the children and her.

What did that mean? Throwing back the covers, she swung her legs out of bed.

"It means he is occupying far too many of your thoughts, and it must stop."

That kiss had disturbed her, and not just because it was the first one that had not repulse her. Her reaction to that man was terrifying. Lilly didn't touch people; she'd learned early in her life that the results were not pleasing, so she kept her gloves on at all times. But him, Lord Sinclair, he had touched her face and neck, kissed her lips, and Lord, the sensations had been beyond anything she could describe. A thousand tiny feelings had traveled through her body, and

Lilly had been a slave to them, to him, within seconds. *Never again*, she vowed.

"I will have a tray in my room, Bee," she said as her maid opened the curtains.

"Your brother wishes you to come down for breakfast, Miss Braithwaite."

Groaning, Lilly buried her head in the pillow.

"Why? What is Nicholas doing out of bed at such an hour?"

Her maid was tall and willowy, but Lilly had realized that in the case of Beatrice Moulds, appearances were deceiving. The woman was as strong as a carthorse.

"As to that, I am unsure. However your aunt will also be there."

Lilly stripped off her nightdress and stepped into the steaming tub of water. Her family rarely ate together. She and Aunt Vi usually, but never Nicholas, as he was sleeping off whatever night of depravity he had participated in.

"We leave for Temple Street immediately I finish my morning meal, Bee, so please be ready."

They were to meet Essex Sinclair there. And while Lilly was not comfortable about the fact she was Lord Sinclair's sister, there was little she could do about the matter, as her hand had been forced.

She dressed and walked to the breakfast parlor.

"Your family are seated, Miss Braithwaite."

"Thank you, Hopkins."

"You are late!"

Ignoring her brother because she knew it would annoy him, Lilly kissed her aunt's cheek.

"Good morning, Aunt Vi."

"Hello, darling. I trust you slept well?"

"Indeed I did."

Their mother's sister, Lady James, had come to live with

them after Lilly's parents' deaths, as her children had set up their own homes and had no need of her. Gentle and sweet-natured, she was the perfect chaperone for Lilly, because she was happy to let her come and go as she pleased from the house.

Taking her seat, she nodded to the maid to pour her tea.

"I have gathered everyone here this morning to make an announcement."

"One hopes it takes you from the house for an extended period of time," Lilly said, reaching for the toast.

She and her brother had once been friends, but all that changed when their father had passed away and Nicholas began to believe himself too important to spend time with her.

"I will ignore that statement in favor of my own," he said in a haughty voice. "I have decided, Lilliana, you will marry before this season is over, and I have selected your bridegroom."

Lowering her knife, Lilly looked up. "I beg your pardon?" *Stay calm, Lilly.*

"You are twenty-five and it is well past time for you to marry."

Where she was fair, he was dark, his eyes almost black. Taller than her, he was a man who carried no spare weight, and clothes sat well on his lean body. She knew plenty of women who certainly thought so.

"Why the concern for my unmarried state now, Nicholas, when you never usually care for anyone but yourself?"

"It is time," he snapped. "You are a disgrace to me."

Lilly's grandmother had left her money that she received in a small yearly sum until her twenty-sixth year. This she spent on the children and Temple Street. The rest would come to her as long as she did not marry first. If she did, it stayed in her family, as she would have no need of it—or so her grandmother had believed.

This was why Lilly had taken pains to remain unattractive when she entered society, not entirely sure whether Nicholas would force her to wed whoever he wished simply to get his hands on her money.

One more year and she would receive her money and set up house on her own. Then she would be rid of him, and could live her life as she chose to. Until today, her plans had been working well.

"Lord Danderfield has inferred he will offer for you soon, and I have told him you will accept."

"What?" The toast she had just swallowed threatened to choke her. "You cannot force me to wed, Nicholas."

Her brother's eyes narrowed.

"I can, actually. As no one has offered for you in three seasons, sister, I have decided to take control of the matter. It is time you were taken in hand."

Stay calm, Lilly.

"Why all of a sudden does this concern you, Nicholas?" Lilly looked at her brother. There had to be a reason; she just needed to find out what. "Father left behind plenty of money; surely you do not need mine also?"

He kept his eyes steady on hers, but she saw something flicker, and then it was gone. Shooting her aunt a look, Lilly noticed she did not look happy. However, she would never naysay Nicholas. He scared her; Lilly was sure of it.

"I have no wish to marry and have my sister still in my household. Therefore, I have decided you will wed Danderfield, and that is all that I will say on the matter."

"What's happened, Nicholas? For two years you were more than happy with me running your household and ensuring the right amount of starch was in your neckties, and suddenly now you are happy to marry me off to a man old enough to be my grandfather."

"It is my duty as your brother to see you comfortable and well cared for."

"Well cared for," Lilly scoffed. "With Danderfield? Surely you jest."

"My mind is made up!" he roared.

She realized then. "You've spent it all, haven't you?"

"Lilliana," this came from her aunt. "I think you have said enough. Your brother wishes only your happiness."

"No, he doesn't, Aunt Vi. He cares nothing about you or me, only himself, isn't that right, Nicholas." Her brother would not meet her eyes. "And he has now gambled every cent of my father's money away and wants mine. But he won't get it," Lilly vowed, climbing to her feet. "I will fight you with everything I have at my disposal, Nicholas. So if you pursue this, be ready for a battle!"

"I am your guardian!" he thundered, rising also. "You will do as I bloody well say!"

"I will not be sacrificed on the altar of your greed, brother, so you can continue to live your licentious lifestyle. If you think I will marry a man old enough to be my grandfather, you can think again."

Lilly then walked slowly to the door and left the room with her brother roaring at her to stay.

By the time she had reached her room, her hands were shaking and her knees weak. Lilly had never had an encounter like that with her Nicholas, simply because she took the path of least resistance, and before today, he had left her alone. He could do as he said, she knew that. He had the power, but she would not let him win.

"Are you unwell, Miss Braithwaite?"

"I'm fine, Bee, just thinking," Lilly said as she paced around her room.

"What did your brother say to take the color from your cheeks? You're whiter than a ghost."

"He said lots of things, as he always does. Now don't fuss, and let us get ready to leave."

Bee helped Lilly into her coat and bonnet. Grabbing her gloves and reticule, she then left the room with her maid on her heels.

Nicholas was about to leave the house also as she arrived at the front door. Ignoring him, Lilly walked past.

"Where are you going?"

"None of your business," she snapped

"Lilliana, as your brother—"

"Brother? That statement is laughable, Nicholas." Lilly kept her voice low, having no wish for the servants to over-hear their conversation. "Brothers care for their siblings. You, however, care only for yourself."

He reached for her, trying to stop her leaving the house, but she stepped to the side, out of range, and continued walking. She did not stop until she was seated inside the carriage her grandmother had left her. She felt her brother's eyes on her as the carriage pulled from the drive, but she did not look back.

Lord Danderfield, the man her brother proposed she wed, was nearing seventy and natured like Nicholas. Lilly could imagine her existence should she yield and marry the man. Why did he want her? Surely he did not need the money of her dowry, as she knew he had wealth and estates, so what was his motivation? Or more importantly, what bribe had her brother offered him to offer for her?

Thoughts spiraled in hopeless circles around her head on the short journey across town. Finally she forced them aside as the carriage pulled up outside the little house. Taking the five steps up to the neat brown front door, Lilly looked up at the property that she alone owned. *Mine*, she thought, feeling the cold knot inside her begin to unravel. *He can never take this from me*. Lifting a gloved hand, she knocked.

"Miss Braithwaite, the door is always open, especially to you."

Mr. Davey stood before her with his perpetual smile in place. Short and stout with a sprinkling of gray hair, the man could lift her spirits with just a look.

"This is your home, Mr. Davey." Lilly stepped inside. They had this conversation every time she called. "I own it, but you live in it. Therefore, you deserve to open the door to callers who knock."

He harrumphed, as he always did.

"A Miss Sinclair is due to call in an hour. I shall be in the parlor by then, going over the accounts, so show her in there, please."

"Of course."

After removing her coat and bonnet, she handed both to him.

"Come, Bee, we should have time for a cup of tea before Miss Sinclair arrives, as I missed breakfast."

The kitchens at Temple Street were one of Lilly's favorite places to visit. Walking down the long pale blue hall, she noted the table with a vase bursting with a jumble of flowers. Such a small thing, yet beautiful in its simplicity, unlike the flowers arranged to perfection in her brother's house. Turning left, Lilly took the stairs down.

"Good morning, Mrs. Davey," Lilly said, smiling to the woman standing at the bench with her hands in a bowl of something. Built like her husband, she had thick red hair and bright blue eyes that never missed a thing.

"Good morning, Miss Braithwaite, Bee."

Pulling out her flour-covered hands, she wiped them on a cloth. "You take a seat and I'll have you both a nice cup of tea and cinnamon bun ready in minutes."

Lilly loved this room; it was always warm and smelled of so many delightful scents. Often Mrs. Davey was singing or laughing, and it was a place she had spent many happy hours in. It was a hive of activity, even though only one person worked in it.

"I would love a cinnamon bun, if you have one spare."

"Of course I have one spare for you, Miss Braithwaite."

After securing the house in Temple Street, Lilly had had Wilson seek out the perfect couple to run it, and it had been he who recommended the Daveys. The couple had been the perfect fit.

"Sit."

Lilly ignored the seat Mrs. Davey waved her to, and moved to sit on the bench. With a small leap, she landed on the surface.

"I'm sure sitting on a bench swinging your legs is not proper behavior for a young lady of your station," Mrs. Davey clucked.

"And yet I have been doing it for many months now," Lilly said, moving her legs slowly back and forth. She wasn't sure why she enjoyed sitting up there, but she did. Perhaps because she rarely got to behave in such a way, or perhaps because this house was hers, and she could do as she wished in it. "Besides, being a lady is not always easy. There are so many rules and etiquette to follow. It is just nice to swing one's legs occasionally."

"I'm sure there is a deeper meaning in there," Bee said, taking down cups.

Lilly just being allowed in this room had been a major step. The Daveys, at first, had treated her like royalty, and drinking tea with a woman of noble birth had taken something of an adjustment. The first time she'd leaped onto the bench, Mrs. Davey had nearly had conniptions.

"Here's your tea, Miss Braithwaite."

"Thank you, Mrs. Davey."

"That mark on your chin has faded some, but it's still a nice plum color."

Sipping tea, Lilly was soon chatting with the ladies and realized that if one day this was the place she was forced to flee to, she would be quite happy about that. Because one thing Lilly knew with absolute conviction was that she would not wed Lord Danderfield. To ensure her brother did not force her, and that she remained single until she reached her twenty-sixth year, she may have to hide, and this would be the perfect place.

CHAPTER 7

"*M*ust you come inside, Dev? You can see it is not a house of ill repute or some seedy establishment that I will never return from," Essie said, exasperated as Dev followed her up the stairs to the little brick house. "Miss Braithwaite was not happy that I knew of its existence, so I can only imagine how she is going to feel now you know."

She had been singing this particular tune the entire journey across town, and he had told her in no uncertain terms that he was not leaving until he had seen inside. Of course his main reason was to see Lilliana again, but he wasn't telling his sister that.

"I see a brick façade, Essex, behind which anything could be housed," Dev said in a reasonable tone that made her teeth snap together.

"She may not have even arrived yet. Then what will you do?"

"Who?"

"I will slap you in a minute, Devonshire Sinclair, just see if I don't!" Essie snapped.

"Such unladylike behavior, Essex." Dev tut-tutted, because when a Sinclair had an opening to needle a sibling he took it.

"You, sir, are a dastardly cur!"

"I do believe that hurt, Essex."

"Oaf."

"Now that's more like the sister I know and love," he said, and then gave a bark of laughter as she poked her tongue out at him.

Standing back as she knocked on the front door, he watched it open. The man who appeared was neatly dressed and wore a gentle smile that made his own lips twitch to respond.

"Surely a murderous individual," his sister hissed at him. Dev smiled, but did not reply.

"My name is Miss Sinclair and this is my brother, Lord Sinclair. We have come to see Miss Braithwaite."

"Miss Braithwaite told me to expect your arrival, Miss Sinclair. Please come this way. She is at present taking tea in the kitchens, but told me to see you to the parlor. I shall collect her."

"Tea. Dear God, run for your lives," Essie muttered. "Taking tea is such a dangerous pastime."

"Careful you don't cut the inside of your mouth with that tongue, sister."

"Oh, please do not disturb her. Perhaps we could simply take tea there also?" Essie said, smiling.

"Oh, I-I'm not sure that would be right." He looked worried, and Dev thought he was unused to receiving visitors such as they. Deciding he wanted to see Lilliana Braithwaite taking tea in the kitchens, he said, "Please lead on, sir. My sister wishes to take tea in the kitchens."

The man moved at his command, and Dev motioned Essie to follow. He heard a woman's laughter as they drew near, the sound carefree and light, and he knew it was her because his body tensed in expectation. Drawing in a deep breath, Dev forced himself to appear calm as he walked into the kitchen.

Miss Lilliana Braithwaite was seated on the kitchen bench, swinging her legs like a child while eating a large bun. Her face was turned in profile, but even with his limited view he saw the genuine smile she was bestowing on the two other women in the room. It was open and natural and held him motionless.

God, she was sweet.

"Miss Braithwaite."

She turned as Essex spoke, the smile falling from her face as she saw him. The heat from the kitchens had put color in her cheeks, and sugar dotted to her lips. Dev battled the impulse to close the distance between them and lick it off.

"Wh-what are you doing here?"

The bun fell from her hands as she scrambled to climb off the bench. In her haste she nearly landed in a tangle of limbs on the floor. Stumbling several steps, she managed to remain upright.

"Forgive me for bringing him."

Dev watched his sister hurry forward to clasp Lilliana's fingers, but she quickly pushed them behind her back so Essie was forced to touch her arm instead.

"I know you have no wish for anyone to know of Temple Street, but he forced me to tell him."

Dev withstood glares from both women.

"He wanted to check that I was not going anywhere dangerous."

She still did not face him directly, but Dev kept his eyes on the delightfully flustered Lilliana. Unlike her choice of gowns in the evenings, this one was a simple cream muslin day dress with small blue flowers. The material did not swamp her figure, and allowed him to see what he had already guessed: Lilliana Braithwaite was a curved and lush bundle of woman. Her hair was pulled back into a bun and adorned with nothing more sinister than a blue velvet band that circled her head.

Dev watched as she retrieved her gloves from the bench behind her and hastily pulled them on, then her glasses.

"Oh please, don't—"

"I like to wear gloves in company."

She cut Essie's words off, and Dev wondered at her need to cover her hands. Were they scarred in some way, or was she simply a lady who did not like to have people touching her?

"Oh, well then." Essie looked uncomfortable. "I am truly sorry he is here." She scowled at Dev once more.

"Please do not fuss, Miss Sinclair. Your brother is protective toward you, and I cannot fault that."

"Essex, please."

Dev watched as she smoothed the fingers of her gloves in little agitated movements.

"My secret is out, it seems."

"Secret?" Dev queried, realizing that once again her voice appeared different from the high, grating tone she used in the evenings.

Reluctantly she turned to face him. "I run a high-class brothel here, Lord Sinclair, and as you can see Mrs. Davey is my highest-paid girl." Enjoying her new role, the housekeeper erupted into giggles. "And it is my intention to recruit your sisters."

Dev's eyes went to the bruise she had received that night he had caught her. The night that had started his intrigue with this woman.

"It is changing color," he said, moving closer and running his thumb over her chin. He wanted to touch her, needed to see if his reaction to her had been merely a single experience.

It wasn't. He dropped his hand. It tingled.

"You can leave now, my lord, your sister is safe here." She backed away from him.

"I protect what is mine, Miss Braithwaite, and I will not apologize for checking my sister's movements."

Her eyes were amazing this close. Even through the small round lenses, he could see the pale lavender color.

"Well as you can see, I am not bent on anything that will harm your sister, so you may leave."

"Take your guests to the front parlor, Miss Braithwaite, and I will bring tea."

"That won't be necessary, as Lord Sinclair is leaving."

She wanted him gone, and as far away from her as possible.

"I have nothing pressing until this afternoon, Miss Braithwaite, and if Mrs. Davey has a spare cinnamon bun on hand then I would very much like to stay for tea." Dev followed up his words with a smile, and the housekeeper giggled, as did the maid.

"Stop flirting with Lilliana's staff," Essie hissed.

"Lord Sinclair is leaving," Lilliana said, standing still.

"He wishes for tea and one of my cinnamon buns, Miss Braithwaite. Surely you can allow him that?"

Dev could see she did not want to allow him anything.

"Will you show me around your house, Miss Braithwaite? Perhaps I can offer my assistance in some way to aid your charitable works?" he said.

"No," she said, and then she sighed. "Follow me," she added ungraciously and turned to leave the room.

She stomped up the first and second steps, and Dev felt it was time to extend the hand of friendship and hope she did not use it to beat him over the head repeatedly.

"I know you would never hurt my sister, Miss Braithwaite, and ask that you forgive me if you believed otherwise."

Her shoulders remained rigid, and she did not respond to his overture.

"I'm sorry I misjudged you for so long. Essex has told me of your good deeds."

"And I am supposed to fall at your feet in gratitude." She rounded on him at the top of the stairs. "You are an arrogant, judgmental man."

"All true, to be fair," came his sister's reply from over his shoulder.

"Yes, thank you, Essex," Dev muttered. "You judged me too, Lilliana," he added, looking at her, their eyes now level.

Her eyes narrowed. "How?"

"You just said I was rude and judgmental, yet have never spoken to me to find out if indeed that was true." Dev congratulated himself on his comeback as he stopped on the step below hers. All he had to do was lean forward....

"I have watched you, as you no doubt have watched me, and you are a man who likes his own way... always. And we have spoken, just a few nights ago."

She blushed at the memory, but did not look away.

"Also true."

"Yes, thank you, Essie, I don't think she needs your encouragement. Will you show me around your house, Lilliana? Please?"

"I gave you no leave to call me Lilliana." She then turned and walked down the hall and into a small parlor.

"Perhaps, seeing as you are meant to be on my side, sister, you could endeavor to paint me in a more flattering light?"

Dev took Essie's arm as they followed.

"What do I get?"

"I'll take you to that exhibition in the park with all those herbs and flowers you have been harping on about."

"Done."

His sister patted his arm and sailed past him into the

room, leaving him shaking his head at the mercenary nature of his siblings.

The parlor was painted in pale blue as the hall had been, and furnished simply yet comfortably.

"Will you tell me about the boy you rescued the other night, Lilliana?" Dev and Essie sat while Lilliana moved to stand behind a chair, her gloved hands gripping the back. It was a protective pose, and he hated that she felt the need to do so in his company, yet understood why. A few nights ago he had kissed her senseless.

"You have obviously furnished your sister with the details of that incident?"

She wasn't pleased about that.

"I do not have secrets from my siblings."

Essie, for once, held her tongue.

"You must know it was reckless of you to be out at such an hour, on those streets, with only a footman at your back."

"How I conduct myself, my lord, is of no concern to you. Therefore I would ask you to keep your opinions to yourself. In fact, unlike the ballrooms, this is my property, and I do not have to tolerate your presence. Therefore I wish you would leave."

"I did not know you owned it."

She realized how much she'd given away in anger, her eyes going from him to Essex. But the thought did not subdue her for long. "Of course I own it. I would not be taking tea in the kitchens otherwise!"

Dev wasn't sure how one led to the other but instead smiled politely. How had she raised the funds to purchase this place? He doubted that fool she had for a brother gave her a penny toward it.

"I think you should leave."

"I would rather stay," Dev said politely, which made her teeth snap together.

"Will you show me around your house, Lilliana?" Essie threw her brother a look he could not interpret, which was nothing new; his sisters were a constant mystery to him. "My brother will follow but keep his comments to himself, and let me assure you that, while he can be annoying, he is the best of men most of the time."

Lilliana's eyes darted from Essie to him and back again. So many emotions chased through the lavender depths it was impossible to decipher each.

"All right, I will show you around. However I have no wish to hear any words of criticism or condemnation from you, Lord Sinclair."

Essie laughed with delight as Lilly finished speaking. "Oh, what a treat it is to have another female put you in your place, brother dearest."

"I shall endeavor to behave," Dev drawled. He then mouthed, "D*eal's off*" to his sister when Lilly turned away.

"Please follow me."

Temple Street was three floors. The lower housed the kitchens, and the second was Mr. and Mrs. Davey's living accommodations. The third, where they currently stood, was for the children who came to be cared for. Everything was scrupulously clean and bright, Dev thought, looking at the green curtains in the room they had just entered.

"Hello, Sam, how are you feeling today? Is your leg still hurting you?"

The small boy was dressed in a blue nightshirt and tucked into the third bed in a row of five. Behind him were plump, colored pillows, and over his legs a blanket of red wool. Beside him lay several books and an odd-shaped soft thing that looked like a multicolored pillow; however, Dev was sure he noted a set of ears poking out the top. He was pale and thin and his eyes held more shadows than a child's should. He had existed on streets filled with sights that would make most people shudder, and his face bore the markings of that struggle.

"Sam had an accident and hurt his leg as he fell from a rooftop," Lilliana said.

Dev had two weaknesses in his life: his family and children. Looking at Lilliana, he had a feeling deep inside that he was about to expand those to three, but as yet was unsure how he felt about that.

He couldn't cope with children in pain, and often struggled to mask his emotions when he saw a child dressed in rags on the streets, or one being mistreated. He gave money where he could, did whatever was in his capacity to do, yet knew the problem was far greater than that. The issue needed to be brought to the attention of those who woke daily in soft beds and large houses.

"It is not hurting near as much, Lilly, and Mrs. Davey says I'll be up out of bed in a while. Mr. Davey read me a story last night."

Lilly. The name suited her, Dev thought as he watched the boy's eyes shoot first to Essie then him. He wasn't comfortable in their presence, and who could blame him? Gentry in his eyes were people who cared little for the plight of the child who lived on the street.

To his surprise, Lilliana sat on his bed and stroked the boy's hair, then examined the pillow with ears. Sam leaned into her and Dev could see trust in the gesture. They shared a genuine delight in each other's company that should not have been there. A boy from the streets and a lady born into society. He wondered what had forced her onto this path. What secrets was she hiding? Shame washed over him again for his treatment of her. The woman before him was far from empty-headed. She had simply been hiding the real Lilliana from society.

"By any chance, Sam, is that a Bulgularas two-eared

Daturmond?" Dev pointed to the squishy thing with ears. "You see, I have twin sisters and a small brother who would be delighted to own one just the same."

Sam snuffled and then lifted the squishy thing for Dev's inspection.

"Good grief, it is," Dev said, reaching over Lilly's head to take the offering. "What you have here, Sam, is very rare indeed."

This time the boy giggled, sounding like every small boy should, and the sound made Dev's heart lighten.

Lilly didn't want to feel any harmony with the dark and dangerous lord, but watching Sam smile as Lord Sinclair continued to tell him a ludicrous tale about the Bulgularas two-eared Daturmond, she felt something unfamiliar stir in her chest.

Lilly did not feel things for people other than her children. Yes, she cared for her aunt, Mr. and Mrs. Davey, and Bee, then there was Wilson, but no one had ever really made her fingers and toes tingle the way looking at and touching Lord Sinclair did.

"They eat only the rarest form of Daturmond seeds, found only three nights a year on the first three days of the Bulgularas Festival."

"Where do the seeds grow?"

"Well now, that's the real problem, Sam."

She watched Lord Sinclair take the seat Lilly vacated.

"Dev is very good with children, Lilliana." Essie led her to the window. "He is a master storyteller and believe me, he has had plenty of practice over the years."

Lilly sat at the small table in one of the chairs and watched Sam laugh as Lord Sinclair continued with his tale.

She didn't want to like him, yet she had to admit he was good with children.

He was disturbing, and unsettled her. Finding her in the kitchens, swinging her legs as she ate a cinnamon bun had not been an ideal start, especially as she was determined after what they had shared in that conservatory that he would see only the persona she donned for society. That idea had not worked. Lilly couldn't find it in herself to be silly here. No simpering or gushing, not at Temple Street. Here, she was simply the person she wanted to be.

"An ideal elder brother, then."

"Oh yes, I cannot fault him, even though his faults are many."

Lilly tried to stifle the flash of jealousy she felt as Essie threw her brother a fond look. Her brother cared nothing for her.

"I am knitting some hats with scarves as a trial for your children, and will send them over when they are finished."

Lilly turned her attention away from the disturbing nobleman and equally disturbing thoughts running through her head to focus on his sister. She and Essie discussed the children's needs.

"How many children do you watch over, Lilly?"

"In truth, there are many who need help. However, some of them are too scared to come forward when they are in trouble or unwell. Those that do are usually desperate and have little choice."

"Do they come here or must you always go into the streets to find them?"

"One of the boys, Toby, lives here with Mr. and Mrs. Davey. He was injured and has stayed ever since," Lilly said, shooting a quick look at Sam. He would not stay here; she would see him safe to one of her family's estates. Unlike Toby, he would not refuse to go.

"He is my eyes and ears. The children go to him if they need me, and he takes things to them. Sometimes I will go to a place that I know is safe to see them. When winter arrives, some of the cold nights send them here. Mr. and Mrs. Davey will feed them, and let them sleep in the kitchens when the beds are full."

"It must be hard for you to leave here after the season," Essex said.

Lilly nodded. In fact, it was unbearable to leave London with her family and retire to her brother's estate. Mrs. Davey wrote with updates on how the children were doing, yet it was not enough. One more year and she would be able to do as she wished—if she could stay unmarried, that was.

They talked for a while longer and then Sam called her back to the bed.

"Did you enjoy that story, Sam?" Lilly said.

"Yes, and Lord Sinclair is going to come back soon and tell me another one."

"Is he?"

"I have promised the boy. Therefore I will deliver on that promise, Lilliana."

He had moved to stand beside her and Lilly fought the urge to shuffle away. This man had kissed her—really kissed her—and she had felt it to the soles of her feet.

"Toby was here this morning, Lilly, and he says another boy is missing."

"When did it happen?" Lilly took Sam's fingers and held them tight. She had not stopped this happening as she had promised.

"Last night. They got little Teddy this time. He just vanished like the others, and no one knows where to."

Aware that the Sinclairs were listening, Lilly lowered her voice.

"It's all right, Sam. I will pay another visit to the local

Watch House to look into it, and demand that someone investigates the matter at once. But right now it is most important that you rest and heal."

"Toby said to tell you he was going out to see if anyone had heard anything. He'll come back later and tell you what he's learned or send you a message."

"All right. Now, you sleep and I will come and see you before I go."

She hugged Sam and kissed the top of his head. Unlike the adults in her life, her children expected nothing from her but what was in her power to give.

"Good day, Sam."

"Good day to you, Lord Sinclair, Miss Sinclair."

Lilly closed the door softly behind them as they left Sam to rest. She led the way back downstairs, and this time she would insist Lord Sinclair depart. She did not want him in her house a second longer.

CHAPTER 8

"What was Sam talking about, Lilliana?" Essex asked as they reached the parlor door on their way to the front door. "Is it connected with what took place the other night with Dev?"

"It matters not." She dismissed the words and took another step, but a hand stopped her.

"Perhaps we could help with this problem?"

"It is my problem, Lord Sinclair."

"I have brought the tea."

"Lord Sinclair was just leaving, Mrs. Davey." Lilly tried to head off her housekeeper.

"I cannot leave without eating one of those buns, Mrs. Davey. In fact, I am half tempted to move into Temple Street myself, if this is the standard of fare I would be assured."

Lilly doubted the housekeeper would fall for such obvious flattery, yet when she glanced at the woman, her cheeks were flushed and she was beaming.

"It is an honor, my lord, to have a healthy appetite in the house. We do not have many visitors."

Lilly could hardly stay in the hall when he and his sister were making their way back into the parlor behind Mrs. Davey, but she wanted to. In fact, she was tempted to walk out the front door and leave them there.

"Can I pour you a cup, Miss Braithwaite?"

"No thank you, Mrs. Davey."

"Does not eat near enough," Lilly heard the woman mutter as she left the room.

She did not want to sit, because that gave Lord Sinclair a target to look at and she did not feel comfortable under his disturbing gaze, so she walked around the room. Surely the height of rudeness when her guests sat, and yet she cared little about that. This was Temple Street; here she did not cater to the whims of others, only the children.

"How long have young children been going missing off the streets of London, and how came you to be chasing that man and rescuing one of them?"

Lord Sinclair asked the question.

"If I tell you, will you leave?"

"Tell us and then we shall see."

"Come, Lilliana. We only wish to help, nothing more. Tell us what is happening to those sweet children."

Lilly told them then, because of Essex Sinclair's words. They were children who needed all the help they could get, and perhaps in telling their story she would achieve that. Much as he unsettled her, Lord Sinclair had powerful people at his back, and with a word from him, those people may champion her cause also.

"Six children have now gone missing over the last four weeks. Wilson and I have called at the local Watch House after each abduction to alert them and ensure someone would look into the matter. However, I was dismissed each time as a hysterical woman. I then demanded to see whoever was in charge, but was merely waved away as if I were some addlepated woman with few wits."

"Well, it is fair to say that I, and others in society, believe you just that, Lilliana."

"Dev!" Essex Sinclair looked at her brother, horrified. Lilly, however, had the ridiculous urge to laugh. She swallowed it.

"I have no idea what you speak of."

He studied her.

"Your dresses are hideous, your hair would please any bird looking for a nest, and you speak like an empty-headed fool."

"Please do not hold back, my lord. It is my fondest wish to receive unwanted fashion advice from you. Not to mention slurs upon my character." Lilly was sure she should be angrier at his attack, and yet she wasn't. Perhaps because, for once, someone was seeing the real her.

"Dev, you are being rude."

"But truthful." He did not look at his sister but kept his eyes on Lilly.

"I have no wish to discuss this matter further. You wanted to hear about the missing children, and so I told you. I did not do so to offer you the opportunity to assassinate my character."

"Perhaps if you had stayed calm when speaking with the men at the Watch House, it may have helped."

Essex Sinclair groaned at her brother's words.

"How do you know I did not stay calm?" Lilly demanded. "It is extremely hard to stay calm when dealing with idiots. One of the men had the audacity to say it was a blessing to get a few of the children off the streets, like you would rid a home of vermin!"

He raised one hand. "I am not accusing you, just pointing

out that you will get nowhere if you do not stay calm and rational."

"I was entirely rational!"

Lilly looked at Essex when she snuffled.

"If you were this calm and rational, then I can imagine how the meeting at the Watch went, Lilly."

"Miss Braithwaite," she snapped. "Not Lilliana or Lilly!"

"Forgive me," he said, and the wicked look in his eyes did not appease her.

"I do not like people patronizing me, nor do I like men believing that because I don't wear pants I am therefore a fool."

"I shall remember not to make the same mistake."

Lilly did not like the way he phrased those words, as they suggested the future included more time spent in each other's company.

"He is always calm and rational," Essex then said, nodding to her brother. "It is most frustrating for the rest of his siblings."

"Someone has to be. We would continually be arguing if I did not put a stop to it."

Lilly watched him swallow another mouthful of what, by her count, was his third cinnamon bun. He would be an uncomfortable husband for whoever he married. Intimidating just by his large presence, and he would want control.

"Have you any idea at all about who has the children? Are there no whispers on the streets?"

"The other night, Toby heard a rumor that they were to take another child from the area we were in. So Wilson and I arrived to attempt to keep the children safe, and this time we succeeded. But we cannot watch them all."

"That was extremely foolhardy of you, Lilly. You could have been hurt or abducted yourself."

She waved his words away. "My concern is for the children, not myself. Toby is spreading the word that I will offer a reward for any news about whoever is behind this."

"Is that wise? Surely you will have any number of people calling here hoping to claim the reward?"

"I am not a fool, Lord Sinclair. All information will come through Toby."

"I never suggested you were a fool, Lilly."

His usual drawl had become more clipped as she challenged him. Good. Perhaps if he knew she was no meek and mild lady, he would stay away from her.

"My name is Miss Braithwaite," Lilly said. "Your sister can call me Lilliana, but that is because I like her!"

"I do believe that hurt." He rubbed his chest and tried to look wounded. Lilly was not fooled.

"Do you know all the missing boys, Lilly? It must be distressing for you," Essex Sinclair said, ignoring her brother.

"I know a few of them. But Teddy, the latest boy to go missing, was here last winter when he became sick."

"And you believe the children selected are random? Not all boys, or girls. Short or tall, large or small?"

"Randomly," Lilly said, looking reluctantly at Lord Sinclair as she addressed his question. "Are you thinking they are being taken for a specific reason?"

"What does your brother say on the matter? Perhaps if he were to intervene on

your—"

"My brother is a busy man, and knows nothing of this, and I would beg you to keep it that way. Lord Sinclair."

Lilly withstood the intense and searching look he leveled at her. She wondered what was in his thoughts.

"I understand, and of course my sister and I will say nothing on this matter to anyone, including your family. However, someone must accompany you to the Watch House today, preferably a man, as you have already determined that you alone, with a servant, will not be taken seriously."

"There is only your brother, aunt, and yourself, Lilliana?" Essex Sinclair sighed. "Imagine that, Dev, having only one sibling."

"There are a lot of you?" Lilly asked before she could stop herself. These people intrigued her.

"Seven in total."

"So many?" Lilly could not imagine sharing a house with seven people.

"I assure you there are benefits," Lord Sinclair drawled. "If you look hard enough."

Lilly looked to Essex. Surely he had just insulted her? But no, the woman was smiling at her brother.

"If your family is unable to accompany you, then I will."

Lilly took a few seconds to realize what he had said, as her thoughts were still on what it would be like to have so many siblings. But when she did, everything inside her rebelled.

No, no... no!

"Thank you, but I can manage on my own, my lord."

"I cannot let you travel to the Watch House on your own, Lilly."

"What a wonderful idea, Dev." Essex Sinclair smiled at him and then Lilly before she could once again refuse. "He is quite handy in most situations, and I'm sure he would excel in this one also."

"Thank you, darling."

"No, I have no wish for you to accompany me."

"We shall take your carriage, Lilly, and Essie will take mine, as she is to return home to our younger siblings."

"Oh, yes indeed." Essex Sinclair jumped to her feet, and her brother followed. "I had quite forgotten I am to take the children to the park this afternoon. Please forgive me, Lilliana, for not accompanying you."

"No, wait." Lilly followed. "There is no need for anyone to accompany me. I am not your concern, Lord Sinclair, and am more than capable of going on my own."

"I would never allow a woman to go into a Watch House on her own. As none of your family is here to protect you, I will accompany you."

Stay in control, Lilly.

"I need no protection, Lord Sinclair, and please address me correctly. I have dealt with many things on my own with some success, and this will be the same."

"And yet I will accompany you. I was there the other night, and can possibly be of some help."

He was smiling at her now, yet those eyes were darker. Perhaps he was not as composed as he appeared.

"No, I have my footman and maid, so I really must insist that you escort your sister home, my lord."

"I will accompany Lilly and her maid to the Watch House and then I shall summon a hackney and return home, Essex. Please tell the children I will visit with them then."

"No—"

"Argument is futile once he has made up his mind, Lilliana, and besides, he may prove useful in some capacity, even if it is to stand behind you and intimidate whoever you speak to. I wish you every luck, and will hear the details when Dev returns home."

She trailed behind the siblings to the door, wondering if it would be wrong to lock the door if she could get him to step outside.

"Our sister and her husband are due to return soon, and I am hoping you will come for dinner one evening, Lilly," Essex said, pulling on her gloves.

"Oh well—"

"Excellent."

She heard Lord Sinclair's deep laugh as she stood looking at the door his sister had just sailed through. They were incredibly forceful, these people.

"Argument is futile, I am afraid."

Frustrated, she glared at him. "This is highly improper, and I have no wish for you to accompany me. Should we be seen it would raise any number of questions."

"And running about London streets with children at dusk is the correct behavior for ladies, is it?"

"Are you threatening to expose me, my lord?"

He looked genuinely surprised by her words, followed by annoyance.

"I'm not sure how you came to that conclusion, but let me assure you that I do not tell tales. No matter how much I question your activities."

"You have no right to question anything about me!" Lilly felt her temper rise. Lord, this man was insufferable... and exhausting to be around.

"Perhaps not, but I am now aware of your reckless gadding about London streets, and I would be lying if I did not say I was concerned."

Truly baffled, she asked why.

"You are a lady of my acquaintance, and as such honor dictates I ensure you are safe."

"But we don't even like each other." His words made absolutely no sense.

He moved closer, taking one of her hands in his.

"We didn't like each other, but now we do."

His gentle smile disturbed her more than it should, and Lilly had a sinking feeling that she was on the precipice of something, but had no idea what. The tingling feeling in her fingers had her snatching back her hand.

"No." She shook her head. "I don't want to like you."

"But you do."

Dear God, she feared he was right, and that all the turmoil inside her was not because she loathed and detested him, but in fact because she liked him. Needing distance to draw a deep, calming breath, Lilly hurried to the kitchens to tell Bee they were leaving. Distance, she reminded herself. Distance would heal whatever madness was currently taking up residence inside her head.

Lilly looked out the carriage window as they journeyed to the Watch House. Lord Sinclair had attempted to converse with her, yet she had been equally determined to get their relationship back on the footing it had held for the last two years.

His words before they left Temple Street had disturbed her, and she knew he was right. She could like him, but she would not. Could not. Therefore, she would retreat.

"Those buns were the best I have tasted."

She looked at him, but his eyes were on Bee. A maid, for pity's sake. Did the man not know that noblemen did not converse with maids—not that she didn't converse with staff, but still, he was a lord.

"I could get the recipe for you, my lord. Mrs. Davey would not mind, I am sure."

"Could you indeed? I should be most obliged."

His eyes lit at the prospect, making him look less like an intimidating peer and more like an eager young boy.

"My younger siblings would enjoy them."

"How many of you are there, my lord? If you don't mind me asking?"

"Not at all, Miss…?"

"Just Bee, my lord."

Lilly watched her usually stoic maid smile. It took a great

deal to get such reaction from her in the normal course of a day.

"Well, Bee, I'm the eldest. My sister Essex comes next, and then Cambridge and Eden. We have a jump then to the twins, Dorset and Somerset, aged nine years, and lastly Warwickshire."

"And you are called Devonshire," Lilly said, intrigued despite herself.

"Yes, we are each named after a location in England. My parents traveled a lot." He finished with a shrug, looking at her.

"It must be very noisy."

Lilly saw the small laugh lines bracketing his mouth as he smiled, and those emerald-green eyes sparkled like the brightest gems. He was dangerous. Very dangerous, and she must always remember that fact. Men were not to be trusted.

"That, Bee, is an understatement. The noise is sometimes deafening, especially when we play games. It's the squealing; it gets into your eardrums and is mighty hard to dislodge."

"And you would have it no other way, my lord."

"Too true, Bee. I am indeed blessed to have so much love in my life."

It was petty of her to hate him for that statement, yet Lilly did.

"We have arrived," she said minutes later, relieved that she could get out of the carriage and away from him. He took up too much room with his long legs and large feet. Not to mention the smell of the man. Her brother wore some over-powering cologne, as did plenty of other men she knew, but not him. For some reason it reminded Lilly of the country-side. The trees, grass, earth. Inhaling his scent made her feel... alive.

.   .   .

Dev stepped down before Lilly, holding out a hand. She was forced to take it, and he lowered her to the ground.

"Come, Bee." She did not acknowledge him, instead addressing her maid.

"Yes, Miss Braithwaite."

Together they stood looking across the road at the brick façade. It was not a building that made a person take a second look. The windows were clean but unadorned, the five front steps painted gray.

"I understand your reasons for being here, Lilly, yet would caution you that it is highly unlikely you will receive the answers you seek yet again."

He would do what he could for her, yet she needed to know that it was very likely another fruitless endeavor they were embarking on.

"Perhaps if you have that attitude then it would be best if you stayed in the carriage. I shall leave Bee with you, so you may continue your cozy chat with her, Lord Sinclair."

"She is a most excellent conversationalist, to be sure. However, I have said I will accompany you, so I shall leave further discussions about cinnamon buns for another day."

"Don't laugh at me!"

"Then don't be ridiculous, and I shall not be forced to."

He reached for her arm as she stepped away from him, but she was too quick and started across the street. Dev turned to look for any approaching traffic. He saw the carriage and the intent face of the driver. Raising his whip, the man urged his horses faster. The street was busy, so he had no cause to be traveling at such speed.

Looking to where Lilly was in the middle of the road, Dev started in her direction. The carriage would not touch her on its present course, yet it would pay for her to increase her pace.

Throwing the driver another look, he then felt it again,

that sudden surge of desperation he had experienced twice in his life before. The carriage changed direction and veered toward Lilly.

"Run, Lilly!"

"Miss Braithwaite!" Bee's cry did not reach her either.

Head down, she continued walking. Dev started running, desperate to reach her and keep her safe. Seconds later she was in his arms. He took a huge leap that carried them to safety before the carriage flew past.

He cursed as his knees wobbled, but he managed to remain upright. Heart thudding so hard Dev felt breathless, he tightened his grip on her.

"Dear God, Lilly, tell me you are all right?"

"Y-yes, thank you, my lord. Pl-please put me down." Her voice was unsteady.

Dev lowered her to the ground, but he couldn't let her go because he needed to touch her. Holding her upper arms, he steadied both of them.

She was safe now, he reminded himself.

"I-I didn't hear them, I'm sorry."

"You are safe; that is all that matters."

Dear God, the desperation inside him had been palpable. He'd experienced that sensation when he had saved the Duke of Raven at Quatre Bras, and then the other night when he had caught Lilly as she'd fallen. What did that mean? She wasn't a Raven. Could his reaction to her simply be because she had his colors?

"Yes—I'm sorry I d-did not hear the carriage coming, Lord Sinclair. It came upon me so quickly."

She was shaking, so he ran his hands up her arms before taking one hand in his.

"Come, take my arm and we shall walk a while before we enter the building. I for one need the time."

Her fingers gripped his sleeve, and Dev fought the urge to wrap his arm around her waist.

"I-I…. please allow me to thank you, my lord."

"I was unsure if I would reach you."

"It was very brave of you to take such a risk for someone you barely know."

"You were about to be run down, Lilly. Of course I took the risk."

"Some would not."

Dev had a feeling there was more to that statement, but he left it for now.

"I did not hurt you?"

"No, I am quite well, thank you, just a little unsettled."

"And forever in my debt."

"Pardon?" She looked up at him, her lavender eyes wide. She was pale, and Dev did not fight the need to close the distance and brush his lips over hers.

"My lord!"

"Excellent, you now have color in your cheeks once more."

"You c-cannot do such a thing out here where anyone could chance upon us!" Her eyes were shooting left and right behind the lenses of her glasses.

"All right, I shall wait till we are alone then."

"No, you shall not!"

"Lilly—"

"Call me Miss Braithwaite!"

"No."

"Why?" She looked up at him once more.

"Because you are now Lilly to me."

She shook her head as if to clear it. "I really do not understand what is happening. We dislike each other, and until a few nights ago, did not even speak."

"Come, you can mull over that later. Neither of us is still

breathing like a racehorse, so we shall take on the local Watch."

"Don't call me Lilly."

His siblings always had the last word too, Dev thought, opening the door and ushering her inside.

CHAPTER 9

The interior was as unassuming as the exterior. A narrow hallway led to a half wall behind which a man scribbled into a small book. He looked up as they approached, and rose with a polite smile on his face. Dev let Lilly go first, and stood at her back as she spoke.

"Good day to you, sir. My name is Miss Braithwaite, and I came here a week ago for my fifth visit and spoke with Sergeant Blacklock, yet again, about the matter of missing boys. I wish to follow up and see what is being done about this problem, as one more child was taken just last night."

It wasn't a position he was used to, yet Dev did not intervene as she addressed the man. His siblings usually let him deal with things; it had just always been that way, yet not this woman. He had a feeling she had dealt with a great many things in her life, and wondered again at the relationship she had with her brother.

His thoughts returned to the driver of that carriage. He had seen his features clearly, and was sure he had directed his horses deliberately at Lilly. But why?

"Well, I can honestly say I know nothing about the

matter, Miss Braithwaite. Where have these boys disappeared from? Are they in your service perhaps?"

"They are children who earn their living on the streets of London, sir. Young, helpless children who have fallen prey to some sort of—of foul play."

Dev watched the man lower his eyes before once again lifting them. He was sure there had been an eye roll in there somewhere.

"As I'm sure the previous officer told you, Miss Braithwaite, the young street urchins are transient. They've probably just moved on to fleece someone else."

"Fleece?"

There was little doubting to anyone present that Lilly was not pleased with the term. Ice had formed on the word as she said it. Dev noted her elevated chin and rigid shoulders. Small and perfectly formed, she almost quivered with indignation.

He wondered again how he'd been so foolish as to not see the woman beneath the exterior she portrayed to society. Possibly because most evenings she was hiding in the corners of the room and he never cared to look for her.

"Ahhh, well, as I see it, Miss Braithwaite, there is little we can do to find these boys, as in all honesty them disappearing is nothing new."

"Six boys have simply vanished and this is nothing new to you?"

If her spine became any more rigid it would snap. Fearing she was about to launch a stronger attack on the helpless man, Dev stepped forward.

"My name is Lord Sinclair. My uncle, the Earl of Wynburg, is a man most interested in the workings of the Watch, as is my brother-in-law, the Duke of Raven. They are both eager to hear the outcome of today's enquiry, as the children who are forced to make an existence on our streets are a particular concern to both."

Dev felt Lilly's eyes on him. She didn't glare precisely, but he thought it inferred. The man looked from her to him, and then nodded. His demeanor had changed at the names Dev had dropped into the conversation. He sat up straight, and the pitying look on his face had vanished.

"If you will wait through here, my lord," he said, opening a door behind him. "I will speak with one of my colleagues over the matter."

"Excellent. Take a seat, Bee. We shall return shortly." Dev waved the maid to a seat and then placed a hand to Lilly's back and urged her forward. Her muscles tensed, as if to stop him, but he used enough force to propel her forward or end up on her face.

"I should have my maid with me."

"She is just outside the door, which is open."

The room was gray and stark, one table and two chairs. A small window high in the wall afforded dull light and Dev thought that perhaps enough time spent in here under interrogation and he would tell them his secrets too.

"Why do you hide behind that facade in the evenings, when it is clearly not who you are?"

"Pardon?"

The hands that were fussing with her skirts stopped as she looked at him.

Dev positioned his chair close to hers before lowering himself to sit. She attempted to shuffle sideways, but he wasn't allowing that. Leaning close, he braced a hand on the back.

"I cannot work out why you are trying so hard to stop society seeing how beautiful you truly are. And that inside that lovely head is an intelligence to rival many."

She trilled out a little laugh.

"La, Lord Sinclair, I do declare it is wondrous to hear you speak of my intelligence."

"It's too late to take a step backward, Lilly. I have seen through you." Dev cupped her chin, then brushed a finger gently over her lip.

"Stop touching me," she hissed, trying to remove his hand.

"Tell me the truth."

She pushed his hand aside.

"You have no right to speak to me so intimately. No right to demand answers from me. We are strangers."

She was scared, and he knew how she felt, as he was too. This, what lay between them, had sprung to life too quickly, and they were both reeling.

"I have no wish to hurt you, Lilly."

"If that is indeed true, then being here alone with you will harm my reputation irreparably. Plus, were anyone to hear you speaking to me so intimately, word would spread with haste, and I have no wish for my reputation to be compromised."

"All true, and yet your activities already do that regularly. Walking about talking to your urchins with only a servant at your side on seedy London streets after dark. Having that house in Temple Street, and what goes on there. So I think my being in this room alone with you is of little concern when the rest is taken into consideration, don't you?"

"I must insist you keep that information to yourself. Were it to get about that I have Temple Street, and have done the things you say, many will not be pleased."

"I will keep your secrets."

Their eyes held, and he was suddenly aware of every breath she drew.

"God, you are a beautiful woman." Dev closed the distance between them.

"Please don't kiss me again." Her words were a frantic whisper.

"Because you want it as much as I and that scares you."

She placed a hand on his chest and pushed.

"I am scared of nothing, and most especially not an arrogant nobleman with far too high an opinion of himself."

"Liar." Dev kissed her cheek, then sat upright as he heard the door squeak.

"That"—she waved her hand about—"is improper behavior, and I wish you to stop it at once."

Before Dev could reply, in walked a man.

"Lord Sinclair, I am Sergeant Gavell."

"Sergeant." He rose to shake the man's hand.

"Miss Braithwaite."

"Sergeant." Lilly nodded.

The man made a lot of fuss about placing his chair on the other side of the desk. Short and round with a bald head, the inspector had a bushy mustache that took up a great deal of his face.

"I understand that you are concerned over the disappearance of six boys who make their living on the streets of London?"

He didn't look at Lilly as he spoke, eyes firmly fixed on Dev, and this, he knew, would not please her.

"As this is my sixth visit here, I wonder you do not know more about this matter. I can also hear the disbelief in your voice, Sergeant Gavell. Do you believe I am making this story up?"

Dev didn't sigh, but he thought about it. The woman had no idea how to deal with a man like the sergeant, who had absolutely no respect for women, even ones of noble birth.

"Sergeant Gavell," Dev began after shooting her a look that he hoped she interpreted to mean *be quiet*. "As you are aware, my uncle, brother-in-law, and I are actively involved in helping those less fortunate than ourselves, and we believe these children fall into that category."

"I hardly think that—"

"And as such when it was brought to my attention that the boys were suddenly disappearing, I decided to accompany Miss Braithwaite on this visit to this Watch House, to lend my weight behind her enquiries. Not of course that I needed to add any weight; after all, a woman's word is equally as strong as a man's, don't you think, Sergeant?"

Sergeant Gavell didn't see his argument at all. His mustache was now quivering with indignation.

"My men have very important work to undertake, my lord, and running around looking for those little... little feral creatures is, I am afraid, not a high priority for us."

Dev felt Lilly tense, no doubt getting ready to fire a volley of insults at the sergeant's head. He placed his hand over hers where it gripped the edges of the seat. Giving it a warning squeeze, he hoped she understood his need for her to keep quiet.

"Of course, if you are unable to spare the manpower for such an important task, I could hire several Runners. I'm sure they will do a thorough job. Understandably, my brother-in-law, the Duke of Raven, and uncle, the Earl of Wynburg, will be very disappointed not to have the Watch behind this investigation, however...."

"That will not be necessary, my lord! I am sure we can spare a few men to investigate the matter."

Sergeant Gavell's color had deepened and Dev could tell he was not happy that he had used his connections to apply the pressure.

Minutes later Dev escorted Lilly outside the building. She reluctantly took his arm as they walked back to where the carriage waited.

"I'm sure you could have used the Earl of Wynburg and

the Duke of Raven's names at least twice more in that conversation, had you tried harder."

"I do believe that was sarcasm, Lilly."

"How astute of you."

"A simple thank-you will suffice."

"Thank you," she muttered. "Loath as I am to admit it, I see now that I would not have achieved the same result had I come alone."

"I accept your apology."

"I did not apologize!"

"Foolish me, I had believed that was exactly what you just did."

She huffed out a loud breath.

"I am going to rethink my earlier thoughts about you and your family, my lord."

Reaching the carriage, Dev opened the door and assisted her inside. "How so?"

"I had rather envied the close relationship you and your siblings appear to share," she said, settling herself on the seat and then making those small, elegant, ladylike gestures all woman did when you seated them in a carriage. "However, having been the recipient of your taunts and dominating behavior, I realize now that I had a lucky escape."

"I do not taunt, I tease, and surely you must allow me some defense against the barrage of insults and abuse I receive daily from my family."

He was subjected to a very thorough look and Dev felt suddenly exposed, as if she were really seeing him, the man beneath the façade, the man who had very real fears and insecurities. The man who had struggled with the weight of supporting his family for so long. It was disconcerting to be inspected by those eyes, unwavering in their intensity.

"You would lay down your life for your family, wouldn't you, my lord?"

"In a heartbeat," he answered her soft words.

"Then they are indeed lucky to have you as their protector."

He heard the longing in her voice and wondered again if she had anyone at her back, and the uncomfortable thought followed that he wanted to be that person.

"I am sure your brother feels the same about you, Lilly."

"No, he does not."

She looked away from him then, and as her maid was seated across from him, he did not do as he wished and pick her up and hold her on his lap, to soothe away the sorrow that lay behind those words.

Dev studied the lines of her body and sent up a silent prayer that she had not shown herself to any other men. Had anyone truly looked and seen what lay beneath the surface of Miss Braithwaite, she would have been inundated with suitors. And the idea of another man anywhere near her made him want to roar.

He didn't think about that anymore, as what lay between them was new for them both. But he would, Dev reasoned. He would think about it long and hard, and the end result would surely be that she was his.

CHAPTER 10

*D*ev watched Lilly's carriage drive from his street, and then made his way to his aunt and uncle's house.

"The Duke and Duchess of Raven have called, Lord Sinclair."

"Thank you, Pennyroll," Dev said, heading for the stairs. "Are my aunt and uncle also returned?"

"No, my lord. Not for another week is my understanding."

He climbed the stairs two at a time, eager to see his sister —and James. The man had grown on him, but he would admit that to no one.

He wasn't sure why he insisted on living next door with Cam when he spent so much of his time, and sat down to most of his meals, here. Perhaps it was the peace, or perhaps it was that he had no wish for his family to know what he did and when he did it.

"Eden missed you all so much that she begged me to return to London early."

Hearing his brother-in-law's deep voice made some of the

tension inside him ease. His family were all here, and they, like nothing else, could calm him when his head was in turmoil.

"Do not believe him. Yes, I missed you all." Eden laughed. "However, he also missed his sisters and badgered me to return to London."

Pushing the door open, Dev was greeted with noise and laughter. The twins were standing on Cam's feet while he attempted to walk around the room. Warwick was sprawled on the floor reading a book Dev guessed Eden had brought him. His family, he thought; God how he loved them one and all.

"Dev!"

He caught Eden as she launched at him. Wrapping his arms around her, he held her tight.

"I missed you, brother!"

"And I you, sister."

Moving back a few steps when he released her, she looked up at him. Unlike the other Sinclairs, who all had green eyes, Eden's were gray, and like Lilly's they saw too much.

"What is wrong, brother?"

"I am well, don't fuss." He kissed her cheek.

"You don't look happy."

"And yet I am, because you have returned. Unfortunately you brought your husband with you."

"You love him as do I, admit it." Eden tapped his arm.

"You could not pull a confession like that from me under any form of torture."

"We had a wonderful time at Raven Castle, Dev." Eden looked at her husband. "Truly wonderful."

"If you don't stop throwing smoldering glances Raven's way, I shall be ill."

She always had a way of looking at Dev and really seeing

what he felt.

"I wish you would tell me what has you out of sorts. Although perhaps I can guess, as Essie told me you've changed your opinion of Lilliana Braithwaite and that in fact you seem rather enamored with her."

Dev glared at Essie, who shrugged back at him, her eyes twinkling and unrepentant.

"How can a man be enamored with a woman who looks like she pulled her clothes from her deceased great-grand-mother's trunks and speaks like a brainless twit?"

"Yes, that's true. However, Essie informed me that she saw her dressed normally this morning, and she is rather lovely. And that she had none of those traits today. Which is odd, don't you think?"

She was stunning.

"Yes, it seems odd, and she certainly looked different. I'm sure Miss Braithwaite has her reasons as to why she behaves as she does, but it is not for us to ask why."

But he wanted to know why.

"What are you not telling me?"

Dev felt cornered. His sister would pick and pick until she had all the answers she wanted, and he was not ready to talk about his feelings for Lilly yet. Hell, he had no idea what they were, other than the fact that they were fierce.

"Essie said you and she had an incident a few days ago, but did not elaborate. Perhaps now you can?"

That would have to stop, Dev thought. He wouldn't have Lilly gadding about in dangerous places with only a servant at her back. He just wasn't sure how to go about achieving that. He'd only been on speaking terms with her for a few days, so he really had no right to feel as he did. Was it so brief? Lord, it felt longer. The woman seemed to have turned his emotions upside down in such a short time.

"Perhaps James would like to be in on this discussion also?"

Dev looked at the Duke of Raven, who was talking with Cam.

"I doubt he's interested in Miss Braithwaite, Eden."

"Normally you would be right, but Lilliana is his cousin, and furthermore, after what I found at Raven Castle, it seems she is also related to us. Although that tie dates back several hundred years."

"What!" Dev roared over the buzzing in his ears.

"Pardon, I believe you meant to say," Eden rebuked. "Did you not know?"

"Of course I didn't know, because no one has told me!" Dev felt like his head was about to explode. Christ, was it possible? Lilly, a Raven and a Sinclair?

"Hello, Sinclair. Care to tell me why you are roaring at my wife?"

The Duke of Raven now stood at Eden's side, one arm around her middle. Where there had once been a cool, aloof expression that hid a wealth of pain, there was now happiness. The man was transformed from the Duke they had first met. Eden had done that, Dev thought. She had brought him into the light.

"He wasn't roaring at me, darling." Eden patted her husband's hand. "He was just surprised that Lilliana Braithwaite is your cousin, and that she is related to us. It seems he is quite taken with her."

"I never mentioned I was taken with her." Dev felt he needed to clarify that point quickly for his sister.

Even if I am.

Raven was one of the few men who rivaled him for size. Dev tried to scowl, but the Duke merely smiled back.

"You never mentioned she was your cousin before, Raven."

The Duke shrugged. "I hadn't realized you needed a detailed account of all my relatives. Believe it or not, there are quite a few, and the list is growing. Furthermore, I thought I remembered you saying that Lilliana was a brainless twit with no fashion sense."

Dear God, say it isn't so. Dev couldn't take it in.

"Is she from your mother's or father's side of the family?" Dev grappled with the knowledge.

"Father's. What does that signify?"

She was of Raven blood. "But you have very little to do with her—"

"We were close as small children. Her father was my father's brother. Nice man, as was my aunt. But eventually, as with everything good in my life, my father decided to cut all ties, so now we are strangers."

"We shall reforge that bond, my love."

Dev watched the Duke smile down at Eden then kiss her briefly on the lips.

"I have no doubts, love." James looked at Dev once more.

"But what is the business about her being a Sinclair also?" Dev asked his sister, still grappling with what he had learned.

"I found this." Eden picked up a fat tome from the table beside where they stood. It was bound in black leather, and Dev could see it was old by the condition. "It is an accounting of some of the Raven history. I found it when we looked for the scroll, which as yet we have not found."

"There are many places to hide things in Raven Castle," James added.

"Miss Braithwaite?" Dev said in a terse tone. "Tell me of her connection to us."

"Don't use that tone with me, brother."

"Sorry," Dev said. "Now speak."

"In 1608, the third son of the then Baron Sinclair saved Lilly's great-great, I'm not sure how many greats, but quite a few, grandmother from a certain death by fire. She was married, but she and the Sinclair fell in love and they had a liaison. The result was an illegitimate child, but her husband was never told, so believed the babe was his. It was then raised a Raven."

"Christ." Dev ran a hand through his hair. He wasn't sure he could take much more of this.

"You've gone pale, Sinclair. Need I catch you when you faint?"

Dev cursed at the Duke.

"What appears to be the problem here? To the best of my knowledge you and Lilliana... oh, no, no, no." The Duke of Raven suddenly looked fierce. "Please tell me you have not saved her from some life-threatening event, Sinclair? I have no wish for another member of my family to be beholden to you."

Dev knew his siblings were listening, as the room had gone quiet. A rarity for the Sinclairs.

Something must have shown in Dev's face, as the Duke clapped a hand over his eyes.

"For Christ's sake. Will this bloody curse never end!"

"Pardon me, James, but were it not for this bloody curse, then some of your ancestors would be dead, along with you."

"Thank you, Dorrie, for enlightening the Duke," Dev said, placing a hand on his little sister's head as she leaned into him. "I am sure for one brief moment he forgot about our family's history. However, I would ask you to refrain from quoting him verbatim, especially when he curses. "

"As if that would ever be a possibility," the Duke groaned, then grunted as his wife elbowed him in the ribs. "Please accept my apologies, Dorrie. I should not have spoken thus in your presence."

Luckily, the children's tutor, Mr. Linues, arrived at that moment to take them away for their afternoon lessons. After being promised a game of hide-and-seek later, they left the room.

"You saved Miss Braithwaite, Dev? What happened?" Cam said after the door had closed.

"She narrowly missed being hit by a carriage."

"Good God, is she all right?" The Duke looked worried.

"Yes, shaken but all right."

"Does this mean we have all your relatives to watch over now?" Cam sounded disgusted. "I mean, if we are talking about cousins, then how far removed will this get? Second cousins, nephews?"

"I am sure it happened simply because Dev was with Lilly," Eden soothed her brother.

"Would certainly keep you busy," the Duke drawled. "Perhaps I should put you all on a full-time retainer, just in case your services are required."

Cam snorted. "I never say no to money. However, I object to being pulled from bed to rescue a foolish Raven who should have a care where he or she walks."

"Did the driver stop, Dev?" James asked him.

"No, he just kept galloping past. It was odd because I remember when she walked across the road, I looked left and right and saw that carriage. I thought it was going too fast, and the driver's face is clear in my head. He seemed determined, and then I turned away. When I looked back, he had changed course and was heading directly for Lilly."

"Lilly?" James said. "Since when is she Lilly to you?"

"Be quiet, darling, Dev is now about to tell us of another incident, and if my hunch is correct, I am sure this is where everything started." Eden patted her husband's chest, and the scowl left his face.

"I need to sit," Dev said. He felt as if he'd been standing out in a storm being battered for hours.

"Would you like, tea, Dev?" Essie asked him.

"A brandy is what he needs, I think." Cam smiled at his sister. "Come, you hold the glasses while I pour."

Soon they all sat, some with brandy, others with tea. Dev swallowed a mouthful and enjoyed the burn as it slid down his throat. He then told James and Eden about Lilly chasing the man who had attempted to abduct the child.

"Good Lord, for the years I had believed that Lilliana had become something of a simpleton, with disastrous fashion sense. It seems I was wrong," James said.

"I'm sure she will not be pleased that we all know what is going on with her, and yet someone needs to watch over her," Essie said.

Amen to that.

"Do you believe what happened today was deliberate, Dev?" James asked him.

"The more I think on it the more I believe so."

"I wonder if it could be connected to those missing children in some way?"

"There are plenty of women helping children around London," Dev said, "but yes, I wondered at the connection also."

"Perhaps Lilly has been getting in the way of whoever is trying to abduct those children. She has the boy Toby out there poking his nose about, and she has been to the Watch House several times," Essie said. "She also foiled that abduction attempt."

"Someone would have had to know you were going to the Watch House to attempt to run Lilly down," James said. "And if that is the case, then someone would need to be watching her."

"You have a suspicious nature, husband," Eden said.

"After what we have just endured, my love, are you surprised?"

Dev wasn't. The Duke had received several attempts on

his life before they had found the culprit, a half-brother he did not know he had.

Around him conversations broke out while he sat silently contemplating what they had discussed. Lilly was a long-distant relation, and a Raven. It was enough to turn a man to drink.

"Pensive is not a word one usually associates with Sinclairs, although perhaps you can carry it off better than the rest of them."

Dev watched James as he cradled his cup in one hand and bit into a large square of cake that he held in the other. He now stood beside Dev's chair, leaning on the windowsill. The Duke was a man who had lived with the burden of a cruel father, a man who knew his share of both physical and mental pain; he was also someone Dev would trust with his life and that of his family. He needed to talk about Lilly with someone who knew her, even if it had only been for a few years.

"I was wrong about your cousin, Raven."

The Duke nodded. "I think she had most of us fooled, from what you have all told me."

"Tell me what you know about her brother, James. I do not like the man, but surely he has not always been a wastrel?"

"No, he was a friend when they visited. But that all changed when his father died. He started drinking and gambling. He kept company with the wrong people, and soon he had become the man you see today."

"I wonder at his relationship with his sister," Dev said. "Surely he can know nothing of what she does?"

"I doubt he'd care anymore. From what I gather, his life is spent in gambling hells and with prostitutes."

Dev had grown up with love. Yes, his father was not a nice man, but he had found that out later in his life. It always made him feel sad when James spoke of his childhood, but to hear that Lilly's brother did not love her as a big brother should made him angry.

"It might pay for you to become reacquainted with your cousin, Raven. It appears she could do with a relative she trusts."

Dev held the Duke's gaze as the man studied him.

"You really are worried for her, aren't you, Sinclair, which suggests to me you also care?"

"Would it do me any good to deny it?"

"Not a bit," the Duke said with a snort of laughter that fell from his lips as quickly as it had come. "I have not thought about Lilliana much over the years, as my own problems were enough to occupy me and because my father seemed hell-bent on keeping us apart, but if she is suffering in any way I would like to know."

"I wonder why anyone would go to such lengths to disguise who they truly are."

"I know that her grandmother left her money, but don't know the details of the entitlement. Perhaps in some way that is the reason? Something to do with reaching a certain age unmarried before receiving it?"

"You need to find out, Raven."

"I shall try, Sinclair." He smiled at Dev. "I can imagine how pleased you are she is related to me."

"An understatement, I assure you," Dev said. "Had it been anyone but Lilly, I would have walked the other way at a rapid pace."

"But you can't," the Duke said softly with his eyes on Eden. "Because something about her has settled inside you and nothing will dislodge it."

"I can dislodge it anytime I wish," Dev said quickly. Surely he wasn't that enamored with the woman yet? Surely what he felt for her was a mild affection based on the simple fact that he wanted to ravish her on the nearest available surface.... Dear God, he was in trouble.

"There is nowhere to run, Sinclair," the Duke said to his back as Dev rose suddenly from the chair and headed for the door as if Satan himself dogged his footsteps.

CHAPTER 11

"*L*ord Danderfield is here this evening and he will ask you to dance, Lilliana. Of course, you will accept."

I would rather eat lumpy porridge, Lilly thought, looking anywhere but at her brother.

The ballroom was filled with primped and pampered guests. Most she knew by sight if not acquaintance. She had been a part of this world for so long now that the scene before her no longer roused more than a sigh from Lilly. The colors and jewels, the decorations that each hostess took months ruminating over, just so they outdid last year and anyone else hosting an event this season, no longer thrilled her.

It was amazing really, that surrounded by so many people she could feel so alone.

She had dressed in dull gray with a black lace trim, which made her appear as if she were in mourning. Bee had reluctantly put a small stuffed bird in her hair, after pulling it back severely, which by the end of the evening would give her a headache.

"He will be a suitable husband for you, Lilliana. I want to hear no more on the matter."

Lilly reluctantly returned her eyes to her brother. He looked pale, and she realized he had lost weight. Was he sick? It would serve him right if he was. It was probably all that alcohol he consumed pickling his liver.

"I will not marry him, Nicholas, no matter what you and he say." Lilly kept her voice low, wishing no one to overhear them. "And I will not be sacrificed because you could not manage father's money and are now in debt."

"I am not in debt!"

"I am no fool, brother. You have never cared if I married before, or for that matter anything about me. Why now?"

He evaded her eyes.

"You look hideous tonight. How can you hold your head high? For pity's sake, Lilliana, you have a bird in your hair!"

"It is a robin, not just a bird."

"Why, Lilliana?"

"Why what?"

"Why do you dress like that and talk as you do when we enter a ballroom or function?"

Lilly wondered why now people were suddenly aware of the facade she had worn for so long. What had changed in her, to make them notice?

"I have dressed and talked this way for years; you were just too self-absorbed to notice. I am shallow and silly, and I like my taste in clothing. If you do not, that is your problem, Nicholas."

"That old crone should never have given you her money. I am sure that is why you have never wed. But I will see you do, and before your next birthday, sister."

"Ah, so you admit you want my money, brother, as you have run through yours, or should I say the family's. And never again speak of my grandmother in that way, or you shall regret it!"

"Bitch!"

"Greedy reprobate!"

Nicholas's snarl turned to a smile as he looked over Lilly's shoulder.

"Lord Danderfield, how opportune. My sister and I were just discussing your flattering proposal, and of course she is so enchanted by the prospect of becoming your wife."

Scrunching her eyes closed, Lilly took a deep breath and then turning, she opened them once more.

"Of course she is. For pity's sake, I would be doing the girl a favor, Braithwaite. Why, she is positively on the shelf, and look at her. A shameful creature. But you may be sure I shall take her in hand."

She turned back to her brother. "And you hate me this much you would make me wed this man?"

"Greet me, girl!"

Lilly turned back to Danderfield before her brother replied. She had never really seen Lord Danderfield up close. Old and craggy was her first thought. His skin hung in folds, his hands were long and bony, and gray hair clung stubbornly to the sides of his head while the top was bald. He smelled of tobacco, spirits, and body odor, all of which she could smell clearly from her position several feet away.

"My brother has misled you, Lord Danderfield. I have no wish to marry, and especially not you. I am unsure why you have decided I would be a suitable wife now, but let me assure you that I would not." If she had thought her harsh words would horrify the man, she had been mistaken. Licking his lips, he looked her over, taking especially long over her breasts, which were hidden behind the thick material of her hideous dress. His lips pulled into a thin line that Lilly thought constituted a smile.

"Spirit, excellent, Braithwaite. My last two wives were meek and gave me no fun at all. This one, however, I hold high hopes for."

"I will not marry you, my lord," Lilly said calmly, even though her heart was pounding. "No matter what promises my brother has given to the contrary."

"I'll have you, girl, because no one else will, and your brother has consented."

With these ominous words, he took her hand and led her to the dance floor. Lilly complied, as she had no wish to create a scene. But she would when she got her brother alone again.

"I just watched Lilly having a conversation with her brother and Lord Danderfield," Dev said to James when he appeared at his side.

They were at the Deighton soirée, which was to Cam's mind just a fancy name for a ball.

"It may not have appeared heated, yet there was no doubting the tension in her as the two men talked. Danderfield's now dancing with her."

Dev watched James take a step forward and look over the crowds to where Lilly danced with the old leech. Her face was tight as she tried to mask her feelings, but Dev had noticed everything about her from the minute she entered the room with her brother.

"God, that is a hideous dress, Sinclair."

"It is an act, James. I am certain of that, just not sure why as yet."

"She has a bird in her hair."

"A robin, one would infer from the color of the breast."

James snorted. "I need to speak to Nicholas and find out what the hell is going on."

"He may not speak with you."

"He will, or I will beat what I need out of him."

"Eden just shook her head at that remark," Dev said looking to where his sister danced several feet away. "Mind your business, shrew," he added knowing she could hear his every word clearly.

"Do you want me to run him through, love?" James said, to which his wife nodded.

Eden's heightened sense was hearing, and of all their senses, hers was the most annoying, as she could hear most things, even with her earplugs in, from some distance away.

"So, it seems my suspicions are confirmed, and you are showing interest in my cousin, Sinclair," the Duke said, leaning beside him on the wall. "I must admit that came as a surprise, as Eden told me you have, until now, never outwardly done so."

Dev sighed. "Should have known this particular subject would remain in the forefront of my family's minds."

"I do wonder why you thought it wouldn't, and why your siblings would not be interested in any woman who interests you," the Duke said.

"A faint hope, Raven, nothing more."

James snorted, his disbelief obvious. "Discretion, in your family?"

"True. As I said, it had been a faint hope only."

The men were silent again, James switching his gaze from Lilly to Eden to check on her and back to Lilly again.

"I think tonight is as good a night as any to reacquaint myself with my cousin, Sinclair."

"Perhaps Eden could hear what Danderfield is saying, if she danced close enough," Dev said.

"I'm sure she will. Where you are concerned, my wife will do whatever it takes to make you happy."

Dev grunted. His family always had his back, as he did theirs.

"May I take this brief moment of solitude from your siblings to offer my... congratulations, for want of a better word."

"For what?" Dev dragged his eyes from Lilly to look at the man beside him.

The Duke was silent for several seconds and then he spoke. "For being the father Eden never had and for raising the wonderful family you have. I'm sure there are times when it was not easy."

How did one answer that, Dev wondered? Raven was not a man given to excess emotions; in fact, when first they had met he had been colder than a dead man. Therefore, when he did express himself, it tended to shock the recipient.

"No words are necessary, Sinclair, but please know that now you are not alone in your commitments, and I will make it my life's work to make Eden happy, and be there for your clan should I be required."

"Thank you," Dev said, as uncomfortable with excessive emotion as the next man.

"I suppose if she marries you at least I can keep an eye on her."

Dev's instincts screamed denial, yet it never showed on his face.

"Pardon?"

"Lilliana. If she marries you, at least I know she will be well cared for."

"A lovely sentiment, I am sure, but may I suggest you put your energies into what is troubling your cousin instead of my future aspirations, Raven."

James smiled. "I'm sure I have enough energy for both, Sinclair," he added, holding out his hand.

Dev shook it and then hissed something foul at the Duke as he walked away laughing.

"Hello, cousin."

"Duke." Lilly sank into a curtsey and attempted to breathe as James joined her.

"James will do, I think."

The emotions churning through her body were making her breathless. She could hear the small pants coming from her mouth but could do little to stop them. Dancing with Lord Danderfield had been horrid. He had touched her inappropriately several times and leered at her breasts. Now her cousin, whom she had once thought so much of, was talking with her.

"Lillana, are you well?"

"I-I am, thank you."

"Come, take my arm and we shall walk a while."

She did and slowly felt her breathing return to normal as they made their way through the open doors and out onto the terrace. Neither spoke as they continued to walk in slow measured steps and Lilly was grateful for it, grateful for the time to find herself again, even if it was on the arm of the man she had not spoken more than a handful of words with for many years.

"I have thought of you much over the years, cousin, and wondered how you fared, yet it was not till I married Eden that I realized just what I lost when we were separated as children. I would ask that you try to forgive me for the distance I placed between us, and hope that like me, you wish to change that."

"It is all right, Duke. Your father—"

"Was a bastard, and most likely he terrified you when your family visited, and for that I'm sorry. But the thing is,

Lilliana, those brief moments when you, Nicholas, and I ran wild over Raven Castle were the memories I cherished most."

Lilly remembered them too. She had loved her quiet, stoic cousin almost as much as her brother back then. Even at a young age she had seen he was hurting, but did not know how to reach him, and then it was too late, as they had left Raven Castle for the last time.

"Do you know why you left and never returned that day?"

She shook her head.

"Your father tried to intervene on my behalf. Asked if I could spend more time with your family. My father refused, and that was the end of everything."

"I'm sorry, I did not know why."

"I am happy now, Lilliana. I have Eden, who loves me and I her, and two sisters."

He smiled, and it was possibly the first genuine one she had received from him. She could see his happiness; it made him look younger and more approachable.

"Sisters, Duke?"

"James," he reminded her. "The story is a long one. Will you come and take tea with us soon so you can make the acquaintance of my sisters, and hear our tale?"

"I would like that," she said, feeling a small glow of warmth in the region of her heart. Nicholas may not love her, but perhaps this man could.

"Come, we should return, but before we do, can I ask something of you, cousin?"

"Of course."

"Devon has told me how you were out on the street that night, and about your house."

Of course he had. Bloody Sinclairs; it seemed they kept nothing close. Lilly did not understand that. She had always held her secrets inside, never sharing them.

"I see that angers you, but you must understand he told me only because he is concerned."

"He has no reason to be so, as I am no concern of his," Lilly said.

"Perhaps, but I think in this he is correct. You must take no more risks. No more nighttime ventures onto London Streets."

Lilly nodded but remained silent.

"Promise that if you need help, then you will turn to me, if you cannot turn to Devon."

"Very well," Lilly said, accepting the kiss he brushed over her cheek. And then he was gone and she stood there, bemused. So much change and in such a short time; how was a person to cope?

CHAPTER 12

*L*illy needed time to think. Somewhere she could sit uninterrupted, and work through everything that was happening to her. She walked along the wall until she found two rows of seats upon which sat numerous young women awaiting a man to ask them to dance, and several older ones, watching their charges with narrowed eyes as they danced or stood in circles with men and women. She had spent a great deal of time on extremely uncomfortable seats on the edges of ballrooms just like these.

"Excuse me." Lilly made her way along the row until she got to a seat in the middle. She would be safe here, tucked away. Safe from the loathsome Lord Danderfield, her brother, and Lord Sinclair.

"Dastardly hot, wouldn't you say?"

Damn.

"Indeed, Miss Juniper."

Lilly had seriously miscalculated. Beside her was one of society's leading gossips. Miss Juniper was in her sixties, a woman who spent her evenings digging up tidbits she could then pass on to her friends the next day. Harmless really, but still bloody annoying, as the woman had no idea on "sitting quietly."

"The Duke and Duchess of Raven are the picture of health this evening, wouldn't you say, Miss Braithwaite?"

Short enough to fit under Lilly's armpit, Miss Juniper had sharp features and reminded her of a little bird, not dissimilar to the one she had in her hair. Her brown eyes were always on the move, as were her hands.

"Indeed they are, Miss Juniper."

Lilly wondered if she could slip out again. The other option was hoping that someone took the seat between them, thereby blocking the woman from her sight and becoming Miss Juniper's next victim.

"That is a very unusual arrangement in your hair, Miss Braithwaite."

"Indeed, do you like it, Miss Juniper? It took my maid some time to arrange. The beak, you know, it needed to be placed so it did not dig into my head."

The deep chuckle coming from the end of the row made Lilly's heart jump. She tried glaring at Lord Sinclair to make him leave, but he simply smiled and started down the row, sending the women he passed into a flutter.

"Lord Sinclair!"

"Miss Juniper." He nodded to her, as if a man taking a seat among the women was an everyday occurrence.

"But Lord Sinclair, there are only women seated here!"

He settled on the seat between them. Due to his size and the seats being placed close together, his thigh pressed into Lilly's.

"Excellent, I am rather happy to be the only man surrounded by so much beauty."

Lilly watched the women who heard him turn and smile, tittering. They all blushed and nodded. Lilly rolled her eyes.

She then moved as far from him as she could, which was not far as a woman sat on the other side.

"Hello, Lilly, you look beautiful tonight."

He turned his body, thereby shutting Miss Juniper out of the conversation completely.

"No I don't and what are you doing?"

"Sitting with you."

"But you should not do so."

"Why?"

His face looked calm, as if they were discussing pleasantries, and yet his eyes... there was nothing calm about the vibrant green depths.

"Because this is where women sit," Lilly hissed. She was attempting to slouch in her seat so no one realized he was sitting with her.

"Is that a rule?"

Horrified, she watched as he turned to Miss Juniper to address the question to her.

"Because if it is, I do not remember seeing it written anywhere."

Miss Juniper tittered. "It is understood, Lord Sinclair."

"Ah, well there you have me," he said, smiling once more. "I rarely understand anything."

He turned back to her.

"That is a rather fetching robin in your hair. Quite the picture, with its red breast, and extremely lifelike."

"Go away."

"Do you realize that when you talk with me your voice changes?"

"It does not," Lilly snapped, trying to change her tone back to the high-pitched trill she was known for.

"No, it does, and I much prefer it."

"Go away," Lilly said, desperate now to make him leave.

Others would see him soon. He was not slouching like her, but sitting tall and straight.

"Did you and James have a nice chat?"

She couldn't look away; it was as if his eyes held her in place.

Run! the voice inside her head yelled. *Run and don't look back.*

"Yes, now go away."

"I had believed you and Miss Braithwaite had formed a dislike for each other, Lord Sinclair. What is it you speak of so secretly?"

He held her eyes for a second longer before turning to face Miss Juniper.

"No indeed, we are friends, Miss Juniper. My sisters and Miss Braithwaite spend a great deal of time together, and as such I also."

Lilly searched for an escape route and decided on simply pushing her chair back. There was a small amount of room between it and the wall; she could squeeze out without making the ladies to her right move once more. But before she did, Lilly had to ensure Miss Juniper kept Devonshire Sinclair busy for some time.

"Oh, Miss Juniper. Please tell Lord Sinclair, in detail, about the uses for white horehound syrup. His younger sister, Miss Dorset, suffers horridly from a hoarseness in the throat and a raspy cough. I believe they have tried everything for the poor dear."

He swung to look at her as she spoke, and the look in his eyes threatened retribution, as everyone knew that once started on her cures Miss Juniper would not be stopped until she was good and ready, which hopefully would not be for some time.

"La, Lord Sinclair, I declare it is quite fortuitous that you have sat beside me this night, as I can indeed help you with your poor sister."

The fact that she had questioned his taking the seat beside her was forgotten as she launched into a detailed discussion about the merits of white horehound syrup.

Lilly seized the moment and stood.

"Good Lord, I quite forgot I promised the Earl of Ridgeway the next dance. I shall not feel too bad at leaving you however, Lord Sinclair, as I will be doing so with the knowledge that you are keeping excellent company. Please don't miss out even the slightest detail, Miss Juniper, as Lord Sinclair is most eager to find help for his little sister."

His hand gripped her fingers briefly where they lay between them.

"I shall find you later, Miss Braithwaite, and we will continue our discussion over that matter."

Lilly shivered at these words, but did not look at him. Instead she fled.

"White horehound syrup, Lord Sinclair, is the only way to cure your dear sister."

Witch, Dev thought, watching Lilly disappear into the crowds of people before them. She'd outmaneuvered him and he should be furious with her, but what he felt was admiration. Every minute he spent in her company made him want to spend several more. He didn't see her ugly clothes or ridiculous hair anymore, he saw her, Lilly. The woman who had his colors.

"Of course, steam also helps, Lord Sinclair."

"Indeed."

Dev muttered the right words at the right time and thought about Lilly. He wanted her to talk to him freely, needed her to tell him what the hell was going on in her life.

Why the charade? What was between her and her brother? Was she happy?

"I will have a rub sent round for her chest, Lord Sinclair."

"I'd be much obliged."

He needed to find her, Dev realized. Because she was just as likely to leave before he had a chance to talk to her.

"Excuse me, Miss Juniper, I have promised my sister I would dance with her."

He walked away before she could launch into further cures. Circling the room, Dev looked for Lilly. Finding her, he tacked right and came up behind her. She had not seen him, and was taking a mouthful out of the glass she was holding. Leaning forward, he whispered in her ear.

"You owe me for what I have just endured."

She shrieked, the glass tipped, and the contents ended up over her hands.

"You startled me!" She spun to face him.

"I hadn't thought your reaction would be quite so violent. Forgive me. Come, we shall find somewhere to clean you up."

Before Lilly could stop him, he had her hand on his arm. Dev propelled her along at his side, and she could do nothing but comply. She would not create a scene; that was not her way, so her fingers appeared to rest on his arm, when in fact, they were digging in.

Dev found an open door that led outside and gently pushed her through before him.

"Why are we on the terrace? I can hardly dry my hands out here."

"They will dry in the air, once you have taken off your gloves. It is warm out tonight."

"I have no wish to be outside at this time, Lord Sinclair."

"I wish to talk with you without anyone interrupting us."

"You are always manhandling me. I am not one of your siblings, my lord. Let me go."

Dev kept circling the terrace until they were alone, he then led her to the shadows, where he knew a stone bench sat.

"Sit."

"I am not a dog," she replied, indignant.

"Please sit."

She muttered something and then the little bird in her hair bobbed as she sat abruptly. She made no move to remove her gloves.

"They are soaked in champagne, Lilly. Take them off and lay them upon the seat."

She hesitated, first looking at him still standing, and then at her hands.

"They will be awfully sticky and uncomfortable if you do not."

"My name is Miss Braithwaite." Reluctantly she peeled first one and then the second damp glove from her fingers.

Dev studied her hands and could see no reason for her reluctance to let anyone touch or see them. She did not lay the gloves beside her, instead waving them about, Dev guessed, in the hopes they would dry faster that way.

"I told James about the incident with the carriage today, and what happened several nights ago."

"The Duke told me this, and may I say it was presumptuous to do so, Lord Sinclair." She was trying for haughty again, but now he saw through the facade.

"Have you given thought to the fact that the carriage that nearly hit you outside the Watch House did so deliberately?"

She was surprised by his words. The gloves momentarily stopped flapping as she looked up at him.

"Why would that be the case? I-I have done nothing to warrant such a thing."

"You are trying to stop whoever is taking those children from taking more, Lilly. You have repeatedly visited the

Watch House. Had the boy, Toby, ask questions, and then you foiled the abduction of that boy the night I was there."

"No." She shook her head fast, dislodging the robin and sending it forward. Dev removed it gently from her hair.

"Why are you touching my head?"

"Your robin has flown the nest."

"La, Lord Sinclair, you are most amusing."

It was exhausting watching her slip in and out of personas. Dev could only imagine how taxing it must be for her.

"You must have a care now, Lilly. If what I have said has foundation, then you must not leave the house without at least two footmen and a maid."

"I don't believe you are right."

But he had made her think, and that, to Dev's mind, was a good thing. She needed to show caution.

He sat beside her suddenly, reaching for one of her hands before she could pull away. Cradling the slender fingers in his palm, he felt it again, the wonderful surge of heat from the contact.

"Don't touch me!" She struggled to pull away from him, tug her hand from his grasp. "I-I do not like to be touched!"

"Why do you not like your hands touched?"

She was frantic now, trying to escape him, but Dev opened his fingers, slipping hers through his larger ones until she was trapped.

"You told my sister at Temple Street that you did not like to be touched, and quickly pulled on your gloves when we arrived, even though your hands were sticky from the bun. Why?"

"You don't understand what you are doing—"

"Tell me, then."

He watched as she struggled to breathe as his hand held

hers. Switching his vision, he checked her color, but it was strong and healthy.

"Lilly, stop fighting me. Take a deep breath for me. Are you in pain from my touch? If so I will release you."

She inhaled and then exhaled slowly.

"Again, that's it."

"You don't understand."

The whispered words were desperate.

"What don't I understand?"

Dev took her other hand, turning her in the seat to face him. He uncurled her fingers from the fist they were clenched in and lifted them to his face.

"Don't."

"Do," Dev said gently.

"I can't normally touch people."

"Yet, you can touch me."

She stopped fighting him, and then the hand on his face moved. Her eyes followed her fingers as they traced the edge of his cheekbone, across his brows, and down to his jaw.

She was gentle and left a trail of heat. Christ, his body was a furnace, and she was barely touching him. He could only imagine what would be between them when she lay naked beneath his body. Wrestling that image aside, he concentrated on her.

"Why can't you touch people, Lilly? What do you feel?"

She shuddered, eyes still on her hand as it ran down his nose.

"No." She shook her head. "It matters not."

"It matters to me."

"Y-you have a bump."

"Eden broke it when we were young."

"Make me stop."

"Why don't you touch people, Lilly?"

"Emotions and feelings, horrid feelings," she whispered,

125

letting her fingers trail down his neck. "But with you it feels so different," she added in wonder. "So very different."

"How long has it been since you touched a person?"

"Since my childhood?"

"Is it only your hands that cause this reaction inside you?"

She nodded. "Yes, although I still hate people touching my face."

"Except me," Dev rasped as she ran one finger around the outside of his ear.

"Yes."

Dev knew she wasn't focused on her words or she would not be revealing so much about herself. He wondered if Lilly had a secret that even she did not understand.

Trapping her hand as it moved down his neck toward his necktie, he said, "Why were you dancing with Lord Dander-field when I could tell you did not want to?"

Her hands immediately stilled and her eyes cleared, losing the look of dazed wonder they had previously held.

"I must return, my lord. Please excuse me, I-I don't know what I was doing—"

"You were touching me, Lilly, and I loved every second your fingers were on me. Yet had you continued I would have been forced to lay you on the bench and ravish you, and when I do that it will not be on a cold slab of stone."

"Y-you cannot speak to me in such a manner!"

He watched as she slipped her gloves back on. He then grabbed her hand back and held her in place as she attempted to rise. There was a flicker of something in her eyes, however he knew it wasn't fear.

"I will make you mine, Lilliana Braithwaite."

"Not if I don't want it!" she snapped, and he smiled at her temper. It was far better to see the fire in her eyes than the desperation they'd held before.

"But you do want it, my sweet." Closing the distance, he

placed a gentle coaxing kiss on her lips. "But for now we shall content ourselves with a dance," Dev said, standing upright while he still could. Placing her hand on his arm, he led them back inside.

Dev swung Lilly into his arms and they waltzed slowly down the ballroom with the other couples.

"I would ask a favor of you, Lilly."

He was subjected to a look, her feathered brows lowering as she studied him, and he could see the wariness return as she wondered what he would ask of her.

"I don't want to promise you anything. This, what happens between us, is not right. I don't want or need it, or the complications it brings to my life."

"Yet it is inevitable," Dev said.

"No, we can go back to what we were—"

"No,"—he gave her hand a squeeze—"we can't. But we will leave that for now, and I would simply ask that if you feel the need to tumble headlong into danger, you come to me, and if not me, James, so one of us can escort you to wherever it is you need to go."

"He has already asked that of me."

"Excellent, so you will have no trouble giving me the same assurance you no doubt gave him?"

She huffed out a breath. "Don't you have enough people to care for, my lord?"

"Plenty, Miss Braithwaite."

"Yet you feel it necessary to watch over me also?"

Dev merely smiled.

"You have been successful in caring for and keeping your family safe, my lord, and I commend you upon it, however—"

"Not always," Dev muttered as visions of Eden at the mercy of their father, Essie with her broken heart, and Cam drinking himself close to death filled his head. He hadn't been able to save them until the damage had been done.

"Whatever trials you and your family have endured, Lord Sinclair, it is undoubtedly a testament to you that you are still together, both healthy and whole. However, you cannot save everyone and I will point out to you again, my welfare is not your concern."

No, he couldn't save everyone, Dev thought remembering campaigns and men he had lost who would never return home to their loved ones.

"Why do you look sad?"

The words weren't offered in a sympathetic tone; she demanded an answer.

"I could not save everyone who fought with me."

"Was it your job to do so then, my lord? Are you such a man that everyone under your command should have returned alive and uninjured? Surely even the great Lord Sinclair cannot work such miracles?"

He couldn't believe she was mocking him.

"I led them."

"Then of course you failed in your duty."

"I did not fail!" Dev felt his anger rise. "I was a very good leader."

"Then why do you blame yourself for losing the men you did?"

He could find no response, and battled the urge to place his hand over her mouth before she said anything else that would increase his discomfort.

"Have you always had this ridiculous need to protect people? This controlling nature that suggests no one can expire or become injured if you are in their lives?"

"Be quiet."

"Oh dear, do you not like feeling vulnerable, Lord Sinclair? Is it not easy to have your innermost secrets and fears exposed, then chewed over like a dog with a tasty bone?"

Her face was serious, the high cheekbones flushed. Her eyes were open and honest behind the glass of her round lenses, and the ache inside his chest that he felt continually when she was close intensified.

"I take your point, so there is no need to discuss the matter further." Of course he'd known she would ignore him.

"Being the eldest of six siblings, my lord, I'm sure you have been called far worse than bossy and controlling. However, I wonder if the description, godlike, would also fit?"

"Yes, thank you, Lilly. I believe I said I understood the point you were trying to make…repeatedly."

"Excellent, then we shall both stop annoying each other, and revert to the way things once were between us, as it seems when we are near, we pull emotions from each other that neither of us are comfortable with."

The song finished, and she slipped into a curtsey and left Dev reeling on the dance floor. She had just slit open a vein in his heart and allowed him to bleed a little before resealing it and walking away.

"Damn," Dev whispered. It had to be love.

CHAPTER 13

"Smear the jam on your toast and not me, brat."

"I want to go there."

Dev looked to where the jam-coated finger pointed, read the small advertisement, and wondered if there was any way he could get out of it.

"Dr. Engle's House of Ghoulish Horrors," the youngest Sinclair sibling, Warwickshire, declared. Lounging half on his chair and half on Dev's lap, he eagerly scanned the advertisement in the morning paper.

"You'll squeal like a babe and have nightmares for weeks," Cambridge said from across the table, where the twins were busy retying his necktie while he ate.

"Won't!"

Dev looked around him. They were all present, except Eden and their aunt and uncle. The room was full of laughter and teasing, and he would have it no other way.

"I want a Roman god starting with the letter *P*." Dev shot Essie and Cam a look. They might be able to throw the young ones off the scent of visiting Dr. Engle's House of Ghoulish Horrors if they played a few word games.

"Poseidon, and that was too easy."

"Forgive me, Dorrie, I was just warming you up."

"Try harder," Somer said, her eyes alight with excitement. Unlike other children, his little siblings enjoyed learning, and the harder the challenge, the better. It was due to their heightened senses; for some reason, this increased their learning capacity.

All the Sinclairs spoke multiple languages, as their mother had loved learning them, and read ferociously.

"Who was honored in the temples known as Capitolia?"

That shut them up. Dorrie, Somer, and Warwick all leaned in and he heard whispering, until Warwick was elected speaker.

"Jupiter, Juno, and Minerva."

"In Italian, if you please."

Dev laughed as Warwick spoke in his most pompous tone.

"What herb is most commonly used to aid digestion?" Essie asked.

"The Egyptians said coriander had digestive properties," Somer said. "But you can use chickweed." She then looked at Dev. "And we still want to go to Dr. Engle's House of Ghoulish Horrors, so no matter how much you try to dissuade us, it will not work."

"I won't squeal either, Cambridge," Somer said.

"Neither will I," Dorrie added.

"Of course you wouldn't, my darlings," Cam said, planting loud kisses on their cheeks.

"How about the park?" Dev said, wiping his brother's fingers with a cloth he had dipped into his water glass. Of course he would never have done that if his aunt had been in the room.

"No!"

"Museum?" Cam supplied. He was now wearing his necktie in a bow around his head.

"No!" all three of the little Sinclairs squealed.

He should have had breakfast at his own lodgings, and then this conversation would never have eventuated. The problem was, when he was alone his thoughts went to Lilly, and his body would grow tight and he wanted her with a fury that scared him witless. She was a fever in his blood, an obsession that Dev feared would only strengthen the more he saw her. He had woken numerous times during the past few nights with the feel of her lips on his and the touch of her hand on his face.

Then there was this business of her being affected when she touched other people. Not him; she had loved that. Dev shouldn't feel so good that he was the only one she could place her hands on, but he did, selfish bastard that he was. If his hunch was correct, she would soon be in for a shock when he explained what he believed the reasons behind her sensitive hands were, but that was for another day.

"Gunter's?" he said quickly. *That got them*, Dev thought, as silence reigned around the table. They loved ices.

"No!" they cried in unison.

"I yield," he muttered, raising his hands in the air. "But Cam and Essie will take you and I will meet you there. I have some business to see to for Uncle first."

Everyone agreed, and Dev was immediately covered in kisses from his little sisters and a fierce hug from Warwick. Minutes later, smiling, he left the house.

The drive through London was slow, as horses, carriages, and carts jockeyed for position, but finally he arrived at the docks. Dev stepped down from his carriage and inhaled. He loved this place; he felt alive surrounded by the bustle, noise, and salt air. Having grown up near the sea, the smell was so familiar to him and made him long for Oak's Knoll, his family's home.

Closing his eyes briefly, he reopened them when he was steadier. Looking at the scene before him was almost too much, an assault on the eyes, especially his eyes, as his vision allowed him to see more than most.

Ships rocked from side to side, their wooden hulls creaking and groaning. Masts waved, rigging jangled, and when they were quiet, the sound of men yelling filled the silence. Walking to where one of his uncle's ships bobbed gently on its moorings, he signaled his intention to board.

Dev had only really known the Earl of Wynburg, his uncle, since arriving in London. Previous attempts from their aunt and uncle to make contact with the Sinclair siblings had been rebuffed by their father. This had changed upon his death.

The siblings had been summoned by the Earl and Countess to London, and then they had learned just what a manipulative man their father had been, and that now they were heirs to the Earl's fortune.

"Morning, my lord. Captain Blake is in his cabin," a seaman said as Dev arrived at the top of the gangway.

"Thank you." He nodded and made his way along the decks to where the captain's cabin was located. Dev nodded to crewmen who were busy checking rigging and preparing the vessel to sail on the morning tide.

"Lord Sinclair, Lord Wynburg told me to expect your arrival," the captain said, coming forward to meet him.

The man's cabin was pristine. The wood and brass were highly polished, as were the boots of the man before him. He had a waxed mustache that made up for his lack of hair, and broad shoulders encased in a white shirt.

"Come, we shall begin the inspection of the stock and I will have my man make a list for you to take to your uncle."

An hour later Dev left the ship with an inventory of the stock and where and when it would reach its intended destination. He had been impressed by the way Captain Blake ran his ship and had taken many mental notes during his time on board. Once again back on the dock, Dev felt his heartbeat increase as he made his way to another ship berthed two along.

He had another reason for being here today, other than doing business on behalf of his uncle. He was here to look over his recently purchased first ship. The *Neptune's Lady* was now his. It was the beginning of his fleet, and would carry cargo and passengers to far-off places and return with goods. Silks, spices, and any manner of things. Things he would sell and begin to build his empire. Lord, he wanted to be on board for the first voyage, but he could not leave yet.

"Permission to come aboard!"

A face peered over the railing above.

"Who are you?"

"The new owner of this vessel," Dev said politely.

"Permission to board, my lord!"

Dev shook his head; surely they had heard that cry four ships away. Eden would have heard it many miles away. Making his way up the gangway, he found himself facing three somber-faced men at the top.

"Lord Sinclair, I am Captain Bilberry."

"Captain Bilberry, it is a pleasure to meet you," Dev said, holding out his hand. Surprise flashed across the worn face before him, but he took the hand and shook it firmly.

"I expect you'd like a tour of your new purchase, Lord Sinclair?"

"If you can spare the time, Captain, I would like that very much."

Leaning on the deck of his ship two hours later, Dev looked at the scene below, enjoying the bustle and activity.

He had viewed every inch of the *Neptune's Lady*, from the gleaming brass in the tallest mast, to the hammocks swinging below deck, and loved it all.

When his parents had died and left him as head of the family, he had realized the state of the Sinclair finances, the mess his father had left him. Leaving the army, he had done the best he could with what few options he had available to him, and they had survived—just. But his uncle had given him freedom, and with that freedom he had found the ability to breathe without tightness in his chest. Fear had ridden him for so long. Fear that he would not be able to feed and clothe his family, not be able to educate them and give them the life he wanted for them.

"You have to let me help you," his uncle had said when Dev had initially refused his offers of support. Still reeling from his father's treatment of Eden and the knowledge of what his previously beloved parent had done to his family, Dev had been angry and confused. His pride had refused all offers of help; he had merely wanted to gather every single Sinclair up and retreat to their home, the only place his siblings had known before their parents' death.

"Have you always had the ridiculous need to protect people?" Dev smiled as he remembered Lilly's words to him. She had not offered him sympathy as others would. She had spoken the truth, and for that he could only respect her.

"Will you need anything else, my lord?"

Dev turned to face Captain Bilberry.

"Nothing further, Captain. Everything looks excellent, and I shall look forward to seeing you in a few months."

With a bow the captain departed, and Dev turned to look back over the railings.

His uncle's empire was vast, and Dev had plans to follow his lead. One day he too would own ships and warehouses. Some would come to him with the Earl's passing, but some he would have purchased and paid for himself.

Dev felt a shiver of awareness roll down his spine that had him scanning the buildings before him. He focused on a small room perched on top of a tavern.

"What the hell is she doing here?"

Pushing himself upright, Dev watched Lilliana Braithwaite pace back and forth before a set of windows beneath which was one of the deadliest drinking houses in the area. The Anchor was renowned for drunkards, whoring, and brawls, and that was before the sun set. As she walked, another man watched her movements from the doorway. Dev recognized him as the servant from the day he had first seen her with the children.

"For pity's sake, woman, I expressly told you to tell me if you wanted to court trouble!" Dev muttered, taking the gangway at speed. "What the bloody hell are you about now?"

Lilly walked through the three rooms one more time. They would need cleaning, and the furniture would have to be replaced.

"I'm really not sure about this, Toby. Another location would offer more protection."

"I've told you why it's perfect, Lilly," the boy said. He looked up at her with wise, old eyes that had seen more than any child his age should. "Temple Street is all well and good for when they's sick, but this will offer them a place to bolt. A place to hide and stay warm, close to where they spend most of their days."

"Do they often need a place to hide?" Lilly almost feared the answer, as in her heart she knew it.

"Yes."

One word that said so much, she thought, looking around

the dark, dismal space. She would ensure it was bright and clean. Ensure those children who needed a place to hide would feel safe in it.

"I will be guided by you with what we need in here, Toby, if I choose to lease it."

She and the boy had come up with the idea for leasing more rooms for the children after he had come to her with rumors that were suddenly thick on the London streets. Rumors about a man called Dominus, who was intent on building an army of children to work for him. An army of thieves that would take over all other gangs. No one knew his identity, but they feared him. It seemed his reputation had grown through foul deeds that even Toby struggled to recount to Lilly.

"I heard tell that he will destroy anyone who gets in his way, Lilly. I'm thinking you need to stop going to the Watch, and stop any inquiries, 'cause it must be him who's taking the children."

"Why do you say that, Toby?" She moved to where he stood, placing a hand on his shoulder.

"'Cause maybe he'll come after you."

Lilly remembered what Devonshire Sinclair had said to her.

"Have you given thought to the fact that the carriage that nearly hit you outside the Watch House did so deliberately?"

Was he right?

"I shall be careful, Toby. Do not worry about me, just keep yourself safe."

The boy was far too thin still, Lilly thought as he started moving again, looking around the small room, checking corners for God knew what.

"We shall need someone to watch over this, Toby, should I lease it. I want to make sure it is kept clean and stocked with food and supplies. It will also need a sturdy lock on the inside."

"Perhaps I can help you there, Miss Braithwaite?"

Lilly turned to Mr. Snow, the owner.

"Happens my sister lives nearby. Husband's a sailor and always off at sea. She has two little ones, and could use the extra money."

"I would be happy to meet with her," Lilly said. She wasn't going to say yes until she had checked the woman over thoroughly. After all, others may not care for these children, but she damn well did and she would have no one abusing them.

"We should leave now, Miss Braithwaite. I hear the noise rising downstairs, which would suggest the Anchor's patrons are well down the barrel. I have no doubt that their excitement is only going to escalate. Therefore I suggest we hasten our departure."

"Soon, Wilson," Lilly said, waving a hand at her footman. His face was creased with worry lines and she hated that it was she who had put them there, but before they left she needed to discuss a few things with the landlord.

"The lease will run for ten years, Mr. Snow?"

"I'd only be willing to offer you five, Miss Braithwaite," Mr. Snow said, rocking back on his heels and rubbing his chin.

"Well, never mind then," Lilly placed her hand on Toby's shoulder. "I'm sure there are other places nearby."

"I know of another," Toby winked at her.

"Excellent, well lead on then." Lilly smiled at Mr. Snow as she drew level with him.

"Now let's not be hasty, Miss Braithwaite."

Lilly knew what he thought, that she was a noblewoman who was following one of her pet causes that would wane in time. Someone he could fleece with an exorbitant rent.

However she was nobody's fool, her grandmother had seen to that, and she knew how to get what she wanted.

"Hasty, Mr. Snow? I have told you my conditions and as they are not suitable to you, there is nothing left to be said."

Mr. Snow scratched his sandy head for a few seconds before speaking.

"As long as nothing outside the law happens up here and my patrons are not disturbed, you have yourself an agreement, Miss Braithwaite."

Lilly was sure that with the Anchor's reputation it would be her children who were disturbed, yet she remained silent on that fact. "Excellent."

They spoke briefly, and then she told Mr. Snow that her man would be in touch. Taking Toby's hand, she left the room behind Wilson. The noise level rose as they reached the street below and pushed open the door. They encountered several drunken patrons who had obviously spilled out of the Anchor and were in the midst of an argument of some sort.

"I warned you, Miss," Wilson said softly.

"That you did, Wilson, and this, Toby, is why I am unsure about this place. Surely the children will run into trouble here," Lilly said as they skirted the group of men.

"Compared to most places we go, this is safe, Lilly, and it's easy to get to. Plus a quieter place would make some of the children uncomfortable. As long as the door has a strong lock, the others will come here if they need a safe place to stop."

Lilly understood the logic behind Toby's words, even if she didn't like it.

"Are we still going to that place like you promised?"

"Yes." Lilly shuddered. Toby had a thirst for ghoulish things, and she had promised if he accompanied her, dressed and clean, on her visit today, she would take him to the place he had heard about.

"Don't like this, it's going to blow."

"Blow what?" Lilly questioned Toby as she followed his eyes.

The group of men seemed to have swelled to about twenty, and their argument had increased in volume.

"'Ere, lads. We have a lady present!"

Damn, one of them had seen her before she could slip by. Wilson stepped in front of her and Toby stood at his side.

"Hello, my love, care to have a drink with old Dan?"

The voice came from over Wilson's shoulder.

"I'll move these two, Dan," another voice said, "and then you and I can have a bit of fun."

Lilly opened her reticule and removed her pistol. Stepping around the men, she aimed.

"I have no wish to have fun, sir. I wish to leave, so I insist you step aside."

She'd thought he would be intimidated; instead, he laughed.

"There's plenty more should I go down, lovely, and a bullet may be worth a tumble with a lady."

He lunged at her, Lilly fired, and then hell broke loose.

"Ouch! Bloody hell, she shot me in the toe!"

Lilly watched as more men poured out of the tavern, all heading her way. She, Toby, and Wilson would be outnumbered in seconds.

"Bloody woman. Why can you not stay out of trouble!"

Lilly's head snapped right at those angry words, and there was Lord Sinclair, striding toward her like an avenging angel. She had no time to sigh at the sight he made, instead preparing for the battle that was approaching.

Hands grabbed her and she was once again pushed behind Wilson and Toby. Lord Sinclair made three.

She heard the sound of fists, and then they were moving

forward. A hand grabbed her, but Lilly jammed the handle of her pistol down hard, and it released her.

"The carriage is this way!" Lilly heard Wilson yell.

"My carriage is closer. Get to yours and head home. My name is Lord Sinclair, and I will see your mistress reaches there safely."

After these roared words, Lilly felt herself lifted and thrown over a shoulder.

"Wilson, I—"

Lilly lost the power of speech as Lord Sinclair started to run, and then he wrenched open the carriage door and she was flung onto a seat. Righting herself, she watched Toby leap in nimbly beside her, and Lord Sinclair follow, slamming the door so hard, it rocked the carriage. He then sat opposite her, and the look in his green eyes told her he was in a rage.

"What were you doing in such a place?"

He held up a hand as she opened her mouth.

"Be warned that if you say it is none of my business, I shall not be pleased. In fact, I am bloody furious! I saw you in that window and could not believe my eyes. Have you no regard for your safety at all!"

Where had he been to see her in the window? On the streets below, perhaps? Surely his eyesight must be excellent to see her from down there?

"You promised me you would not walk into danger. Promised to ask James or me to accompany you—"

"Actually, I'm sure I didn't...." The words fell away as his eyes narrowed.

"You," he pointed a finger at her, "are entirely too reckless."

"James was busy," she said, trying to glare at him, when in fact she wanted to touch his jaw, to see what it felt like clenched like that.

"I know you didn't contact him."

"Are you calling me a liar, sir?"

"Yes." He held her eyes, and Lilly had to fight not to look away.

"I have handled myself perfectly well for years, and have no need of a man now or ever."

"God, you are a stubborn woman," he growled. "For pity's sake, I have saved you three times now. Is that not a warning to you?"

He did have a point, and perhaps if she thanked him it would go some way toward appeasing him.

"Please accept my gratitude for your actions on my behalf, Lord Sinclair."

"Dev or Devon," he snapped.

"Very well. Thank you, Devon." Lilly nodded and tried to appear chastened, which she'd never really perfected.

"I cannot believe you pointed a gun at that sailor, and then shot him in the foot." His eyes closed briefly.

"I had not intended to shoot him. He rushed at me, and I instinctively fired."

"You should have asked me to accompany you today, Lilly."

"I don't need your help, or anyone's for that matter."

"Everyone needs help occasionally."

She dismissed his words with a flick of her wrist.

"Please set us down anywhere, my lord. Toby and I can get a hackney."

The last time they had been together, he had taken off her gloves, and she had run her hand over his face. The memory was still very clear in Lilly's mind, and making her uncomfortable in his company.

"Are we still going to Dr. Engle's House of Ghoulish Horrors, Lilly?"

"Of course," Lilly said to the back of the boy's head. His face was pressed to the window.

"As it happens, my destination is also Dr. Engle's House of Ghoulish Horrors, so I shall be happy to escort you there, and to pass the time on the journey you can tell me why you were at the docks today."

"You made that up!" Lilly said, certain she was right, and equally certain she did not want to spend any more time than necessary in this man's presence.

"No, I did not. My siblings are at present awaiting me outside Dr. Engle's House of Ghoulish Horrors. No doubt impatiently," Dev added, pulling his watch from his pocket and noting he was now late.

Dev knew she wanted to tell him to go to hell; he could see the anger in her eyes. They had darkened to purple and her hands were clenched. He was a rational man, always had been. He liked to follow things to their logical conclusions. Everything had its place, but she made him irrational. He wanted to lock her in a room with him so he could learn everything she was hiding behind those pretty eyes.

"Why were you in that room above the Anchor today, Lilly?"

Ignoring his question she said, "Thank you for...."

"Saving you?"

"Aiding us in leaving the scene, my lord."

"Why were you there? Surely you know it is not safe for you—"

"Because I am a woman, my lord, and therefore unable to look after myself?"

"Because anyone who was caught in that today would have been lucky to escape, and yes, because you are an intelligent woman and should know better. For pity's sake, Lilly,

had I not arrived when I did you would have been trampled!"
Dev felt the anger he had just tamped down surge to life once
more. If he hadn't arrived when he had....

"My name is Miss Braithwaite, please use it."

"You are Lilly to me, as you were the night you ran your
hand over my—"

"Yes, thank you." She shot a look at the boy, who had
stopped looking out the window and was now watching
them closely.

"He's right though, Lilly, we shouldn't have gone there
without more men."

He was young, perhaps the age of Dorrie and Somer. But
Dev had a feeling this boy, like the one he had met in Lilly's
little house in Temple Street, had seen some of the worst
things life had to offer a child. He had that world-weary look
in his eyes. Clean and tidy, he was small, as many were who
had lived a tough life.

"Please set us down, Lord Sinclair. We will make our
own way from here," Lilly said, drawing his eyes from
the boy.

"As I have explained, our destinations are the same.
Therefore there is no need to take a hackney," Dev said, swallowing his smile as her teeth snapped together. "What were
you doing at the port today, Lilly?"

"What I was doing there is none of your business."

"How long before we get to Dr. Engle's House of
Ghoulish Horrors?" the boy said as Dev was about to question her again.

"Not long, I am sure," she said, straightening his cap and
shirt.

She was comfortable with him. Dev had never seen her
touch anyone willingly, except children; of course, she still
had her gloves on.

"Five minutes, Toby, and we shall arrive."

Dev was subjected to a frank appraisal from the lad, which he sat calmly through.

"Thank you for saving Lilly, my lord."

Dev nodded.

"It could have got nasty back there, Lilly, like I'm always telling you. You gotta be more careful."

Good boy, Dev thought. The boy was reinforcing his own statement. Lilly didn't like it, not one bit, yet she bore it silently from Toby.

"I shall be more careful in future."

"When will you begin fixing the place up then?"

"What place are you fixing up, Toby?" Dev asked, keeping his voice light. He could usually pry anything out of his younger siblings with that tone.

"Do not bore Lord Sinclair, Toby, he has no interest in our affairs."

Dev watched Lilly wriggle in her seat then adjust her gloves and straighten her skirts. She wanted to be anyplace but here with him, while Dev could honestly say he was quite happy where he was, sitting across from her, smelling her scent, watching her twitch and generally unsettling her.

"You always told me to respect my elders, Lilly, and if I am spoken to then I should speak back."

She glared at Dev as he muffled his laughter behind a cough.

"Of course, and you are right, but I am sure it would take too long to go into all the details, Toby, therefore I shall apprise Lord Sinclair of them when we have more time."

Toby looked at her as only a child who has been fobbed off could, then shrugged and remained silent.

"As I am meeting my family at Dr. Engle's House of Ghoulish Horrors, perhaps we can view the place together?"

"I-I don't think that will be necessary, thank you, Lord Sinclair. We have inconvenienced you enough. Toby and I have no wish to hold up your family, as he has never been there and it will take us some time to observe the exhibits."

"My family has never been there either, and I'm sure they will wish to also take their time. The twins are very thorough."

"Twins?" Toby said.

Dev spent the remainder of the journey telling the boy about his siblings. Lilly, he noticed, feigned indifference, yet he knew she was taking in every word. He liked children; they were open and honest, for the most, unless they were trying to get him to do something.

Further conversation ceased as the carriage pulled to a stop. Dev climbed down with Toby behind him and then he turned to help Lilly.

"Thank you, my lord."

"It was my pleasure, Miss Braithwaite."

She ignored the mocking tone of his voice and followed Toby down the street.

CHAPTER 14

*D*r. Engle's House of Ghoulish Horrors was housed in a narrow alley below the ground. A large black sign with bloodred writing indicated they had arrived at their destination. However, if Lilly had not been sure she was at the correct location, Lord Sinclair's scowling family all standing outside awaiting him would have been a clear indication.

"You're late, Dev!"

This cry came from the young boy standing beside Essex and Cambridge Sinclair, as they approached.

Lilly watched, surprised, as Lord Sinclair reached his family and bent to hug the three children. Whatever he said into their ears had them laughing in seconds.

She felt suddenly off-balance again, as she was when he removed her glove. Men like him were not supposed to be this way. They were aloof and left the raising of siblings and children to nannies and mothers. He wasn't meant to appear human in her eyes.

Yet hadn't she seen him with Sam, and just now in the carriage with Toby, and of course with Bee and Mrs. Davey?

She needed to hate this man, yet was sure the softening in her heart suggested the opposite. *Not a good idea, Lilly*, she reminded herself.

"How lovely to see you, Miss Braithwaite, and in my brother's carriage."

"And you, Mr. Sinclair," Lilly said, looking at the younger brother, who was a smaller version of Devon.

"Cambridge, please," he said, bowing.

"Your brother came to my assistance when I... ah...."

"Became lost," Lord Sinclair said, turning with his little sisters' hands in his. "These are my sisters, Miss Braithwaite, Dorset and Somerset, and my youngest brother, Warwickshire."

The girls curtseyed and the boy bowed, although his eyes were fixed on the entrance of Dr. Engle's House of Ghoulish Horrors.

"How lovely to meet you, and I would be honored if you would call me Lilliana, as Miss Braithwaite seems such a mouthful, don't you think."

She heard Devon Sinclair snort, and knew it was because she had told him he must address her correctly.

"And this is Toby," Lilly said, taking the boy's hand and pulling him forward. His reluctance was obvious and she knew how he felt. She was never very good around strangers, and he had never known children who were raised differently from him.

"Are you going inside too?"

"We are," Lilly told Warwick when he questioned Toby.

"Can I walk with you, because they giggle and shriek and hold on to me when they're scared," Warwick said, his face a picture of disgust as he nodded toward his sisters, who were now poking their tongues out at him.

"Suppose," Toby said, shrugging.

"This is a nice surprise," Essex Sinclair said, slipping her arm through Lilly's. "Another woman to even up the numbers." She laughed, making light of what to Lilly felt like a very awkward situation. What must they think of her, arriving in their brother's carriage?

"That combination of roses and cinnamon you wear, Miss Braithwaite, is really rather stunning on the senses."

Lilly looked at Cambridge Sinclair in surprise. How had he known what her special blend of fragrance was from where he stood, several feet away? Was her scent too strong? Perhaps she should wear less in future?

"I have a good sense of smell," he added, as if reading her thoughts.

"Can we go in now, pleeeeease?"

"Yes, Warwick, however whining like a girl is not very attractive in men."

"And yet if my memory serves me correctly," Essie said to Cambridge, "Mother always said no one whined quite like you."

Even Lilly snuffled behind her hand as Cambridge lunged at his sister, who in turned skipped from his reach with a giggle.

She had never been around family who actually seemed to enjoy each other's company. It was quite a revelation.

Lilly felt Lord Sinclair's large, warm hand on the small of her back, but while she stiffened, she said nothing. His family was nearby, and she had no wish to draw attention to herself.

They walked down the steps and into the small foyer of Dr. Engle's House of Ghoulish Horrors. She then watched Lord Sinclair move to the front of the small party and pull some money from his pocket.

"I can pay for Toby and myself, Lord Sinclair," Lilly said as he held up eight fingers.

"You could, but as I have already done so that would be a shame."

"Oh but—"

"You get used to that."

"Get used to what?" Lilly questioned Essex as they followed her siblings through the door the proprietor had indicated.

"Him taking control. Unfortunately, he has had to do it for so long we just stand back now and let him."

"I don't have to let him," Lilly muttered, following the others into the room and immediately coming to an abrupt halt as the door behind them slammed shut, and she was surrounded by darkness.

"Can I walk with Warwick, Lilly? I know you're scared of the dark, so if you say no that's all right too."

Lilly could feel her cheeks heat as Toby whispered these words loudly as he moved to her side. She hoped no one else had overheard him, as she had no wish to give Devonshire any more ammunition to use against her.

"Of course, I'll be fine," she said, patting his head. In seconds he was gone and she was surrounded by black and Sinclairs, and she wasn't sure which terrified her more.

Dev, unlike the others, could see what was happening before it happened. His night vision allowed him to move freely in the dark. Cam had the twins in hand, and Warwick seemed comfortable with Toby. Essie, he noted, had fallen in behind the boys in case she was needed, which left Lilly to him. He loved his family, but never more so when they were looking after him, and there was little doubt both Ess and Cam had deliberately left them together.

The room was not overly wide but it was long, and he could see wisps of mist before them. The walls were dotted with small indentations in which stood figures, some real, others fake. Large cobwebs draped the ceiling and drips of something that looked like blood fell into pools on the floor. He supposed if you didn't have his vision and were scared of the dark, like Lilly apparently was, it could be intimidating. There were pockets of red light strategically placed to add atmosphere, but only enough to lead the way.

"We have to walk through there, Lilly; the door behind us is now locked. Remember what the man told us when we entered," Dev said, taking her arm to guide her forward. She hadn't made a move to follow the others.

"O-of course."

She took a step forward and then another, but she looked a bit like a drunkard, listing from side to side. Dev kept pace with her, trying to see her eyes; however, her head was lowered and he had a suspicion she was closing them every few feet.

"You really are terrified of the dark."

"No, of course not. Adults are not afraid of the dark."

"Where is that rule written?"

"It just is." He could tell she wanted to snap, but her words didn't have the strength behind them.

"Is this another weakness of the beautiful Miss Braithwaite?"

"No—yes, I... I— Dear God, what was that noise? The children, I must get to them."

"Cam and Essie have them, and they are at present laughing and shrieking in delight at their adventure. You, however, are pale and sweaty and about to pass out from lack of air if you do not slow your breathing down."

"Don't be absurd, I never faint."

That put the poker back in her spine.

"How very well-bred of you," Dev taunted.

"'Tis ill-mannered to rag at s-someone when they are not at their best, Lord Sinclair."

"I am duly chastened," Dev said, leading Lilly forward as the children called for them to follow.

Her body was rigid, the arm he held clenched tight.

"It's funny what scares us. I can't stand to see my siblings bleed. Unmans me completely, and I usually end up on the floor."

"Really?"

Her eyes were going from left to right with speed, waiting to see what horrors awaited her next.

"Yes, it is a weakness, and gives my family no end of enjoyment at my expense, but there is little I can do to change it. Seeing the blood of anyone I care for unsettles me." He remembered how he'd felt seeing the blood on Lilly's chin that night she had saved the boy, and prayed fervently he never saw any on her again in his lifetime.

Dev saw the man lift the ax and get ready to lunge at them, but knew Lilly had not. Placing an arm around her waist, he drew her to his side.

"My lord, unhand— Argh!"

Dev was sure he had just ruptured an eardrum, but it was worth it. Lilly was now buried against his chest. Her heart was beating a rapid tattoo and she was clutching his coat in her fists. He was a cad for taking advantage of her fears. Bad person that he was, watching her come unraveled was as enjoyable as her touching his face. When her defensives lowered, Lilly was extremely hard to resist.

"Lilly, it's all right."

"I... I hate the dark and I hate to be scared and I want to l-leave now."

The words were muffled in his chest. She sounded young and vulnerable at that moment, and he wondered at the experience that had given her this fear. One day she would tell him, along with everything else he wanted to know about this infuriating woman.

"And so we shall, but first we have to find the way out."

Taking a deep breath, she pushed out of his arms and looked up at him.

"You're enjoying this."

"Having a beautiful woman terrified in my arms? Never." Dev laughed as she huffed.

"I will concede to being scared witless, my lord, and I will also concede that I need your assistance to navigate the remaining corridors of this hideous place, yet once we are outside, I will again dislike you intensely."

"Fair enough, forewarned is forearmed. However, I must point out that you don't dislike me at all," Dev said, intercepting her hand as it sought his sleeve and twining their fingers together. She struggled for several seconds, but he won the battle as a cobweb brushed her face and she swallowed a shriek.

"No, I do."

"Of course you don't. We have visited a Watch House together. I am the first person you have touched and enjoyed. Then there is the small matter of me saving you several times."

"About me touching you," she said. "Please forget that incident, as I was not myself."

"Of course you were." He brushed her words aside.

"You are an arrogant and conceited man," she said, moving closer to his side as another axe-wielding man appeared before him.

"Conceited no, arrogant upon occasion," Dev conceded. "But do you honestly believe I could get away with being arrogant around my family? My sisters alone constantly humiliate and belittle me. It is a wonder I have any pride left at all."

"And you would have them no other way," she said softly.

Dev sighed. "How is it that on such short acquaintance you can see through me?"

A fountain of blood erupted from a man's chest and she screamed.

"Bloody bothering hell!"

Dev laughed as she shrieked out the words.

"Well, well, well, not quite as well-mannered as you portray yourself to be, Miss Braithwaite?"

"Go to hell."

Dev was still laughing as they came to a stop behind their party, who were inspecting a cabinet of what seemed to be bloodied body parts. Everyone was talking at once as they pointed and stared; not one of them sounded frightened, he noted.

"How is it that none of them appear even the slightest bit afraid?"

"Well, I can't speak for Toby," Dev said. "But my three have been exposed to darkness and terror by their elder siblings since they were old enough to walk. We used to play hide-and-seek in the dark, and often jumped out at them at any given time. It certainly toughened them up."

"You all love each other very much, don't you?"

The words were quietly spoken, yet Dev heard the longing, and at that moment he would have told her what was inside his heart had he thought she was ready to hear the words. Because everyone deserved to be loved, but he believed Lilly had not experienced the emotion for some time, and that upset him a great deal.

"Dev!"

Lilly hated how she felt when Lord Sinclair released her hand and reached for one of the twins as she launched herself at him. She didn't want to like this man or need him, but it seemed she was in grave danger of both. When he had held her, suddenly the fear had receded, as if in some way he had taken it from her, which of course was ridiculous. She watched him hug the little girl tight as she sobbed into his shoulder.

"W-Warwick said I was a ninny for shrieking."

"Lilly and I never heard you shriek, Somer, and he has called you worse names than that, sweetheart. So what else is upsetting you?"

He was so comfortable in his role of guardian with the girl, his gestures natural as he listened to her tale of woe.

"Yes, but he embarrassed me in front of T-Toby."

"Ah, it all becomes clearer now," he said, kissing one of his sister's damp cheeks before lowering her to her feet.

"You tell Warwick that if he says anything further you will tell Toby about his Dougie. Don't say it out loud, Somer, but make sure he knows you will if necessary, and that will be deterrent enough."

"Why can't I say it out loud, Dev? He deserves it."

Lilly loved watching children. They were just what they appeared. No front, back, or side for that matter. If they were sad, it showed. Of course, the children she knew were different from these Sinclairs. They had learned early not to show emotion, because no one cared.

She watched the smile the little girl gave her big brother before she ran off, happy once again. If only life were that simple, Lilly thought. She hoped the Sinclairs understood how lucky they were to have each other, but most especially to have the man who loved them all so much.

"That seems a very weighty sigh, Miss Braithwaite. Care to share your troubles?"

"No, I have no need to share anything with you."

His chuckle made her shiver, thankful for the dark so he

could not see the longing she felt was written all over her face.

"May I enquire as to the origins of the Dougie?"

"A small dog made of sticks that Eden made for him when he was three. He has never been parted from it and it sits beside his bed every night. We had Eden make four of them in case he lost the original."

"And did he?"

"No, surprisingly he never lost it, and takes better care of it than his teeth."

Lilly was surprised into a giggle.

"You should do that more. Your dimples are lovely."

"Not many people go about laughing, Lord Sinclair."

"No, but many do laugh regularly. I don't believe I have ever seen you do so."

She felt his eyes on her face, but thankfully knew he could not read her expression.

"As we have only been acquainted for a short time, I don't believe you can accurately make such a statement."

"I have watched you, even if we have not conversed."

The breath suddenly lodged in her chest at his words; luckily she did not have to reply, as Toby spoke.

"Next is the murder house, Lilly."

She could tell he was still wary of the Sinclair family, but for all that the boy was enjoying himself. His face had relaxed and he was happy to walk beside Warwick.

"Will the fun never stop," she whispered.

"Sarcasm, Lilly. I am seeing many sides of you in your moment of weakness."

"I am not now, nor am I ever, weak," she muttered, clutching his hand once more, because quite frankly the prospect of walking into a dark room called the murder house without being anchored to someone was terrifying. It could have been any hand, she reassured herself. "I am merely unsettled. It shall pass."

"It is supposed to be the most horrible and gruesome room in all of London, filled with obscene objects, like blood, body parts—"

"You will not scare me with talk of blood and other revolting things, my lord. Unlike you, my weakness is only the dark," Lilly said, wishing she could leave his side and stalk after the children, yet knowing she would then be alone.

"I knew at the time it was folly to tell you about my little issue with blood. However I was fairly certain given your terrified state you would forget. A major miscalculation on my part, I fear."

"A momentary weakness that I shall gladly use against you at the first opportunity, my lord."

"Devon, for pity's sake, Lilly. You have wept piteously upon my chest, groped my face, and yet I am still Lord Sinclair."

"I most certainly did not grope your face!" Lilly said indignantly and followed it up with a shriek as they entered a room cloaked in darkness.

"Something touched my ankle."

"Oh, that it had been me," he sighed.

"Scoundrel!"

"You wound me."

She heard the deep rumble in his chest.

"Men are extremely unpleasant creatures," Lilly said softly, not wanting to alert whoever was lurking in the shadows to their presence.

"Not all men," he whispered in her ear, his breath against her skin making her shudder.

Her eyes began to adjust, as this room had more light, and Lilly felt some of her fear ease. The murder house had severed heads and limbs, all, Lilly gleefully noted, slathered in blood. There were murder scenes reenacted, and the sound of moans and screams wailed around the walls.

"There is certainly a great deal of blood," she said, hoping to unsettle the man at her side.

"I believe I mentioned that it is only my siblings' blood that upsets me, madam. Therefore, you may remove that smirk from your pale face."

"I have no idea what you are speaking of, sir," Lilly lifted her chin.

"Each of these is of a real murder, Lilly!" Toby yelled from his position in front of a gruesome murder scene.

"Will they have nightmares from this, my lord?" Lilly questioned, feeling guilty that such young children were being subjected to so much blood and gore.

"I don't think mine will. And if my guess is accurate, Toby has seen more horror than both you and I, therefore I think they will slumber well tonight."

She looked at Toby as he gave Warwick a small smile.

"He is the one you told Essie about that day at Temple Street, isn't he?"

"Yes. When Mr. Davey found him, he was bruised and beaten, and lying on the doorstep."

"Was he the first of the children to go there?"

"No, there had been three before him. However Toby was different from the start. Mr. and Mrs. Davey love him as their own, and he lets them because they do not smother him. Yet he is still untrusting and will disappear for a few days when he needs time alone, which of course worries us, but we try not to let that show. "

"And you have a special bond with him?"

Lilly didn't answer immediately, choosing her words carefully.

"There is something about him that tugs at my heart. He

is so strong and stoic, and yet sometimes I see the fear in him."

She felt Devon's hand squeeze her fingers gently before once again releasing them. Lilly shouldn't feel warm all over from such a small gesture, but she did.

"Miss Braithwaite, will you come and see this? Somer says it is a severed finger, but I believe it is a severed toe."

Lilly looked at the twin before her then at the man beside her. "Surely your brother would be a better judge?"

"He will try and agree with both of us," the little girl said dismissively. "He likes to be fair." She rolled her eyes. "We have asked Cam, Essie, and Toby, and now we need to ask you."

"You're a heartless little wretch, Dorset Sinclair, to dismiss your big brother so ruthlessly."

Dorset merely poked her tongue out at Dev, and then took Lilly's arm and towed her to inspect the aforementioned appendage.

After it was decided that it was indeed a toe by Lilly, which pleased Dorset hugely, she was then taken in hand by both twins and escorted the rest of the way around the exhibits.

Lilly told herself she was relieved to have left Devon Sinclair's side, yet the truth was she felt bereft. And that alone was enough motivation to keep her distance.

Dev stayed a few feet behind Lilly as the twins dragged her from room to room. She was good with them, teasing them and tweaking a curl here and stroking a cheek there, much better than she was with adults. She seemed to lose her inhibitions around children.

"So do you mind telling me why, when you went to the port to look at your latest acquisition, you picked up a woman instead, and not just any woman, but your Miss Braithwaite?"

"She is not my anything, and stop meddling, Cambridge, or I'll break your nose again."

"Funnily enough, Dev, when you did it last time—after it had healed—my sense of smell was even stronger. In fact, I had this strange smoke smell minutes before our kitchen in Oak's Knoll caught fire, remember? I knew it was about to happen even though I was some distance away."

Dev had realized very early on in his life that you could never insult Cam without him turning it around to the point where you forgot the original insult in favor of the discussion you were being sucked into. So it was important to stay focused.

"Just leave it be, Cam," Dev warned, watching the sway of Lilly's skirts as she swung Somer's hand in her own.

He had seen another side to her today. Her fear of the dark was real, like his of blood. Then there was her humor. He'd believed her silly and brainless, but in fact she wasn't.

"Oh, surely I'm allowed a little more fun? After all, you harassed me for days when I fell in love with Miss Millhouse. I remember waking up one morning to you singing a love song at the end of my bed, and then there was the little matter of that red velvet heart. Eden made it, and Essie initialed it."

"I take responsibility for the song, as I was the one singing it," Dev said. "However, the heart was your sisters' idea."

"Which you happened to suggest," Cam scoffed.

"Can Lilly and Toby come and eat an ice with us, Dev?" Somer said, coming to his side.

"Of course they can. Go and ask them nicely."

"Just so you know, Dev, we like her," Cam said, punching his brother in the arm before he started herding the children toward the exit.

So do I, Dev thought, feeling his chest tighten as she laughed at something Essie said.

Dev had known that when the time came that he found his mate, he would fall for her quickly. She would consume him, and he would want everything she gave and more. Lilly, he now knew, was that person. He thought it may take her a while longer to come to that conclusion, however.

CHAPTER 15

"*C*an I not convince you to choose the lemon with a cream sarcenet overdress, Miss Braithwaite?"

"No thank you, Madam Dupont. I like the mustard, it suits me perfectly, and please add a trim of gray around the neck and cuffs. Plus I think a large collar of the same trim would be lovely, don't you?"

The seamstress made a choking sound but nodded.

Lilly wanted something really ugly to deter Lord Danderfield. She had tried to put the man off, but since that day she had gone to Dr. Engle's House of Ghoulish Horrors with the Sinclair family and Toby, he had been most persistent. Yesterday he had called to take tea, and asked that she go driving with him today. Lilly had quickly refused, stating she already had an engagement.

He was a loathsome pig, and she would never marry him, even if she was forced to flee. She would rather live in Temple Street than be subjected to that man's advances.

His questions were personal and invasive. He wanted to know her every movement, and had told her that when they were wed, he would be curtailing all activities except those he approved of.

"Can I not interest you in something in a lighter fabric, Miss Braithwaite? Perhaps a—"

"I have quite made up my mind, Madam Dupont. Please have the dress made and delivered to my brother's house."

Leaving the shop, she purchased a pair of gray gloves and a silly bonnet that she would have Bee add several unflattering things to.

She had thought a great deal about Lord Sinclair—Devon, as he insisted she call him. The man had infiltrated her head and made her smile at random moments. Lilly did not smile randomly, well not genuinely she didn't. She giggled foolishly in public, and in private she had not had much call to smile.

The most terrifying part of Dr. Engle's House of Ghoulish Horrors, upon reflection, was realizing just how much she had enjoyed it, had enjoyed being with the Sinclair family and allowing Devon Sinclair to hold her hand and lead her through those horrid dark rooms.

Toby had told her in his no-nonsense manner that they were all right, those Sinclairs. High praise indeed from a boy who rarely had a kind word to say to anyone.

Seeing the Sinclairs together as a family, watching them laugh and tease each other, hug and touch each other, had been something special to be part of, and Lilly was not so cynical that the experience had not moved her in many ways. If she were honest with herself, she'd been jealous of the bond they so obviously shared. She had lost count of how many times Devon Sinclair had touched a sibling with a stroke of his big hand on their heads or the brush of his lips on a cheek, and every gesture had made Lilly's toes tingle because she had wanted to be the recipient.

She was not herself, Lilly realized. So much was unsettling

her. First there was this business with Lord Sinclair, and how she appeared to be letting him in to aspects of her life that she let no one in to. Actually, he had forced his way in, but still, had she fought harder, that would not have happened, surely. There was also the concern about Nicholas's insistence she marry Lord Danderfield, and of course, the issue of the missing children.

"Pardon me, Miss Braithwaite, but an urgent message has arrived for you."

A young boy handed her a note. Opening her reticule, she handed him some coins before looking at the missive. The handwriting on the front was not familiar. The content made her heart sink.

Come quick to Lady Jane Street, a boy is hurt. Toby's name was printed at the bottom. Lilly looked at the paper then folded it carefully, and slipped it into her reticule. Something was not right, because firstly, Toby could not write, and secondly, how did he know where to find her, when only Bee was aware of her destination?

She couldn't afford to ignore the message if a child was in danger, yet what if it were dangerous for her, or a trap of some sort? She would have Bee and Wilson with her, so she should be quite safe Lilly reasoned.

She hurried to her carriage with Bee on her heels.

"Jane Street, Wilson," Lilly said before she climbed inside.

"Is it a child, miss?"

"Yes, Bee. It says we are to go to Jane Street, as there is a child in trouble, and it was signed by Toby."

"Toby can't write though, miss."

"I know, but why would anyone else send me a note if there were not a very real danger?" Lilly said. "No, I must take a look. I will think of little else otherwise."

The day was a gray one, but as yet no rain had fallen. When the carriage halted, Lilly stepped down into Jane Street.

"We will not be long, Barnabos," Lilly told the driver as Wilson joined her and Bee on the street.

"'Tis not the best street in London, Miss Braithwaite," Wilson said as they began walking down it.

"No indeed," Lilly agreed. Looking around, she saw rickety old buildings that she was sure housed small children who wanted shelter for the night. London was full of such places. "I don't believe I've been here before, Wilson."

"It's not a place I'm overly familiar with, Miss Braithwaite. Perhaps you should wait in the carriage with Bee, and I'll find the child."

As the last word left her footman's mouth, Lilly felt icy fear grip her body. "We need to leave here; something is not right."

They came from the buildings. Five men; Lilly and her servants had no chance of escape. She struggled as a man grabbed her, and watched in horror as Bee was thrown to the ground and Wilson knocked over the head with a piece of wood, his body crumpling at her feet. Desperate, she fought, but they were too strong. She was lifted, her hands and feet bound, and then a sack was lowered over her head and she was suddenly in her worst nightmare. Alone in the dark.

Dev had walked around the ballroom several times and had still not found Lilly. Bracing himself against a wall, he resorted to his other vision to find her. Color was suddenly all around him, but he forced himself to focus, breathing in and out slowly. He could do this, subject himself to this, for her. Where the hell was she?

He'd been uneasy all day, as if he were coming down with something, or something monumental were about to happen to him or his family. But as the minutes ticked away, Dev had a feeling it was to do with Lilly.

She was nowhere in sight and after an hour of checking rooms, the feelings began to intensify. She hadn't arrived at all, because he had asked the servant who announced the guests, and yet he knew she'd been planning to attend, because she had told Essex of her intentions.

"That scowl is scaring the ladies. What has your hackles up this evening, brother?"

Changing his vision, he looked at Cam.

"Have you seen Lilly?"

"No."

"Something's not right."

"Why do you say that?" Cam straightened from his habitual slouch, eyes intent as he looked at Dev. The Sinclairs understood each other, and their heightened senses fired if one of them sensed danger.

"I don't know, something just feels off," Dev said, shrugging as if he could shake the unease from his body. "I have looked everywhere and in both visions, and still I cannot see her.

"You used your other sight here, with all this color? Are you all right? Why the hell did you not find me first?"

"I am fine, don't fuss. I have the same feeling I had when Eden was kidnapped, Cam."

"And you are sure it relates to Lilly?"

"I am."

"Is there any chance she simply chose not to attend this evening?"

"Yes, there is that chance. Yet it's my belief she has met with foul play, but I have no idea why I believe that."

Cam didn't question him further. Dev's tone told him that his concern was very real, and if the Sinclairs knew one thing about each other, it was to respect their intuition.

"Her brother is here, in the card room."

"I'll go," Dev said, knowing how much Cam hated going

into such a place now. It had once beckoned to him, and he still felt the lure upon occasion, so he stayed away.

"And I shall check once more to see if she actually arrived here tonight, and then left."

Dev nodded and then headed for the card room. His clothes felt uncomfortable, as if lined by hair, and his throat tight.

Lilly, where the hell are you?

Nicholas Braithwaite was sitting at a table with four men when Dev walked in. He looked up and smiled as Dev approached. The smile was insolent and instantly set his teeth on edge.

"Lord Sinclair, have you come to play, seeing as your brother cannot be trusted to?"

As far as taunts went it was said more in the tone of jest, yet all present knew the intent behind Braithwaite's words was to insult. Nicholas had never forgiven Dev for removing Cam from his influence before the man had broken his brother completely.

"I would like to speak with you alone, Braithwaite. I shall need only a few minutes of your time."

"I say, Sinclair, we are in the middle of a hand here, can't it wait?" one of the men said.

"No," Dev held Nicholas's eyes. "It can't."

"You'll have to wait, Sinclair. As you can see I'm on a winning streak, and unlike your brother, I won't be dragged from the table like an errant schoolboy."

Braithwaite was nervous; Dev could see it in his body. His eyes were flitting from Dev to the cards in his hand. They had shared no more than a handful of words since the business that night with Cam, and possibly that was because where he went, Nicholas Braithwaite made sure he did not.

"Braithwaite, I will not ask politely next time," Dev said, not raising his voice, but there must have been something in his tone because everyone at the table grew still. He didn't usually make scenes, but for Lilly he would make an exception.

He needed information about her, and to get that he had to start with those closest to her.

"Gentlemen, it seems I must leave you briefly. I shall return in due course, after my brief conversation with Lord Sinclair."

Dev watched the man rise and move to his side.

"You can bloody well walk me back to the ballroom; that is the only time I will allow you, Sinclair. I had a winning hand, damn you!"

"I think not," Dev said, taking his arm and pushing him toward the doors that led to a hall. He marched Braithwaite down it until he found an empty room.

"Unhand me at once!"

Ignoring him, Dev shoved the man through the doorway and slammed the door shut behind him. He had to give Braithwaite some credit; he did not move away from him, instead standing his ground.

"Be quick. I have little time for the likes of you, Sinclair. Poor country boy who lives off his uncle's coattails."

Dev ignored the taunt and let the silence stretch until he was sure Nicholas's nerves were taut, and then he spoke.

"Where is your sister?"

Surprise flashed across the man's face.

"What has my sister's location got to do with you, country boy?"

There were only so many insults a man could take, especially when worry was riding him hard. It was just a small tap to the face, but it made Braithwaite's head snap back and when he righted himself his upper lip had begun to swell.

"Try that again," Dev growled.

"How dare you strike me! Why, I'll have you thrown out!"

"Not keen on challenging me yourself, Nicholas, like most men would do?" Dev said, putting an emphasis on the word men. "Of course, you like to get a man when he is down, don't you, Braithwaite? Make sure your victims are already weakened before you strike. How terribly brave you are."

Dev was usually a peaceful man, yet he had to admit to enjoying taunting Lilly's brother, partly because of Cambridge, but more importantly, Lilly.

He now cared for her, and after talking with James again, they believed this man had not treated her as she deserved.

Handsome and rich, Nicholas Braithwaite appeared to have it all. Everything that should have made him so much more than he had become. But what got to Dev the most was the fact that this was Lilly's big brother, and it seemed he had failed in that role. To him, that was an unpardonable sin.

"Where... is... your... sister?"

Braithwaite didn't speak quickly enough for Dev, so he took a step closer to him once more.

"Sh-she didn't come home today!"

"Home from where?"

"Shopping."

The fist in Dev's stomach clenched tighter.

"And where have you looked for her?"

Nicholas dropped his eyes.

"I asked you a question, Braithwaite. Where have you looked for her?"

"Her servants did not return either, so it's my belief she has run away. I am simply waiting to hear word to that effect. I will then see she is brought back to London."

Dev clenched his fists and took a deep breath.

"Why would she run away?"

"This is none of your business, Sinclair."

"Answer the question or I will beat the answer from you."

"I-I have consented to a match between her and Lord

Danderfield. My sister is taking some time to understand that I have her best interests at heart."

"You would place your sister in the hands of such a man?"

Nicholas Braithwaite stumbled backward as Dev roared at him.

"What the hell has she done to deserve such a fate? Damn you, she is your sister, for God's sake!"

"Sh-she needs to marry."

"Why?" Dev stood over the man, deliberately intimidating him.

"That is none of your business."

Looking at the guilt in Nicholas Braithwaite's eyes, Dev began to understand his motives. "It's money you want, isn't it? You're selling your sister to save yourself."

"No, it is time she wed."

"You're lying. I know this because like your sister, you drop your eyes. I'll tell you something else, Braithwaite. Sisters are something to be treasured. They are the softer part of us. The part that knows when you need to be hugged. The part that can make you laugh and cry. Quite simply, without my sisters I would be nothing."

"W-we are not like that."

"Like what? Loving? You weak-kneed fool. She is your little sister; she should have to look no further for support than you."

He wouldn't look at Dev.

"If any harm has come to her, Braithwaite, my advice to you is to leave town, because if I ever see you again, you will know fear."

"She is t-testing me," he rasped.

Disgusted, Dev left to find his brother before he beat the man senseless. Had she run away? Would she simply leave her house in Temple Street? Was that where she had run to?

Cam was where he had left him.

"Braithwaite said she did not return home from shopping today, and neither did her maid or footman. He believes she has run away to show him she will not marry Lord Danderfield."

"Good God, he does not mean to wed her to that revolting man, surely?"

Dev gave a curt nod. "It's my belief he is doing so because he has used up all his money and is now in debt."

"He wants Danderfield's money."

"James said Lilly's grandmother left her money, and thought the majority may come to her when she reaches a certain age if she does not wed. Perhaps this money is what he is after, rather than the settlement from Danderfield."

Cam whistled. "Whatever the situation is, we need to find her. I wonder if she is at Temple Street, Dev?"

"Pardon me, my lord."

A smartly dressed servant stood at Dev's elbow. He looked uncomfortable and his face was flushed.

"Yes?"

"A Mr. Davey has appeared at the servants' entrance asking to speak with you, Lord Sinclair. I would normally have turned him away, but he said it was a life or death matter, and you would not be pleased if I were to do so. He has a young boy with him, and both seem extremely agitated. He said they would not leave until I mentioned the name Miss Braithwaite to you."

"Take me to him at once, please," Dev said as the knot in his stomach grew larger. With Cam on his heels, he headed out of the ballroom and down a long hallway, then a set of narrow stairs and through a door at the bottom. Mr. Davey stood with Toby at his side in a small entranceway. Both their faces were lined with worry.

"Lord Sinclair!" Toby called to him as he approached.

"My lord." Mr. Davey bowed.

"Thank you, I know them." Dev handed out several notes he had pulled from his pocket to the two servants who appeared to be standing guard. "I would be grateful for a moment alone with them, if you please."

The staff left to go about their duties, leaving the Sinclair brothers with Mr. Davey and Toby.

"Tell me what has happened, Mr. Davey?"

"I have grave concerns for my mistress."

Dev nodded for him to continue.

"Bee, Miss Braithwaite's maid, and her footman, Wilson, were brought to Temple Street by Miss Braithwaite's driver, as Temple Street was nearby and he knew they needed help immediately."

Dev tried to stay calm, when inside, his stomach was twisting into knots.

"He found them lying on the ground. Mr. Wilson had been knocked over the head, and Bee also hurt. Of Miss Braithwaite there was no sign. Bee managed to tell us that her mistress received a note while out shopping. It said children were in trouble in Jane Street. She went to investigate, and she, Bee, and Wilson were set upon by men."

"Bee said the note came from me, but I can't write, and Lilly knew this, but went anyway," Toby added, his face pale and drawn with worry.

Dev bit back the anger at Lilly's reckless behavior, nodding for the boy to continue.

"I went out and looked for her everywhere, and put the word out for any information, but I ain't heard nothing back yet," Toby said. "I think it's got something to do with the missing children. Lilly's been interfering, and those that are taking them must be aware of that."

"But to take a woman of noble birth is a risk." Cam entered the conversation.

"Not if the man who is taking the boys is of noble birth," Dev said slowly.

"Care to enlighten me as to what the hell is going on?"

Dev turned to see James appear.

"Your sisters had an uneasy feeling all was not well with you, and sent me to find you at once. I asked a footman where Lord Sinclair and his reprobate brother had gone to, and he led me here."

Dev's chest was burning.

"Your cousin is missing, James, and you need to go to the Watch House and alert them, then collect every servant from your house and my uncle's. We need to start searching at once."

"Lilly?" James frowned, his eyes going from Dev to Toby. "How do you know she is missing?"

"She has not arrived," Cam said, "and Dev is uneasy."

"Has her brother, Lord Braithwaite, been notified?" James questioned. He did not doubt Dev's intuition.

Toby and Mr. Davey looked blank.

"I have just spoken with him and he has no idea where she is," Dev said.

"But how can that be?" James looked confused. "She is his sister for Christ's sake!"

"Come there is more, but we need to start looking, because the feeling inside me says she is in danger," Dev urged everyone from the room, Toby and Mr. Davey included. "We will gather everyone and leave at once." They soon found themselves in the front entrance. Wide-eyed, the man and boy stayed close as they took in the elegant surroundings and stares from the guests they passed.

Essie and Eden were called, and soon they were all awaiting carriages while Cam recounted the story once more for his sisters.

"We need to start looking," Eden said to each of her siblings. "All of us, and using our senses."

"Agreed," Cam and Essie said. James and Dev remained silent, both working through and discarding plans.

"Braithwaite, if you don't want me to darken your eyes, I suggest you turn and walk smartly in the opposite direction," Dev snarled as the man appeared before them. To his surprise, he kept advancing.

"What has you all out here so soon after you have arrived?"

"Go away, Nicholas, because what Dev leaves I will finish!" James said, glaring at his cousin.

"If you have information about my sister, I wish to hear it."

"Why would you think we have information about her when you told me you thought she had run away?" Dev said. "Actually, what you said was you think she has run away because you have decided to wed her to Lord Danderfield. And the reason for that is that you need the money to clear your gambling debts." Dev felt no shame in telling everyone assembled what Lilly's brother was capable of.

"What!" James stepped toward his cousin.

"Do you have knowledge about my sister?" Nicholas Braithwaite stood his ground. "If I was wrong in my belief she has run away, I wish to know it, and help find her."

"Pardon?" Dev was sure he'd heard the words wrong.

"I want to help find her."

For seconds no one spoke. Nicholas Braithwaite had lost the cynical look he usually wore, Dev realized, and in fact appeared uncertain, his eyes darting back and forth from Dev to James, who both, he was sure, looked as malleable as stone.

"Perhaps you should have thought of that sooner, Braith-waite," Cam said, placing a restraining arm on Dev's arm.

"Don't create a scene out here, brother. There are far too many flapping ears and wagging tongues about."

"Of course you do, my lord," Eden said, taking a firm hold on her husband's arm in case he had the urge to finish what Dev had started. "And we would be grateful for any help."

"No, we wouldn't," James and Dev growled.

"Do you have news about Lilliana or not?" Braithwaite said again. "I have a right to know as her brother."

"Rights," Dev snarled. "Don't you dare speak to me of rights, when you were about to force her into marriage!"

"We believe she has met with foul play, as her servants were found by your sister's driver, bruised and beaten," James said quickly, cutting Dev off as he opened his mouth to continue abusing Lilly's brother. "Of Lilliana there was no sign."

"Dear God. I-I had no idea, I truly believed—"

"Fear not, Lord Braithwaite, we shall find your sister," Eden said.

"Your brother said some things to me that shamed me, Duchess. For the first time in many years I saw myself as I truly am."

"I would have thought you incapable of that emotion, given that I have firsthand knowledge of your depravity, Braithwaite, not to mention your obvious disrespect of your sister and her welfare," Dev said.

"I am a long way from forgiveness, Nicholas, but as I too have guilt where Lilly is concerned, and my treatment of her, I will allow you to help us," James said. "You will go to the Watch House with Mr. Davey and then return him to Temple Street, and you may go home or to my house and await news."

"But where do you all go?"

"I'm afraid that is as yet undetermined. However, when I

have news of your sister, I will send word to my house. Tell Buttles I sent you."

"But—"

"Braithwaite, so help me God, I will throw you into your carriage if you do not go willingly. Your cousin has thrown you an olive branch. Personally, I would rather beat you with it, but I will respect him in this," Dev said. "But if you do not do as he states and alert the Watch, then never show your face before me again."

"I will ensure it is done, Lord Sinclair," Mr. Davey said, his face grim.

"I will do it." Nicholas gave a short bow before he left with Mr. Davey on his heels.

"Is there any way I can get you to go home, wife, and take your sister with you?" James said, looking at Eden and Essie.

"No, we need to be together to find Lilly. Our senses are stronger that way."

"I could have married anyone, but I chose you," James muttered as he grabbed Eden and planted a loud kiss on her lips, uncaring of the outraged gasps behind him as two of society's matrons tittered in horror at such a display in public.

"Outside now," Dev said to his family, aware of the spectacle they were making.

They quickly left the house and assembled on the street outside.

"Toby." Dev placed a hand on the boy's shoulder. "We need you to take us to anyone who may have information. I will pay handsomely, but do not know where to go."

The boy nodded. "I can do that, but it's not a place for ladies—or gentlemen for that matter."

"Just as well none of those are present then," Cam said.

"Toby is right," Dev said to his sisters. "I'm not sure you

should come, as this will be unpleasant and dangerous. As your brother, I want to keep you safe—"

"Stow it, Dev, we are coming," Eden said, grabbing her husband's hand.

"We tried." The Duke sighed.

"Lead on, Toby," Dev said, taking Essie's hand, and seconds later they were moving.

Hold on, Lilly, I'm coming.

CHAPTER 16

*L*ight from the gas lamps did not offer much illumination as they followed on Toby's heels through the London streets. Dev had to stay alert, as Toby would slip down an alley no wider than an arm span and expect them to be behind him. He hurried up and down small lanes Dev had not known even existed.

No one spoke, as Eden had her earplugs out and was listening to see if she could detect any voices or information that may lead them to Lilly.

They stayed connected, the Sinclair siblings holding hands so their strength was greater and their senses stronger. Dev felt sensations travel through them as they focused, all intent on finding Lilly.

He and James spoke to whomever Toby took them too, and handed over money for information, but as yet none of it led him to Lilly. They frequented small, dilapidated buildings, and talked with people huddled in alleyways. No one approached, and Dev thought that was due to the fierce expression he knew he wore.

Someone knew something, and he was willing to pay

whatever was needed to get her back, but the desperation inside him told him he had to find her soon.

They passed people doing things no child should know about, yet Toby never flinched, his small body watchful and silent as they made their way to another informant, who he hoped would have the information he needed. Dev used his vision in the more sinister areas to determine anything moving or alive; most kept out their way, as they were moving fast and a large group.

Essie and Eden stayed between the men, but when two men tried to grab Essie, Dev's growl and Cam's fist sent them back to the shadows.

"Stay here, my lord, and I shall return shortly."

They had reached the back of a small alehouse. Dev could hear the rumble of noise with the occasional high-pitched squeal.

"The big brother in me demands I shouldn't let you go in there unescorted, Toby, yet I know this situation is not new to you."

Toby snorted and shook his head, but said nothing before disappearing through a door.

"A remarkable young boy," James said, pulling Eden in front of him and wrapping his arms around her.

"Are you all right, Eden?" Dev asked, as this was harder on her than any of them. She would be able to hear every-thing that was happening around her.

"I am, although what is taking place in the rooms some-where in that house is extremely disturbing."

Cam snorted, knowing full well it was a brothel.

"Where the hell is she?" Dev said, giving voice to his fears.

"If anyone can find her, brother, it is us," Cam said. "We will search for as long as we need."

Dev looked at the faces of his family, all there to support him and find the woman he loved. Yes, it was love, he knew that now, because the pain inside him was unlike anything he had experienced before.

Toby came out of the building. "I have just spoken to Split, who has heard from Jessie, who overheard his master, Ely Chit, talking to Delve about something happening down at a warehouse on Dilth Street. It's old and unused and by the water."

Dev's siblings often talked in circles, so he followed with what little patience he had left.

"We has to find her tonight," Toby added. "'Cause Jessie said that Gegan is involved, and that means there's a lot of money at stake. 'Cause he'd sell his mother for a coin."

"Do they know what he's involved in?"

"Jessie said Dominus was at Dilth Street."

"Dominus being?" James asked.

"He's new in town, but mean and done some bad things. But he's starting up an army of thieves, so we have heard."

"And the missing children could have been kidnapped to work for him?" Dev made the leap.

"That's my guess, but there's got to be more, 'cause we all know how to filch, so this had to be more," Toby said.

"Specialized, you mean?" Cam said. "As if he wants them trained for a reason?"

"Not sure what the first word means, but I think the other part's right. Could be he plans to steal from nobs."

"Nobs like us," James said.

The boy nodded. "Strange that no one seen him yet though, and don't know much about him."

"Why strange?" Dev asked.

"Rumors have a way of spreading on these streets. The man must be a mean one, if he's managed to keep everyone's lips tight."

Dev thought about that for a few seconds. Could whoever was taking these children be the one who had Lilly? Was her disappearance a direct result of her interference? If he had her, what did he plan to do to her?

He could not contemplate that, so he focused on Toby again.

"We have to find her now," Dev said, the tension inside him rising.

"Let's go then."

Toby led them deeper into a dark side of London. Buildings rose above them along narrow lanes, blocking even the smallest glimpse of the moon.

"Now," Eden whispered when they reached the end of a narrow lane. "Hold hands now."

Dev and his siblings formed a circle and while they closed their eyes, he changed his vision and focused.

"I hear men, three, possibly four. They are discussing a woman," Eden said. "Where they are to take her, and what is to be done. It's Lilly, I'm certain, and she is in very real danger. We must get to her now."

"She's near, I can detect the faintest trace of her scent," Cam added.

"Fear," Essie whispered. "She's scared because it's dark, and she's alone."

"The warehouse is just down there," Toby said, his eyes wide as he tried to understand what he was hearing.

They trod silently to where the old building stood. Dev looked around for people and saw two men standing at the front of the building. A black carriage stood waiting for someone, and Dev wondered if it belonged to this Dominus Toby spoke of. Looking toward the building, he opened his senses and found Lilly, her unique color among the others inside. She was alone, and relief nearly buckled his knees as he watched her move. She was alive and her color strong.

"I see her," Dev whispered. "I'm going to get inside

through one of the open boards. Cam, you come with me and watch my back. You others stay here."

"I should come with you."

"I know you want to, Toby, but I need you to go back to the end of the street and keep an eye out for anyone approaching."

He didn't want to; Dev could see it in the narrowing of his eyes and jut of his jaw.

"Trust me to get her out safe, Toby."

"I do."

"Can I take your scarf with me? I may need it."

Nodding, the boy quickly unwound it from his neck and then left.

"No risks, Dev, you call to Eden if you need help, and I'll come," James said.

Leaving their family looking grim, he and Cam walked along the building until they found some broken boards and a space big enough to slip through.

I'm coming, Lilly.

Lilly was dirty, hungry, and in the light of day, she had also been bloody angry. Now, however, the darkness was making her fear for her sanity. Moonlight helped, and showed her she was alone in the room, but still the shadows had appeared, and with them the fear.

Her hands and feet were bound, and she had been bundled into a cart and carried for hours—well it had felt like hours—to her current accommodation.

The small room she had been thrown into had nothing to sit on or look at. In fact, it was dark, damp, and airless, with only one window above her in the roof.

She feared for Bee and Wilson, and hoped they had

survived the attack. Where was she? Would anyone come for her?

Looking up, Lilly tried to focus on the glass and the sky beyond, anything to force back the terror that was rising inside her. Could she see stars? Just one that she could focus on.

Biting her lip to stop the moan of terror, she inhaled a deep breath and slowly released it.

"You are strong, Lilly. The dark will soon give way to light, and you will be safe until then." She forced herself to focus on those words. She was intelligent and knew that her fear was irrational, but it had been that way since she was a child.

Did anyone know, besides her staff, that she was missing? Who would come and find her? Toby, definitely, Wilson and Bee if they were unhurt. Mr. and Mrs. Davey, perhaps. Her brother? Definitely not. In fact, he would probably rejoice in her disappearance. A pair of green eyes slipped into her head and Lilly quickly banished them.

Lord Sinclair would come for her if he knew she had disappeared, because he was an honorable man, but who would tell him? Blinking several times, she forced the tears away. She would not think of him now, or the prospect that she would never see him again. It really was ridiculous how she felt about him, and all simply because he had been nice to her.

Liar, there is a great deal more to your feelings for him than that, a little voice inside her head said. Lilly pushed it aside.

Had she been kidnapped because of her interference with the missing children? It now seemed likely. If whoever was taking them had enough power, he could have her removed —as he had—successfully. Yet, she was still the daughter of a nobleman, so kidnapping her would not go unnoticed. Presumably she was a threat that made this worth doing.

Relief filled her as a key fitted into the lock on her door. She didn't care who walked through that door; whoever it was would take her mind off the dark and the thoughts spinning around inside her head. Lilly struggled to wedge her bottom into the corner of the room and lever herself to her feet. If she was to face her captors, it would be standing and defiant.

"I 'ave food."

Not exactly a cheerful face, yet the man was not fearful-looking either. Short and round, he could be everyone's favorite uncle and not their feared jailer, and better still, he had a lamp. Lilly felt the muscles in her body slowly ease as light began to fill the dark spaces in the small room.

"Why am I here?"

"Not my business. Eat and drink or don't, I care nothing either way."

"Charming. I bet you have trouble with the ladies," Lilly muttered, wondering if she antagonized him enough, would he leave and forget to take the lamp with him. "It's not as if you have the physical attributes to fall back on either." Lilly clamped her knees together to stop them shaking. She would not show this man she was terrified. Her grandmother had told her to never show fear when faced with adversity. *"Attack, Lilliana, when others expect you to cower!"*

"There's no call for you to speak to me like that!"

"Oh sorry, were the words to big for you too understand?" Lilly cooed. "I meant that you're ugly."

She watched his face puff up and turn as red as Mr. Davey's nose on a chilly winter's day. Lilly wondered why she was antagonizing the man when she was alone, bound hand and foot, and totally at his mercy.

"I have ladies!"

A man's ego was so fragile, Lilly thought, looking him

over slowly and hoping he couldn't hear the thudding of her heart.

"Come now, sir, we both know the women who spend time with you could not be termed ladies, even loosely." She was pleased with her words, even if they were high-pitched and squeaky.

"My Rosetta is a lady!"

"I need you out here, Joe!" The words came from somewhere beyond the door.

"I ain't untying your hands now."

With a final glare at Lilly, the man dropped the tray at her feet, taking the lamp with him as he left the room. As the door clicked shut, Lilly was once again plunged into darkness.

Slumping to the ground, she pulled up her knees. How would she ever escape from here? The food smelled bad and she had no intention of putting any of it into her mouth; the way she was feeling it would just come out again anyway. She felt the sting of tears begin to slowly fall down her cheeks and was angry for the weakness. Tears achieved nothing but a sore head and tired eyes, yet still they came. Lying on her side, Lilly gave up the battle, letting them flow in the hopes that exhaustion would help her sleep and, let her escape the darkness.

CHAPTER 17

*D*ev, with Cam on his heels, made it through the
warehouse undetected and up to the second floor.
He had seen the colors of several men grouped together in a
small room downstairs, but had managed to keep away from
there. Passing the door that he knew Lilly sat behind, he
noted the lock was large and secure and the door made of
sturdy wood. He had nothing to break it, and even if he did,
it would alert someone that he was there.

Moving past, he did not tell Lilly he was near, but kept
walking to a small door at the end of the hallway. Opening it,
he found a balcony.

"You stay here," he whispered to Cam, then motioned that
he was going up onto the roof.

Climbing onto the railing, he pulled himself up. If his
luck was in, there would be a window in the side of the
building or in the roof and he could get her out that way.
Walking slowly, he hoped it would hold him. Dropping to his
knees when he was above her, he found a window and
looked down. Pressing his face to the glass, he tried to
find her.

"Lilly, it's Devon," he said softly, using his fingers to tap on the pane. He kept tapping until he heard her call his name. He had to take a chance and break the glass—hopefully they would not hear him from below.

"I'm going to break the glass, Lilly. Move away from beneath it."

Standing, he stomped his foot, and the window cracked instantly. Taking off his jacket, he wrapped it around his fist and cleared the glass from the opening.

"Please hurry, Devon!"

He could hear the panic in her voice and remembered her fear of the dark. Add to that everything else she had endured, and he would say she was close to hysteria.

"Soon, Lilly, I will have you out soon. Just a few minutes more."

"I-i-it's dark in here."

"I know, sweetheart. I am going to put a knot in the end of this scarf and then lower it to you. I want you to use both hands and hold on tight while I pull you up." Lord, he hoped she was strong enough. The distance wasn't great, yet it would be difficult for her.

"I-I can't. My hands are bound at the back."

Someone would pay for leaving her bound, helpless, and alone in the dark; he would see to it. Once again on his stomach, he looked down at her.

Dirt was smeared over her face, her clothes were torn, and her hair had come unbound. However, it was the look of utter desperation in her eyes that made him curse. He'd never seen that look before.

"Y-you'll have to get help."

"I won't leave you, Lilly," Dev said, trying to work out how the hell he was going to get her out of the room. She sniffed but said nothing further.

"Bend at the waist and slip your hands under your

bottom. Then sit on it and try and wriggle them under your legs so they are bound in front of you."

He watched as she wriggled, trying to push her hands beneath her.

"My petticoats and bottom are too large."

"Your bottom is not too large, it's perfect. Now wriggle harder."

She did and finally she sat and began a series of maneuvers to try and get her legs through her hands. If she failed he would call Cam, then drop into the room and lift her up to him.

"It-it's hard!"

Her skirts were now up around her waist as she tried to wriggle her hands past her ankles, and if the situation were not so dire, he would take great pleasure in viewing her long, slender limbs.

"Don't you dare look at my—"

"Knickers?" Dev supplied. At least she had some fight back in her voice.

"I did it!"

"Clever girl. Now stand and take the end of the scarf."

Sitting upright, Dev braced his feet on either side of the window frame and began to pull her up.

"Don't drop me!"

"Untrusting wench!" Dev grunted.

"My h-hands are slipping."

"No," Dev wheezed, "they are not."

"Pull, Dev!"

He answered with a grunt. When his hand clamped on her wrist, she sobbed. Standing, he hauled her through the opening and then she was free.

"I–I have you," Dev rasped, breathless as he lowered them to the roof. He sat with her on his lap, wrapping his arms around her. He held her tight and dropped his head to her shoulder.

"Thank you," she whispered, burrowing into him. "I didn't think anyone would come so soon. I-it was dark, and then a man came and I was horrid to him, and he left a-again, taking his lamp."

He let her babble out her fear as he held her, stroking her hair and assuring her she was with him now, and safe.

"Let me untie you," he said when his breathing had begun to regulate and she had run out of words.

"Thank you." She gripped his neck hard. "Thank you for coming to find me."

Dev kissed her cheek, and then easing her back, he untied her feet and hands, rubbing each when he had finished.

"I have you now, sweetheart; no one will hurt you again," he said, cupping her face between his hands. "I have been slowly going out of my mind imagining what horrors you were being exposed to."

"You really mean that, don't you?" she whispered.

"I never say anything I don't mean."

"I-I did not think anyone would come for me," she added, and Dev wanted to go and find Nicholas Braithwaite and punch him, only this time harder.

"My family and James are here, plus Toby, and I would love to tell you how many ways you are special to me, Lilly, but right now we need to leave as quietly and quickly as I came, before any of us is detected."

Lilly nodded. Dev lifted her to her feet. He took her gloved hand and led her to the edge of the roof. Cam was waiting to take her, and Dev lowered Lilly into his arms. He quickly followed. Opening the door, they saw no one in the hallway, and he pulled her through behind him. On tiptoes they walked its length, and then started down the stairs.

"We need to slip past a room where I believe several men

are, and as there could be trouble waiting for us out there you must run if I tell you to," Dev whispered. "My family will be outside, go to them."

"I will not leave you."

"You will do as you are told, Lilly. If I say run, you run to where the others await."

"I—"

"Promise me," Dev demanded softly.

"I promise."

Cam snorted at the unenthusiastic tone of her voice. However, she had promised, so at least Dev had her word.

Dev could see clearly; Lilly and Cam, however, could not, so he led them silently through the warehouse. It was as they approached the hole they had entered through that he heard the sound of feet running toward them.

"Run straight ahead, Lilly, there is a hole in the wall. Once you are through, call James!"

She left his side as the first man reached him. Turning, Dev swung out with his leg as James had taught him to. It connected and the man went down. But seconds later, the next was upon him.

Cam had two on him, and the brothers fought with everything they had.

Dev heard Cam's war cry as he took a fist to the chin that made him see stars. He looked and found James entering the fray, Dev's sisters behind him. He took a right to the jaw and quickly returned the favor with more force.

"Don't touch him, you cad!"

Lilly appeared on his right, wielding a piece of wood like a saber. Dev didn't have time to roar at her, as the man before him was bigger and meaner than the others. He just hoped she stayed healthy so he could kill her for disobeying him when this was over.

"Leave now!" he managed before taking a fist to the stomach that nearly doubled him over.

"Take that!"

Dev watched the man's eyes open wider and then he simply fell backward, landing hard enough to ensure that if Lilly hadn't cracked his head, the floor would have. James did some sort of swinging kick caught his man unaware and sent him face-first into a wall. Cam, with a well-placed punch, finished off his opponent. Nobody moved for several seconds, all dragging in large lungfuls of salty air.

"You, madam," Dev wheezed, pointing at Lilly when he could speak, "promised me you would run when I told you to! Yet I turn around to see you wielding that bloody piece of wood like Zenobia!"

"Wasn't she Queen of the Palmyrene Empire in Roman Syria?" Cam said, grinning.

"Yes, she led a famous revolt against the Roman Empire," Eden added, stepping to Dev's side with a handkerchief, which she pressed to his sorely abused lip.

Ignoring James's snort of laughter, Dev glared at his siblings as best as he could over the white square of linen. He was well aware of what they were doing, but this time it wasn't going to work. Nothing was distracting him from telling Lilly what he thought. He was sure she'd taken years of his life tonight by getting involved in the fighting.

"Shut up, all of you!"

"Now, Dev, you've always lectured us on learning about famous women as well as men in history. Surely Zenobia falls into that category."

"Cam, I will thrash you if you don't cease!"

"I had my fingers crossed!"

Spinning back from glaring at his siblings, Dev gently pushed his sister and her ministrations aside and looked at Lilly as she spoke. The wood was still clasped firmly in her hands and she looked small and fragile, a façade that no longer fooled him.

"What?"

"I had my fingers crossed when I promised you."

Dev stared at her for several seconds—maybe the events of today were catching up with her, because she was making no sense. "What?" he said again.

"Oh, well then, that makes perfect sense," Essie said, rushing forward to take the wood from Lilly and drop it to the ground.

"Yes, it's a code we Sinclairs have always lived by," Eden said, moving to Lilly's other side.

"Eden," James warned in that tone that told Dev he wanted her to shut up and stop interfering. As he was in full agreement, he followed it up with a glare.

"You crossed your fingers when you promised me you would leave?" Dev said as it finally dawned on him what the hell she was talking about. She didn't speak, just nodded. His sisters moved closer, pinning her between them.

"Excellent. Well, I'm glad that's sorted," Cam said loudly.

"Nothing is sorted! For Christ's sake, when we cross our fingers on a promise it is over something trivial like raiding each other's rooms and stealing belongings, not... not"—Dev had never been the type to fly into a rage, but it seemed tonight it was his destiny—"when your life is at stake!"

"I don't know, when Cam took Miss Pound Cake, I was devastated," Eden said.

"She was a doll!"

Lilly's giggle sucked the anger right out of Dev. It was such a sweet, unrestrained sound, and all the sweeter because it came from a woman who had had very few reasons to giggle in her life.

"We need to get out of here," Dev snapped, pointing to the hole in the wall and scowling. "Now!" he roared, which had his siblings scurrying forward, dragging Lilly with them. James, however, strolled. The Duke never scurried.

"Toby, you are coming with us too," Dev said, looking to where the boy sat.

"I-I c-can't."

Dev heard the pain and quickly crouched before him. He had one hand clutched to his side and when Dev pulled it away, he saw blood. "Why didn't you say something?" he said, picking him up and running to the opening.

"It hurts."

It must have been bad if he said that because this stoic little boy was not one to make a fuss. Dev found his siblings in the carriage that had been outside the warehouse. James was driving, with Cam seated beside him. He hoped that between them they could get them home safely.

He climbed in with Toby in his arms and settled him on Lilly.

"What has happened?" Lilly cried.

Dev picked her up and held them both on his lap. "He's hurt. I don't know how badly, but we need to get to the Raven residence now."

Dev heard Lilly's whisper as she talked to Toby on the journey to the Raven town house. Essie was kneeling on the floor before the boy, inspecting the injury as best she could given the circumstances.

No one spoke. All eyes were focused on the boy, and he could feel the fear in Lilly as she held him close. Toby lay against her, quiet and still.

"Cam, take Toby," Dev said as the carriage stopped. He lifted Lilly to her feet and followed.

The house was well lit as they walked into the front entrance, yet like Dev, Lilly did not see her brother standing beside the butler until he stepped before her.

"Are you well, Lilliana?"

"What are you doing here?"

"I came to find you."

"Why?" she asked, and Dev could hear the confusion in her voice. Placing a hand on her back, he reassured her she was safe and he was there at her side.

"I am sorry."

"For what?"

"I—everything."

"I don't know what game you are playing, Nicholas," she said, "and why you look as you do, but I assure you I want you to leave here now and never return."

Dev let her leave then, to follow Cam, who was carrying Toby up the stairs.

"She was hardly going to run into your arms, Nicholas."

Dev stood silently beside James as he spoke, watching Lilly run up the stairs. He would follow soon, but had a few words to say to her brother first.

"At least she is safe, and for that I thank you."

"I almost believe you mean that, cousin."

"Surprisingly, I do," Nicholas said quietly, looking from Dev to James. "She will not wed Danderfield. I will see to it in the morning."

"Dare one ask about this transformation you seem to have undergone in the space of one evening?" James said, the skepticism clearly evident in this tone.

Nicholas didn't answer instantly, and Dev watched as he thought about his next words.

"I loved her once, you know, but things changed with my father's death."

"The fact she was your sister never changed, Braithwaite," Dev said. "And there is much you don't know about your sister, or what she does."

"What?"

"The story is hers to tell, not mine."

"Very well, I will speak with her tomorrow. And I would thank you for your harsh words; they have made me see just what I have become, Lord Sinclair."

"Words will cost you nothing, Braithwaite," Dev said, brushing past him. "Actions, however, now they are worth a great deal more."

Dev helped Essie and Lilly clean Toby's wound. He seemed to drift in and out of consciousness, and the tension in the room grew with each breath he struggled to draw into his small body.

"There is so much blood," Lilly whispered as she once again rinsed the cloth in the bowl, the water now red.

"Dev says the damage inside him is bad and that he is bleeding. Therefore, I must be honest, Lilly, it does not look good."

Lilly's hands stilled as Essex spoke. "Please tell me he will live."

"Essie will do everything she can and James has called for a doctor," Dev reassured her.

Lilly looked up at him, her eyes wide and pleading. "He can't die, Devon."

"We won't know anything until he has been treated, Lilly, but for now, we have to stop the bleeding," Essie soothed.

Dev let himself slide into his other vision. The boy was bleeding from the inside, and he could see his color was weaker, the yellow now almost cream. Unless they stopped that bleeding, Toby would die; he knew it, Essie knew it. Lilly, however, did not.

The doctor came, a ridiculously young-looking man who, as far as Lilly was concerned, did not have enough experience to make an accurate diagnosis. She looked over his shoulder as he checked Toby, and Dev could see the young man was intimidated.

"He has internal injuries I am afraid, and is losing too much blood. I fear the prognosis is not promising."

"Well, then do something!"

Dev intervened as Lilly glared at the doctor, and he quickly pushed him from the room into James's hands outside.

After applying a paste to the wound and forcing several sips of herbal tea down Toby's throat, Essie left, muttering about needing a medical book she had in her room. Toby's breath had grown weak and his face was as white as the sheet he lay upon. Dev took the cup of warm tea and buttered crumpet off the tray, both of which Lilly had refused, and moved to her side.

"Eat this."

"I couldn't," she said, her eyes still on Toby, and Dev wondered where she got her strength. He was wilting and he hadn't been abducted, bound, and left in a small room with no nourishment for hours on end.

"You will eat this, Lilly, because you will need your strength to care for Toby. If you faint, then it will be me he sees when he opens his eyes, not you."

She took the tea and gulped it down, then nibbled the crumpet. He wiped the corner of her mouth when she ate the last bite. The sob came from nowhere, and when she launched into his arms he caught her.

CHAPTER 18

"*T*-tell me he will live, Dev."

"I can't, sweetheart, you must understand that," he said, running his hand over her hair.

She lay against him, looking at Toby. Dev lifted her hands, looking at her bloodied and torn gloves, and slowly took them from her fingers.

"Do you trust me, Lilly?"

"Yes."

Amazing how one simple word could warm him to his toes. He kissed each finger because he knew she liked it, and was rewarded with a gentle sigh. Even exhausted, she responded to him as he knew she always would. Looking at her slender hands, he wondered if his hunch was accurate. It seemed now was the time to test his theory.

"Did you ever touch another person before you took to wearing gloves, and feel strange sensations, Lilly?"

She looked at him for several seconds and then slowly nodded. Lord, she was beautiful. Her hair was everywhere, her clothes dirty with bits torn here and there, yet he had never wanted another woman like he did Lilliana Braithwaite. He wanted to take her home with him and keep her safe, lock her away from anyone who would harm her, and that simply confirmed just how important she had become to him.

Only his family made him feel such emotions, yet now it seemed Lilly could too. Brushing his lips over hers, he kept the kiss light, and then turning to the bed he looked at the small boy lying motionless. Switching his vision, he could see Toby's color was now white, and Dev feared he did not have long to live. Essie had tried everything and was even now looking for something to save the boy, but Dev knew death better than most, and Toby was close. His breathing had grown shallow and he lay still in the big bed.

"Will you try something for me?" Dev said, once again taking Lilly's hand in his. "Just place your hands on Toby and tell me what you feel." She didn't speak, just turned and laid one palm flat on Toby's forehead, the other on his chest. The boy twitched instantly and then calmed.

"What do you feel?"

"He's so cold, almost like he's—"

"No, Lilly, he's not dead," Dev said, placing his hand over hers. If what he suspected was true and Lilly could heal with her hands, then maybe he could help her in some way, use his strength to support her.

"Now we're going to move your hand slowly down his arm."

"I'm scared."

"I know, love, but I'm here and I will keep you safe. You said you trusted me, remember." She nodded as he moved as close to her as he could, his front now pressed to her back, and then cupping her hands with his, he began to run them over the boy. The heat from her hands made his tingle, the sensation not unbearable, but he could feel it traveling up his arms.

"Focus on your hands, Lilly. We are going to move closer to Toby's injury now."

He kept his voice calm.

"I-it feels as if I am being stung by a thousand bees, Dev."

"I have you, love, my hands are right there with yours," he soothed as her body tensed.

He felt her hands get hotter as she reached the boy's injury. Beneath her fingers Toby grew restless and color filled his face as he began to murmur and thrash about in the bed.

"I-I... it's—"

"Are you in pain, Lilly?" She shook her head. "Tell me what you feel."

"M-my hands feel hot, like I am being stung by stinging nettle, but my body is cold."

"Pull your hands away if you can no longer stand it."

"Am I.... Are my hands healing him?"

Dev was watching Toby's color to make sure his light didn't go out completely, and saw the yellow steadily grow brighter. The tension in Lilly's body worried him and he wondered what effect this would have on her. He could feel the tingling she spoke of beneath his fingers and the chill that was creeping into her body. Wrapping his hands around hers, he lifted them and saw the wound had healed significantly. There was only a cut that would easily heal.

"Dear God! He... it is nearly healed," Lilly gasped.

Dev felt the boy's head and checked his pulse, and then looked inside him and saw the bleeding had stopped. Toby was still sleeping but this time it was a healing sleep, and his color and breathing were strong. Lifting Lilly into his arms as her knees buckled, he walked around the bed and lowered her onto the other side, beside Toby. Her color was strong, yet he could see that in doing what she had for the boy she had used the last of her reserves and was now exhausted.

"Wh-what just happened?"

Framing her face, Dev kissed her again. "Do you want to discuss this now, or sleep?"

"Dissscusss."

She was asleep before she finished the word. Dev watched her, taking in the long sweep of her lashes, the pallor of her cheeks. He loved her because she was his mate. The other half to him. He had the gift of sight and she touch. She was the piece that completed his family's circle. Dear Christ, he could hardly take it in.

Pulling the covers up, he tucked them both in. Toby slept, his face young and innocent, the woman beside him looking remarkably similar. Stroking a hand over her hair, he then gave her a last long look and left the room.

A maid waited outside the door, so Dev told her to have a room and bath prepared for Miss Braithwaite and one for him, and he would return soon to escort her.

"I have the herb here, Dev, and have instructed the kitchen to bring more boiling water."

Dev took Essie's hands as she appeared before him, her face creased with worry. She stilled, looking up at him.

"No, Dev, please tell me Toby is alive!"

"Yes, he lives, and he is sleeping the sleep of a tired yet recovering young boy, Ess. Now I need you to come with me. I have something to tell you all, but I want to say it only once."

"I-I don't understand." She gripped his fingers.

"You will, love. Come."

She let him lead her to where the others waited in James's study. Nicholas Braithwaite was the first to gain his feet as Essie and Dev entered.

"How are Lilliana and the boy doing, my lord?"

His lip was now puffy and purple and his hair stood on end, and at some stage, he had removed his jacket and necktie. He looked vastly different from the previously elegant and pampered Nicholas Braithwaite.

"I think the boy will make it through the night, and your sister has been taken to a chamber to sleep, as she was both exhausted and hungry," Dev said, telling the lie as easily as he took his next breath.

Perhaps Braithwaite was changing, yet Dev was still not about to trust him completely and most especially not with both his family's and Lilly's secrets.

"She asked me to request that you go home and tell your aunt you have received a letter from her stating she has left London briefly to visit one of your estates, as she is in need of fresh air."

"But she has never done that before. Aunt will be suspicious."

"Braithwaite, you are foisting a seventy-year-old reprobate on her, which I may add you had no issue with until this evening. Surely you can use that to your advantage when telling the tale."

Dev had believed there were no similarities between Lilly and her brother, but the glare he got suggested they both had the same backbone.

"There is no need to keep reminding me I have neglected my sister, Sinclair. I will go home at once and tell our aunt. She will believe me, as she would have no reason not to," Nicholas muttered as he prepared to take his leave. "I will return in the morning with some of Lilly's things. I hope one of your sisters will care for her until I return?"

"They will," Dev said, pleased that at last the man seemed to be aware of his duty to his sister. "But remember this while you sleep, Braithwaite. Your sister will not forgive the years of neglect and abuse easily, and she will wonder at the abrupt change in you, as do we."

Nicholas didn't say anything, just nodded.

"Be ready to beg, Braithwaite. With four sisters, this is the best advice I can give you."

When the door had closed, Dev went to sit before the fire with the rest of his family.

"Eat now, Dev," Eden said, handing him a plate, "and then tell us what's happening."

"You probably heard most of it anyway," he said around a mouthful of buttered toast.

"Most, but not all," she said with a cheeky smile.

James frowned at her. "I thought you put your earplugs in when you returned?"

"James, James, James," Cam said, shaking his head. "When will you learn not to believe her when she says that?

"You lied to me!" James roared, glaring at his wife, who looked totally unrepentant.

"Not lied, darling, exactly," she said, kissing his cheek. "I had them in and then I took them out. Anyway," she quickly added as James opened his mouth to continue the discussion, "we have much more pressing matters to discuss regarding Toby and your cousin."

Dev realized this was his cue, so he took a large swallow of his brandy before beginning. "None of you have probably noticed, but Lilly always wears her gloves. I discussed it with her one night and she told me she had always worn them, since childhood."

"That's true," James added. "I used to question her on it when we were playing but she usually just fobbed me off."

"Christ, she's one of us!"

Dev had known it would be Cam who worked it out first, and he wasn't disappointed. Essie followed seconds later. Eden of course, already knew.

"Good God!"

"Christ!"

"As you know, I don't like to hear those words coming from my sisters, but if ever there was a time they were acceptable, now is it," Dev added.

"What the bloody hell is going on?"

Looking at James's bewildered expression, Dev laughed. For once the mighty Raven brain was not working.

"Lilly has sensitive hands, Raven."

"So do a lot of people. One of my drivers is allergic to.... Mother of God!"

"Yes darling, your cousin has the heightened sense of touch, just as I have hearing, Cam smell, Essie taste, and Dev sight. She is the fifth and final sense, it seems. How strange that it was you who uncovered this, brother," Eden said, giving Dev a pointed look that he ignored.

"She healed Toby tonight. It exhausted her and now she sleeps, but she did it."

"How did you know, Dev?" Cam queried.

"I took off her glove one night. She rebelled, but I grabbed her hand, and she told me she had never touched anyone before without it causing her pain."

"Like I cannot hear, James," Eden said with a sly smile. "Love dulls the senses."

Dev ignored her.

"Another one." James groaned, falling back into his chair. "But how is it possible? Surely her blood tie to the Sinclairs is weak?"

"Apparently it's not," Cam said, still looking stunned.

"She is also a very special lady with special colors meant for the strongest of us all," Essie said, grinning at Dev, who in turn glared at her.

"For what it's worth, brother, I like her," Cam said, taking the last piece of apple pie off the plate.

"Of course you like her, she's my bloody cousin!"

"As do we all," Eden said, taking her husband's hand and giving it a hard squeeze as he opened his mouth again. It closed quickly.

"I will go and see her and have the maid take her to a room, Raven." Dev got to his feet.

"I will do it!"

"No, you won't, James. Dev is more than capable."

Leaving the room before another word was said, Dev made his way to Lilly's side. He was eager to see her, eager to know she was well. He loved her. The thought nearly dropped him to his knees. Another to love, another to care for. But this one would be different, he knew. This one was a part of him.

CHAPTER 19

*L*illy woke aware that she was in her cousin's house. She was relieved to find the room was lit by the glow from the fire. It was bad enough waking in her own room in the dark, but to do so in a strange house was terrifying.

She thought briefly about looking for Toby to check on his injuries, and then discarded the idea. James's house was huge with many rooms, and Lilly had visions of walking in on James and his family while they slept. She lifted her hands and studied them. Had they really healed Toby? How had Devon known she could do that?

He had told her, when she lay beside the boy, that he was sleeping peacefully. Could it be true? Her head hurt just thinking about it. How was it even possible for one person to heal another?

Pushing herself upright, she saw the bath not far from the bed, and the tray of food on the small table beside it. Throwing the covers aside, she tried to decide which she wanted more: food or cleanliness.

Both.

Standing, she felt her legs wobble. She felt weak after healing Toby, as if the action had taken all her strength.

"Did I really do that?" Lilly said to no one. Yet she knew it was not a dream.

She dragged the small table closer to the bath, then stripped off her dirty clothes, and removing what pins were left in her hair, she sank into the still blissfully warm water. After scrubbing her skin pink with the soap that smelled of lavender, she then washed her hair. Finally clean, Lilly lay back, exhausted, and reached for a piece of cheese. Popping it into her mouth, she let her thoughts return to the night's events.

As if being abducted had not been traumatic enough, now she had to think about what her hands had done to Toby. What did healing a person without medicine make her? Was she a witch or a freak who should reside in a circus? The cheese suddenly felt leaden in her empty stomach.

Her thoughts were interrupted by the door opening. His head appeared first, followed by his body. Devon stepped inside and looked to the bed, then turned toward the fire. His eyes held hers and then he simply closed and locked the door behind him.

He wore a robe, his dark hair damp, bruises forming on his face. He looked almost savage and lord, he looked wonderful.

"You.... We.... You shouldn't be in here, my lord."

He didn't speak, just advanced, his eyes running over her face and down her body. Lilly could feel each place they landed. Heat seemed to be spreading through her with speed.

"You should leave, Devon."

"I know," he said, dropping to his knees before her.

"Wh-what are you doing?" Lilly whispered, and then she shuddered as he ran the tip of his finger from her shoulder to her fingers.

"Touching you," he said, his eyes holding hers as his hand moved back up her arm and onto her chest. "Looking at you like this drives every rational thought from my head."

"This is wrong. We shouldn't—" Lilly moaned as he reached her breasts.

"I will leave if you ask me to, Lilly."

She couldn't; the words would not form in her throat.

"Are you finished eating?"

With her lip trapped between her teeth, Lilly could only nod.

"Excellent," Dev said, rolling up the sleeves of his robe. He slipped his hands into the water beneath her. Lifting her out, he reached for the drying cloth.

Lilly felt color heat her cheeks as he held the cloth at his side and simply looked at her. "Please, Dev, I—"

"I have dreamt of you every night since that first kiss we shared, yet nothing could compare to this. You are perfection, every lush inch formed to drive me wild. Let me love you, Lilly."

Lilly didn't speak; instead, she climbed to her toes and wrapped her arms around his neck. "Kiss me, Devon."

Their lips met in a fevered joining. When one kiss finished, another started; they drank from each other. He ran his hands over Lilly's spine, the large palms mapping her body, then cupped her bottom, urging her closer.

He lifted her into his arms and carried her to the bed. She reached for him as he set her on the edge. Lilly's fingers shook as she released the tie at his waist and slid the robe from his body.

Lord, he was magnificent, the muscles on his shoulders, the strength of his forearms, the ridged planes of his stomach... what lay beneath. The jut of his arousal stood proud between braced thighs, and Lilly knew what would follow, yet she felt no fear. With one hand she traced the length of his broad chest, twirling her fingers in the sprinkling of hair and then moving lower to run her hand over his ribs. Her fingers tingled from the contact, the sensations traveling through her body.

"Your touch is beyond pleasure," he rasped, closing his eyes as she moved lower.

"To touch freely…." Lilly closed her eyes briefly. "It has long been a dream of mine. To feel another's heat. The texture of skin, the feel of hair, the curve of a cheek."

"I am yours to feel, Lilly, my love. Whenever you wish it."

"Only you," she whispered, pressing her lips to his chest. "Anyone else causes me pain, but not you."

She found a scar beneath his belly button and leaning forward she placed her lips on the small line and was rewarded with another groan, his hand fisting in her hair.

"H-how did you get this?"

His eyes were brighter than any jewel; the green depths ablaze with sensual heat. "Cam stabbed me with his toy sword," he said, tugging her hair and urging her upright. He once again joined their lips and Lilly could only feel. He kissed her neck and shoulders, each touch of his mouth an exquisite caress, and then licked his way down the slope of one breast and took her nipple. Lilly cried out her pleasure. He feasted on her as she writhed against him, heat pooling deep in her loins as he slowly heightened her pleasure.

"It is almost too much," she whispered as sensations caught and held her.

"We can never hurt each other, Lilly. Let me touch you, let me show you what is between us."

"It scares me how much I feel when you touch me," Lilly said honestly.

"Because you have never been close with another person before?" He looked into her eyes.

Lilly nodded. "The emotion is so strong, Dev. I don't understand these feelings between us."

"I feel no different, and given time you will understand what they mean as I do."

Before Lilly could ask what he meant, he lowered his head to kiss her once more.

Searing heat built inside her as his hands traveled to her waist, and then lower. He touched the soft hair and then eased a finger between her thighs.

"Oh my," Lilly whispered as she shuddered at the wonderful sensation.

"Just feel, love," he urged, leaning forward to place his mouth on her breast. He slowly stroked her as he laved her breasts with kisses.

"The sensations, Dev."

"Let go, Lilly."

She did, her body arching back as she felt the powerful release consume her.

He eased her back onto the bed.

"Open for me, Lilly, let me make you mine."

Lilly had never wanted anything more than to be possessed by Devonshire Sinclair. She let her legs fall open and felt him slowly enter her.

"Wrap your legs around my waist."

His jaw was clenched and sweat glistened on his body. He looked like a fierce warrior. Her warrior, Lilly thought, and then she could think no more.

"Kiss me, Dev," she whispered at the bite of pain as he sank deep inside her.

"You are mine now," he breathed against her lips.

"Yes, and you are mine."

Slowly withdrawing, he re-entered, and while there was pain, there was also pleasure, and then she felt it building again. That wave of pleasure she'd ridden just moments before. He was gentle, easing in and out of her slowly, the effort to hold back showing in his body.

"Let go, Dev," Lilly whispered, and he thrust into her until they both found their release.

He lay beside her, breathless.

"T-Toby?" she whispered.

"Is healed," he said, yawning as he moved them to lie on the pillows. Lilly kissed his chest and closed her eyes as he pulled up the blankets and in seconds she was slumbering, as was Devon.

Lilly woke to darkness. The fire was out, yet she felt no fear because beneath her cheek beat the heart of the man she now understood she loved. She felt no need to hurry as she usually did upon waking—in fact, her body felt the stirrings of need as he stretched beneath her. Last night had been a revelation to Lilly. Previously she had believed men used women to meet their own needs, and that the women gained nothing from the union, but now she knew better. His fingers skimmed her shoulder, and she felt like purring. To wake every day like this would be heaven.

"Do you want me to light a candle, Lilly?"

"No, I'm not afraid when I'm with you."

His hands lifted her high for a slow lingering kiss, and then lowered her down beside him. He turned on his side to look at her.

"If you stay on top of me like that I will want you again and it will be too soon, love," he said, answering her unspoken question. "We also need to talk, Lilly, and I need you to hear me out before you ask questions."

"All right."

Needing to touch him, Lilly placed her palm on his chest.

He covered it with his own, twining their fingers and then lifting hers to his lips.

"Do you feel well this morning; any niggles of pain from your adventures yesterday?"

"I am well, Devon. Should we check on Toby?"

"He has someone sitting with him until we rise."

They lay in silence for a while, and then he began to speak.

"My family is different." He laughed as she snorted. "In more ways than one," he added. "They have special senses like you."

"I don't understand?"

"I need to tell you the entire story, Lilly, so bear with me."

"All right."

"Supposedly, hundreds of years ago one of our ancestors saved the Duke of Raven from certain death. It is believed by the Sinclairs that our gift was the result of this event."

"By gift, you mean the special senses?" Lilly grappled to understand.

"Yes. The Sinclairs were given the job of protecting the Ravens for future generations, and it is also said that we were given our title as a gift by King Edward III in 1335 for our protection of the Ravens. Our land sits beneath Raven castle."

"And have they... Sinclairs, I mean. Have they saved Ravens?"

"Yes, many of them. Both Eden and I saved James, and then I you."

"Tell me of these senses you speak of?"

"I have the gift of sight, Cam has the heightened sense of smell, Essie taste, and Eden hearing. My younger siblings also have them."

"It is almost beyond belief and yet I have to believe it, don't I, because I saved Toby. How is that possible, as I am not a Sinclair?"

Lilly closed her eyes as Devon traced the line of her brow.

"You are, actually. Someone from your family line, hundreds of years ago, was saved by a Sinclair. They had a liaison, and the child was raised a Raven."

"If I read this tale I would not believe it," Lilly whispered. "The fact that it is true is hard to grasp."

"I know, but you will in time."

"But I am not a true Raven either."

"You carry their blood, Lilly. You are a Raven."

"When did you find out I was James's cousin?" Lilly whispered.

"The day I saved you outside the Watch House."

"And you were unhappy about what you learned, weren't you, Dev?"

"I was not unhappy about saving you, my love."

Lilly accepted the kiss he brushed over her lips.

"You have to understand that my family has lived with a secret for many years, and supposedly we are what we are because of the Ravens, and yes, it came as a shock to know that the woman who unsettled me was one of them, but only because I did not see it coming."

"I can see that would be unsettling," Lilly conceded. It was certainly a great deal to take in, and had she learned of it even yesterday, she would have doubted his words, but after healing Toby, she did not.

"And you believe I have the heightened sense of touch?"

His hand traced her cheek, then moved to her neck. Lilly closed her eyes, enjoying the sensation.

"Yes. You healed Toby, love. We both saw it and I felt it through your hands."

"It just seems so... so amazing and yet we are here in this room talking about it as if it were a common occurrence."

"But it is for me, Lilly. I have lived with it since birth."

"Tell me of your gift. What do you see?" Lilly questioned, intrigued.

"Everyone has a color. Cam is orange, Essie is pink, and Eden and James are blue. If you want to continue this conversation, madam, then stop moving."

She hadn't realized she was wriggling closer to his body, eager to feel him against her. Lilly stilled at his harsh tone and then she felt it, the tension in his body and the hardness against her thigh. She had done that to him. Her, Lilliana Braithwaite. The knowledge was heady indeed, considering she had never produced so much as a smile in other men.

"These colors, what do they mean?" Lilly said. "Does it matter if a blue person is married to a green person, for example?"

"Ah, no."

Lilly had the feeling he was reluctant to continue with the discussion.

"Devon?"

"Yes. It is my belief that a marriage is stronger if the couple has the same color. I have not done extensive studies to that end, but the few I have seen seem to be happier."

Lilly touched his jaw, making him look at her. The green of his eyes was bright.

"What color are you?" she whispered, her breath brushing his lips.

"Green."

"And me?"

He was silent for several seconds and then he said, "Green."

"Are there lots of people like us?"

"I know of only two people."

"You and I."

It wasn't a question, just a quietly spoken statement.

"Yes."

Lilly slowly mapped his face with her fingers, as she had that night when he had first removed her gloves.

"I love touching you, reading your face with my hands, finding each line and curve. It is as if my hands have been covered all these years just waiting until you came along."

He opened his mouth to speak, but she pressed her fingers to his lips, shaking her head.

"No more, Devon. I don't want to talk of things that once we step outside this room we will have to confront. For now just let me touch you."

He lay still as her hands touched his shoulders, each stroke building the smoldering embers of passion higher between them.

Lilly rose to her knees beside him, and then placing both hands on his chest, she learned the body of Devonshire Sinclair. She found that his breath hissed as she brushed his nipples, so she took her time there, and he moaned when she touched the planes of his stomach. Bending over him, Lilly placed small kisses on his skin while her hands ran up the sides of his ribs. Kissing the scar she had touched last night, she questioned him on its origins once more.

"If it was a toy sword, how has it left a scar?"

"He sharpened the end," he rasped. Then his entire body clenched as she laughed, brushing hot air over his stomach.

"Lilllllly."

Smiling at the groan, she took a deep breath and moved her hands lower, skimming her fingers up the length of his arousal, the skin smooth and silky beneath her fingers. His body went rigid and his breath came in harsh pants as she moved her hand up and down.

"Dear God, that is exquisite," he gritted out. "But I fear I cannot take too much more."

"I wanted to touch your legs, feel the hair with my fingers. I have much to make up for."

"No more touching, shrew, it's my turn now."

Lilly felt herself lifted, and then he had her flat on the bed and loomed over her. His hair was tousled, jaw shadowed, and she wondered at the emotion inside her, the ache deep in her chest that she had never felt before.

He nibbled her ear and kissed her lips and continued in that vein until he reached her breasts; once there, he pleasured her until she could think of nothing but him. Her fingers wrapped around the bedsheets and held on as he licked and kissed each one slowly, thoroughly, until she was moaning just as he had.

Lilly's stomach quivered as he reached there. She shivered as he circled her navel, and then his lips skimmed to the soft hair beneath, and then lower, to deliver the most intimate kiss of all. Shocked, Lilly grabbed a handful of his hair.

"Should you be.... Dear Lord!"

Devon trapped both her wrists in one hand as she tried to push him away and then he simply feasted on her, licking the soft folds and biting softly down on the hard little button between her thighs. Lilly gave up fighting him as he took her back there, to that wicked place where the tension built inside her. When she thought she could take no more, he stopped and braced himself above her.

"If you are sore, I will stop."

"Don't stop," Lilly whispered, holding his gaze as he slid inside her body. She was tender, but she wanted this, him.

He started moving, keeping his thrusts gentle, and Lilly felt the wave of sensual pleasure grip her body once more. She shuddered, as did he, and her last thought as they scaled the heights of passion was that it was too much. She felt far too much for this man, and that would surely lead to trouble.

CHAPTER 20

"*I* feel fine, Lilly, you don't need to keep touching my head."

"I'm just checking you are not over warm, Toby," Lilly said, removing her hand and fussing with the covers instead. She had on a pair of Eden's gloves that had appeared in her room, along with a clean set of clothing.

"Essex said I'm nearly well, just a few more days of rest and I'll be fine again. I was sure I was going to die, Lilly, felt like it anyway, and my wound looks like barely a scratch. Devon says it's all the fine living I've had. It's making me weak."

"Very possibly." Lilly didn't look at Toby. How could she when her hands had saved his life? She couldn't tell him, or anyone for that matter. Surely they would lock her away in Bedlam if the news came out.

No one would believe her anyway, and if they did she was sure they would want her to heal them. Shuddering, Lilly thought about the sensation she would create if anyone realized just what she could do.

"Do you want anything else? Food, drink? Or maybe a

216

story?" Lilly said, giving Toby's head one more pat as he shook it. She stood silently beside his bed as his eyes grew heavy, and soon he was asleep, and she knew there was no longer any reason for her to stay in the room, yet she was reluctant to leave it.

She and Devon had fallen back to sleep after their.... Dear Lord, she was blushing just thinking of the things they had done to each other in her cousin's house. Unsettled, she wandered around the room. What would he expect from her now? Could they just resume their life as it had once been? *Don't be a fool, Lilly.* Devonshire Sinclair was a gentleman; he would never treat her so shabbily.

But if he offered for her, could she accept? Would he let her continue with her children, or try to stop her going to Temple Street? Would he try to control her? Did she want to marry him?

Yes.

Oh Lord, she had complicated the entire situation by falling in love with Devon and then making love to him. She did love him, and that was a revelation, because Lilly had thought herself incapable of the emotion.

But if she wed him then surely it would be better for her, as he too had heightened senses, and would understand what she was capable of.

Knowing she could not stay in this room indefinitely she gave Toby a final look to check he still slumbered, before quietly slipping out the door.

"Good morning, Miss Braithwaite. My name is Buttles, and if you will follow me I will escort you to the breakfast parlor."

Lilly gave an unladylike squeal as the butler appeared suddenly before her. "I-I did not hear you, sir."

"Please forgive me, Miss Braithwaite, I have been told I am very light-footed."

"Surely an excellent thing if you are a butler." Lilly fell in behind the very straight back of Buttles.

She took the time to steady her nerves and look around her cousin's home. She saw touches of Eden everywhere in the flowers and furnishings. Dark paneling was complemented with pale walls and lovely paintings. Rich carpets muffled her footsteps.

"It is a very nice home, Buttles."

"The Duchess has an eye for color, Miss Braithwaite, and with help from Lady Samantha and Miss Emily, she has brought the house to life once more."

Lilly smiled. It was nice to hear how proud he was of both the house and the family who resided in it, and again it made her feel sad that such warmth and love did not fill her brother's house.

The hum of voices told her they had reached their destination.

"Thank you, Buttles, I will be fine now."

"Very well, Miss Braithwaite."

Lilly watched the butler leave. Running her hands down the skirts of the dress Eden had lent her, she hoped she could get through the next few minutes without making a fool of herself. Rubbing her forehead, she wondered briefly if the words Scarlet Woman were written all over it, because surely if she so much as glanced Devon's way everyone would know what lay between them. Dear Lord, imagine if he saw it too, saw with his sharp eyes the love she felt for him. Perhaps she should simply leave, without anyone realizing? Yes. Lilly turned; she would—

"And where are you going? The breakfast room is this way, Lilly."

When she turned back, she found Devon now standing in the doorway.

"I, ah, I thought to...."

"Leave?"

The bruise on his jaw looked angry this morning.

"No, I had—Yes, I was going to leave."

"Why?"

He didn't touch her, and for that she was grateful. He destroyed her concentration.

"I feel like everything has changed now, as if I have lost control and don't know how to regain it."

"I will help you if you'll let me."

"I'm not sure how to do that, don't you see?"

He moved closer, and Lilly fought the urge to retreat.

"I don't, actually." He touched her cheek. "You're not alone now, sweetheart. We will work it out between us."

Shaking her head, Lilly tried to dislodge his hand from her face, but it simply slipped to her shoulders. "Please, Devon."

"Please Devon, what?" he said, pulling her slowly toward him.

"I must learn how to deal with all of this now. There is so much to take in. Plus, those children are still missing and I must find out who has taken them—"

"You will not be doing that alone, Lilly. I need your assurance on that."

"I am no fool."

"If that were true, why did you go to Lady Jane Street when you knew that note was not from Toby?"

"I had to."

"No, you didn't. It would have been a simple task to send me word of where you were heading."

"I am not used to consulting others about my actions."

"However, you will get used to it," he said, giving her a final tug so she fell against him. "And I won't let you run from me now, not after last night."

"There is so much to take in," Lilly whispered again. "What you told me and what I have learned about myself—"

"May I enquire what is going on in my hallway?" James drawled, appearing behind Devon.

"Your cousin was about to run away, and I was attempting to dissuade her."

"Was she just. We cannot have that," James added. "There is now danger out there for you, Lilly. You will be running nowhere. Measures need be taken to keep you safe." He ignored Lilly's scowl. "Bring her into the breakfast room, Sinclair. We need to talk."

"And I have no say in the matter?" Lilly said loudly.

"None," both men replied.

Devon led her into the room behind James. Around the table sat Eden and two others; Lilly guessed they were her cousins.

"Samantha, Emily, this is your cousin Lilly," James said.

"Hello, Lilly," the youngest said. She was blonde and blue-eyed with ringlets with a big floppy yellow bow tied in her hair.

"Hello, Miss Braithwaite." Lilly knew with just a glance that Emily was not quite as comfortable in this setting as her younger sister. She remembered James telling her she was his half sister, the bastard child of his father. She was thin—too thin, Lilly thought, looking at her wrists, and her gray eyes looked weary as they looked from James to Eden and then back to Lilly.

"Please call me Lilly, Emily, especially as we are family." The girl nodded, yet remained silent, once again lowering her eyes to her plate.

Yielding to the pressure on her arm, Lilly fell into the chair Devon directed her to. "There is no need to use force, my lord. A simple, 'have a seat,' would have sufficed."

"Of course it would, and that's why you were running out

the front door like a scared rabbit," he said, moving to the sideboard.

Lilly watched as he loaded two plates. He then returned, lowering one before her and placing the other in front of the seat to her left.

"Be a good girl, Lilly, and eat now. Talk later," James said.

"Yes, do as your cousin says," Devon added.

She was not usually rebellious, as it got her nowhere with her brother. But call it tiredness, or uncertainty. The last few days were obviously taking their toll on her sanity, as Lilly poked out her tongue—and instantly regretted it as Samantha clapped and giggled. Eden hooted with laughter and even Emily made a small snuffling sound.

"Lord save me from impertinent females." James winked at his sisters as he spoke, and then grabbing his wife's chin, he kissed her loudly on the mouth.

Lilly's jaw dropped at the display of emotion. She had always believed James was like her, someone who kept their emotions firmly in check at all times.

"Eat, cousin." James gave her a gentle smile of under-standing.

"I visited Toby this morning, Lilly. He said he would teach me to use a slingshot."

"Not until he is stronger, Samantha," James said, which again surprised Lilly, as surely Toby was not fit company for the sister of a duke, not to mention that a slingshot was hardly ladylike.

"When will he be stronger, James?"

"When he is."

"What sort of answer is that, husband?" Eden said.

"The only one she's getting until we are sure he is healed."

"One more sleep, Samantha, and he should be fine," Dev said.

Lilly felt his fingers brush hers as he reached for his cup, and hated her betraying shiver.

"You will not fire a slingshot inside these walls, Samantha. There will be a target set up out in the gardens for you. Furthermore, Buttles will not be used for practice."

"Yes, James," Samantha said, looking sincere. However, Lilly wasn't so sure; the child had a look in her eyes she had seen in the children she knew a time or two.

"It appears we are in time to partake of breakfast. Excellent, I am famished."

Lilly watched Cambridge and Essex Sinclair walk into the room. Essex took the seat to Lilly's right, while Cambridge wandered to the sideboard to raise the lids and sniff. Now that Lilly knew about his nose she understood why, although he did look remarkably like a hound.

"I suppose he just had a full breakfast less than an hour ago," Eden said, looking at her sister.

"Of course," Essie said, pouring tea.

"Hollow legs," Dev grunted.

"Another stunning dress, Emily. I shall sit here and bask in your beauty," Cam said, taking the seat beside James's sister.

"If my dress does not meet your high standards, sir, it is of no concern to me. Furthermore, you should have a care not to poke out your eyes with those ridiculously high points should you turn too quickly."

"They are always like this," Dev said in Lilly's ear, as she studied the previously quiet girl and Cam. "From their first meeting they have antagonized each other, and while initially James and I tried to stop them squabbling, he now leaves them to it, as it is the only time Emily appears to come out of her shell."

Lilly turned to face Devon before she spoke. "It must be hard for her though, don't you think?"

"Hard in what way?"

His eyes really were startling, green with gold flecks, and they appeared so alive, almost sparkling. "Living this life, knowing—"

"None of us care about Emily's birth, Lilly. She is now just one of us, as are Samantha and James."

Lilly thought about that as Emily and Cam continued to argue. To love unconditionally as these people obviously did was a rare thing indeed.

"I wear them when I know I am meeting you, Emily. I use them to shield me from your rapier tongue," Cam said with his mouth full of food.

"You have the manners of a barnyard animal!"

Even Emily's lips twitched as Cam neighed like a horse.

Lilly didn't see the communication, but she was sure there was one between Emily and James, because seconds later she left, taking Samantha with her and leaving Lilly to face the Sinclair/Raven clan. Lord, they were a terrifying group. So vibrant and alive, they made her feel... well, gray and dull.

"As you all know, Lilly healed Toby last night," Devon said, and Lilly felt the jolt of his words. Looking around the table she saw no censure, only understanding, and some of the tension left her body.

"We also know after last night that someone is trying to harm her, and it is the belief of both James and I that this is due to her investigations into the missing children."

"You did not tell me you had come to that conclusion." Lilly looked from Dev to James. "Furthermore, perhaps you should talk to me about these matters before announcing them."

"Toby told us of this man called Dominus and what he believes he is about."

"Yes, I knew of him," Lilly said.

"And yet you did not tell me?"

The dark raised brow indicated Devon was not happy.

"I'm not sure why I would, when at the time we were barely speaking to each other."

"Bravo," Eden clapped her hands. "We have an ally, Essie dear. It seems Lilly too will stand up to these dictators should it be required."

Lilly watched James and Devon sigh.

"We are merely trying to ascertain what is the next step, wife," James said.

"Excellent, and of course we shall help you with those steps."

"Obviously," he drawled.

Lilly felt Dev's fingers stroke the outside of her thigh, and the resulting heat that washed through her made her cheeks flush.

"Lord Braithwaite wishes to speak to Miss Braithwaite, your Grace," Buttles announced from the doorway.

"Unhand my sister, Sinclair!"

Lilly turned to watch her brother storm into the room; his eyes focused on Devon's hand beneath the table.

"A little late to play the role of big brother, don't you think, Braithwaite?" Devon drawled from beside her.

"Nicholas, why are you here? I told you last night not to return." Lilly got to her feet to face her brother.

"Why was he touching you?"

She could hardly believe his words. He had cared nothing for her, ever, and now he was the outraged older brother. If she could dredge up a laugh, she would have done so.

"Enough, Nicholas. Unlike you, these people actually care about me and I will not have you coming into our cousin's house and behaving in such a manner. Now leave."

"I will not leave! Someone must protect your honor."

"Protect my honor? Where was this protection when you

wished to wed me to a man old enough to be my grandfather? Go away, Nicholas. I will be home when I am ready. Tell Aunt Vi not to worry. I am well."

Lilly looked at Devon as he came to stand at her right. James then moved to her left. It was a show of support and she swallowed down the lump in her throat.

"I have no wish to discuss this here in front of these people. Come, Lilliana, we will leave at once."

"She is going nowhere with you, Braithwaite. You had your chance to look after her and failed," Devon growled.

"My office, I think," James said, leading the way. "Move, Nicholas," he ordered, and her brother surprisingly did as he asked. "I think we need to clear a few things up before anyone leaves this house."

"What are we clearing up?" Lilly said, running to keep up with the long strides of the men, who were stalking down the hall before her. No one answered her. Devon, however, stopped, took her hand in his, and led her into James's study.

"Do you trust me?" he said, lowering Lilly into a seat and bracing his arms on either side to look at her.

"I-I, of course." And she did, Lilly realized, and not because of what had happened between them. She knew that to the toes of his large feet, he could be trusted. He would lay his life down for his family, and she had the feeling he would do the same now for her. It was a humbling thought.

"And I will treasure that gift always, my sweet," he said, straightening. "Just remember those words."

CHAPTER 21

*H*ad Dev his way, he would have left Lilly with his sisters, and yet he knew she would never have allowed that. She sat, hands folded in her lap, appearing calm on the outside. But he knew her now; she was anything but calm. Her lovely eyes were moving between the three men constantly.

James sat behind his desk, Lilly across from him. Dev paced instead of doing as he wanted: punching Nicholas Braithwaite. Lilly's brother also stood.

After last night, his need for this woman had, if possible, grown. Just looking at her twisted his insides. She looked delicate this morning, her eyes haunted, face fatigued. She wasn't delicate, however. She was strong and resilient.

He'd made love to her last night because he could not resist her. She was a fire inside him now, a part of him. He wanted to protect her and keep her safe. Lilly, of course, would never allow that. She had been protecting herself for some time.

"Firstly, I want to know why you contemplated marrying

Lilly to Danderfield. Is it, as Dev suspected, because you need money?"

Devon was pleased to see that at least Nicholas did not lower his eyes when James spoke.

"To my shame, yes, that is the truth."

James gritted his teeth.

"That is unpardonable, Nicholas. How could you treat your own blood that way? Your parents were good people. You have no excuse for your behavior."

"I know my behavior has been reprehensible, but I want to change... will change."

"Yes, well, we'll deal with your behavior and subsequent debts later. Now is not that time."

Nicholas Braithwaite's lip was swollen from Dev's fist yesterday, and he looked different; his eyes had lost their insolence. Today he, like his sister, looked young and uncertain, but Dev had no intention of feeling anything but anger for the man.

"I have made this mess I now stand in. I will deal with it, and my debts."

"Very noble, I am sure, cousin, but I will not let you fall on your sword when both your sister and aunt rely on you, and you have your parents' reputations to uphold."

"One thing has come clear to me, Braithwaite." Dev entered the conversation, as standing in silence and letting another speak for him had never been something he was comfortable with. "Your sister's life is in danger, and living with you she has no protection. Therefore, she will move in here with James and between us, we will keep her safe."

"I understand the gravity of what has occurred, Devon," Lilly said. "I am of course indebted to you all for saving me, but I am sure that as long as I now exercise caution, I will remain safe living in my family home."

"No you will not, now please be quiet, Lilly, while we discuss this matter further," Dev said.

"No, I will not be quiet, damn you! Do not speak of me as if I am not seated right here several feet from you."

"Lilly!" her brother said in shocked tones, which told Dev that Nicholas knew nothing about his sister. She was outspoken when required, and used several curses, also if required, to prove her point.

She spun to her brother. "Don't you dare censure me for using the word damn when you have used that and worse in my presence. You are a drunkard, gambler, and whoring wastrel. At least I can lay claim to doing something worthy with my life."

Had she sprouted wings and flown across the room, the effect on her brother wouldn't have been greater.

"I-I know my past behavior has been wrong," Nicholas said slowly, as he looked at Lilly as one would a fire-breathing dragon. "Yet, I ask that you allow me to make amends."

"No." She shook her head. "I want nothing from you."

"Me, however," Dev said, moving to her side and placing a hand on her shoulder, "she will wed, and I will ensure she is loved, protected, and safe, Braithwaite."

He felt the tension beneath his hand.

"No, I will not marry you."

Yes, you bloody will.

Dev was about to open his mouth when he looked at James, who shook his head. He was right, of course; this was not the forum to pursue the matter of their futures, and seeing the firm set of Lilly's jaw, he wished he had held his tongue and spoken to her first. She made him lose reason, which while understandable considering how he felt about her, was not a practice he should continue. The problem was, he wanted her bound to him so tight she could never leave.

"I do not know what has happened or why she was abducted, yet when I am furnished with all the facts, I will change everything from this day forth. She will be protected, and I will ensure she feels no pressure to wed. She will not be forced, Sinclair," Nicholas Braithwaite declared.

"Why would you do that?" Lilly questioned. "What gain is there in any of this for you, Nicholas? I am trying to understand your motivation."

"Before you answer that, Braithwaite, perhaps you should beg your sister's forgiveness for her treatment at your hands over the last few years," Dev said.

"I want no apology from you simply because you are intimidated by James and Devon, Nicholas." Lilly regained her feet. She had a feeling she needed to stand tall to deal with what was about to unfold.

Her brother seemed different today. His face had lost that arrogant expression it perpetually wore. Yet Lilly knew him well enough to know he could play any part should he need to.

"I understand you do not trust my words, Lilliana, but in this Lord Sinclair is correct. I do need to beg your forgiveness, but I will not do it here."

"You know nothing about me, Nicholas. You know not what I do from one day to the next. You cannot simply apologize to me and expect everything to be all right."

"I know that too, and hope you will tell me what I do not know about you. Tell me the things I have missed out on in your life."

Lilly's laugh held no humor. "Believe me, brother, you will not support them, but be warned you will not change the direction I have taken, nor will you get my money if that is still your agenda."

"I do not want Grandmother's money, Lilliana."

She almost believed him, but not quite. Not yet.

"I don't believe you, Nicholas."

He looked sad.

"I did not expect you to do so immediately, but hope in time you will see that I want to change."

James rose from his seat and stepped to Lilly's side and held out a hand. The gesture surprised her, as neither of them liked to touch or be touched. She placed her fingers in his, and let him lead her across the room until they were alone and the others could not hear.

"I know that like your brother I have given you no reason to trust me, Lilly, yet I would ask that you try."

She nodded, but remained silent.

"I know what it is you do with the children, just as I now know about your house in Temple Street."

"Sinclairs cannot keep secrets," Lilly said.

His smile was gentle.

"Actually they can, but only if they believe they need to be kept. If they believe that in the telling, the words will help, they will do so without hesitation. In this, my brother-in-law was right, Lilly. You are my cousin, and I have neglected you for long enough. I want to be more involved in your life."

"I do not expect society to care about what I do. They will look on it as my charitable works. But I had no wish for my brother to know. Appearances were everything to him, and that is why I have kept my life a secret."

"Is that why you dressed and acted as you did also?"

She nodded. "I had no wish to wed, and Grandmother's will stated that if I reached twenty-six years still unmarried, then I could get the full amount she left me, and set up house on my own."

"Ah, it all makes sense now. I must admit to wondering what had become of you. How you had changed so much from the intelligent child you were to the simpering, brainless, badly dressed woman I saw in society."

"People see what they want, and once I had established the facade, no one questioned it."

"Not even your brother."

Lilly looked at Nicholas, who was watching her, and then her gaze moved to Devon, who was doing the same.

"I had not planned to wed, James. My life was to be my children."

"But you care for Devon, Lilly. I can see that."

She could not lie. "I do, but that scares me."

"As it did me, cousin, when Eden stormed into my life. I was terrified when she began to tear down the walls I had placed around myself, the barriers I had erected because of my father."

Lilly nodded, knowing she had built those barriers also.

"But love is worth the risk, Lilly. You and I were only living a half life before these Sinclairs stormed our defenses and made us feel."

"It hurts to feel."

"But to not feel is not living, cousin. So now I must ask if you love my brother-in-law."

Lilly didn't miss the significance of the word brother-in-law. James was telling her he counted the man as family.

"With all my heart," she said, looking at him.

"Then we shall make it happen," James hugged her briefly.

"I feel as if I no longer have control over my life, James. For so long I knew the direction I was taking, yet lately...."

James laughed as he guided her back to the two men who waited silently across the room. "Yes, at first it is like being on a runaway carriage with no means of getting off. The Sinclairs are a protective lot, Lilly, who encompass you, but in time you will learn to like the feeling."

"Like you do?"

"Like I do," James acknowledged. "But I would ask you never to repeat that to any of them."

231

Lilly sighed. "I am unsure how to let go of the control, James, as for so long it is what kept me going."

"You need not let go of the control, Lilly. Just relax the reins slightly and the rest will fall into place. You will see." He hugged her once more and she rested against him, enjoying the steady beat of his heart. She felt a small kernel of warmth that he was in her life now, that if she needed him, he would be there for her.

"Remember that I am always here for you now, Lilly. I am not going anywhere."

"Thank you," she whispered when he released her.

"Lilliana, I need to talk to you."

Nicholas sounded urgent, and Lilly knew that if she was to return home with him, then yes, she should at least talk to him. Especially if he was going to try to change.

"Please let me speak to my brother alone."

Devon didn't want to leave her with Nicholas; Lilly saw that.

"Let me talk with him, Devon. I promise to call for you if I need you." Lilly touched a finger to his chin, which she could see surprised him. She was not someone who did such things with others watching.

He nodded, glared at Nicholas, and then accompanied James from the room. No doubt to stand outside the door and listen.

She stood four feet away from her brother, looking at the man who should have been so important to her, and once had been, until she realized the person he truly was.

"What happened to your lip?" Lilly asked when the silence grew uncomfortable. She could not remember the last time she had conversed with Nicholas; usually he talked at her.

"Your dark lord pointed out the error of my ways."

Lilly could do nothing to stop the small smile at his

description of Devon. He would protect her, even when she did not want him to do so.

"I lay in my bed last night reliving our lives since our parents passed. Each memory that came and went shamed me. My treatment of you is unforgivable. I'm not sure when it started, or why—"

"They were not bad years, Nicholas, just lonely ones." Lilly decided that only honesty would do now.

"Christ, you must loathe me." His words were hoarse. "I could find no sleep last night thinking of what I had become and how I treated you. And then I wondered how to ask your forgiveness when I know if I were in your situation, I would never give it."

Lilly thought she saw honesty, but many years of division lay between them.

"I am having trouble believing that you would change suddenly, Nicholas. Why now? It makes no sense."

He ran a hand over his face.

"I don't know why now. Perhaps it took Sinclair to point out the error of my ways. Aunt Vi told me last night when I spoke with her about you that she was ashamed of the person I had become, but she was never brave enough to stand up to me." He closed his eyes briefly. "I became a bully in the eyes of the two people I should love most."

"Words, Nicholas," Lilly whispered. "These are just words to me, which I struggle to believe."

"When you were born I was instantly enamored. In fact, for the first year I would visit you and carry you everywhere, and I would beg your nurse to let me hold you."

He took one of her hands in his and gripped it tight. Lilly thankfully had on her gloves, as she did not want to touch anyone but Devon. Perhaps one day soon she would try with someone else she cared for, but not yet, and especially not her brother.

"I loved you very much, but as the years passed I had forgotten that."

"Perhaps I did not make it easy for you," Lilly conceded. "I dressed as I did, and wore the glasses and behaved in that silly manner, so I would reach twenty-six unwed."

The shock on his face was genuine.

"Did you really? Strange how I did not see what you were doing."

"You saw nothing but yourself," Lilly said, pulling her hand free and walking to the window. "And my fear was that you would force me to marry, when I had no wish to."

"Will you tell me about yourself, Lilly? What you have become, and about the abduction? I have a feeling you know why you were taken."

She did, because she wanted nothing to lie unsaid between them anymore. He could no longer hurt her; James and Devon would see to that. She was free to speak to this man as she wished.

"I had no idea. How have you kept this from me?" He looked shocked at her revelations. "You purchased this house in Temple Street alone?"

"You showed no interest in me, Nicholas. Therefore, it was easy for you to believe what you wished and not see what was really happening."

"I can see that now, and am ashamed of what I have become. But that is my burden, not yours. Now I need you to tell me if it is your wish to marry Sinclair, as I will not consent to the match otherwise."

"Yes, I wish it with all my heart." Saying the words out loud confirmed what she thought. It was a step she was scared to take, but Lilly knew that being parted from Devon was not an option.

"Then I shall honor your wishes, sister," he said, leaning

forward to place a kiss on her forehead. "Will you return home with me now?"

Lilly shook her head. "I will be there later today. Please tell Aunt Vi I shall take my evening meal with her."

"And I shall be there also."

He rarely ate with them.

"Of course, if that is your wish."

He looked at her for long seconds. Lilly wondered if it was the first time he had really seen her. Shaking his head, he bowed deeply and left the room.

Lilly heard the murmur of voices outside the door and then Devon opened and closed it behind him. She heard his footsteps as he moved to her side, where she still stood at the window, looking at the garden below.

"Are you all right, Lilly?"

"So much has happened." Lilly faced him, let her palm rest on his chest. The strength in this man calmed her.

"You have been abducted. You healed with your hands." Lilly closed her eyes as he cupped her cheek. "And I'm sure what just transpired between you and your brother was not comfortable."

"I just don't know if I should believe him."

"We will deal with it together, love."

Lilly sighed as he kissed her softly. She then rested her cheek on his chest. It was a wonderful place to be, safe and secure in his arms. She had capitulated, she realized. She had given herself completely to this man.

"I love you, Devonshire Sinclair, and yes, I will marry you."

She was lifted then, high in the air, and twirled. Laughing, she wrapped her arms around his neck as he lowered her down his body, his arms holding her tight.

"You will not regret it, my love."

"I'm sure I will," she said, smiling down into his face. "Yet, I doubt I can live without you now."

"I know I cannot live without you," he said gently.

"I am used to being alone, Dev, but now... now I no longer wish for that. In the space of a few days, I want to be part of this, part of your family."

"Our family," he amended. "I will call upon your brother tomorrow."

"I need you to understand something, Devon." Lilly tried to sort through the words that she wanted to say.

"Tell me then, and I will try."

"My children, the house in Temple Street, I will not give them up."

He cupped her face, lifting it so they looked at each other.

"I would never ask you to, but what I would ask is that you let me help you with them."

She nodded, daring to believe that he actually meant those words.

"Trust me."

"I do." She raised her chin for the brief kiss he brushed over her lips. "I am going home this afternoon, Devon, and in this I will stand firm. I need to see Aunt Vi, and it is not right for me to stay here."

His expression darkened, and she knew this was the first of many battles they would wage.

"I want you safe."

"And I will be. I will take no more risks, and go nowhere without alerting you or James if I believe there is danger involved."

"And that is supposed to appease me?" He was scowling now.

She kissed him this time, softly, their lips lingering.

"I won't let you go now, Lilly. You are mine forever."

"I-I don't want you to let me go... ever."

"Do you know what my first thought was when those men abducted me?"

He led her to a chair, then sat and pulled her down onto his lap.

"Tell me."

"I wanted you. I had never turned to anyone before, but at that moment I needed you so much."

"And that scares you?"

"Yes, it scares me because I don't like to rely on people anymore."

"You can rely on me, Lilly, because I will try to never willingly let you down. There may be times when I make you angry because I can be a bit overprotective and.... Did you just snort?"

She smiled. "A bit overprotective?"

"I am the head of my family now, love. It is not always an easy job keeping them all safe."

Lilly brushed the pad of her thumb over his lips. "And yet you have, Dev. And now I will keep you safe and help you chase away those demons that you keep locked inside you."

She watched the unease gather in his eyes as his body stiffened.

"What do you know of my demons?"

"I know you carry the pain of every soldier who died while they fought beside you, and I know that any pain your family suffered, you blame yourself for not shielding them from."

"I believe you said I thought I was a god?"

She smiled. "It is not a fault to put others before you, Devon. But you cannot blame yourself for things that are not in your control. You are a protector, it is in your nature, I understand that, and it will be my job to ensure you do not take the role too seriously."

"I do have demons, love, it comes with my nurturing

nature, so my mother always told me," he said with a wry smile. "Our father was not a good man, and I did not realize how bad he was until he died, yet part of me still worries that I should have known what he was doing—"

"No, Dev." Lilly pressed her fingers to his lips. "I know you will tell me what he did when you are ready, but I also know that you are the most honorable, wonderful man I have ever known and that you did everything you possibly could to make your siblings happy and that is enough. Now, take some of your own advice and leave the past behind you."

Resting his forehead on hers, he said, "How have I lived without you for so long? I love you, Lilliana Braithwaite, more than I ever believed possible."

"And will you let me share your burdens?"

"I will."

"I love you, Devonshire Sinclair."

He kissed her, a thorough meeting of lips that Lilly felt to her toes. Slowly the flames of passion licked at her as he deepened the contact. She needed this man so much it terrified her. Throwing her arms around his neck, she kissed him back.

"We have to stop, Lilly," Dev groaned, pulling back.

"Why?"

"Because if this continues I will throw you on top of your cousin's desk and ravish you, and it is too soon. Not to mention that it is your cousin's desk."

Lilly looked at James's desk and nodded.

"Perhaps that would not be wise."

CHAPTER 22

"*H*ello, Lilly."

"Hello, Samantha, you look very pretty today." Lilly had arrived to visit with Eden, but the woman had been delayed as she was tending to a staff member who had fallen ill. Lilly had decided to sit in the library with a tray of tea and wait for her.

Samantha was dressed in pink with ruffles and frills where young girls should have ruffles and frills, and with a matching band in her hair. Lilly marveled at the resilience the child showed. Like James, Samantha had been raised by a tyrant, and yet showed no signs of it.

"Emily and I are about to go to the park. We are taking Mr. Whiskers for a walk, and wondered if you would like to come?"

"Mr. Whiskers?"

"My dog," the girl said, smiling, which showed her little white teeth. "He spends most of his time with me, so you have probably not met him yet. James does not like him to run every-where because he still chews and does naughty things, so I only let him loose when he's out." The last was said with a cheeky smile which Lilly felt herself responding to. "We call him Whisky most of the time, which James says suits him as he forces him to drink when he has chewed another of his neckties."

Two weeks had passed since Lilly had returned to her house after the abduction, and every day when she woke, it was to find her brother had indeed changed. He now shared his meals with her and Aunt Vi, and a great deal of his time. The household was happier, and for that Lilly could not fault him. He had also allowed James to help him with his debts, but had said he would be repaying every cent.

For the first time in many years, Lilly was happy, and it was a wonderful feeling.

"James said a notice appeared in the papers announcing your betrothal to Devon yesterday, Lilly. Dorrie and Somer are excited that they get to be bridesmaids again."

"Yes, I believe they want pink dresses."

"I enjoyed being James's bridesmaid and everyone said that three little girls looked better than two."

"Did they now?" Lilly was not fooled by the winsome expression on Samantha's face."

"Yes, and we were so very well-behaved, unlike Warwick."

"What did Warwick do?"

Placing both hands on her hips, the girl narrowed her eyes, making her look like a ferocious pixie. "He tied the laces of my pretty blue boots together so I fell on my face in front of all the guests."

Lilly pressed her lips together to stop from laughing. "What did you do to him?" she asked, knowing there would have been retribution.

"Dorrie kept him talking while I sprinkled some of Essie's herbs that Somer got me on his meal. He had a troubled tummy for two days after."

"Oooh, you're clever," Lilly said in awe.

"What color are they going to wear?"

"Who?" Lilly blinked at the change in conversation.

"Your bridesmaids."

"I believe I have already mentioned they will be in pink."

"That's my favorite color."

Lilly laughed. "Would you do me the honor, Lady Samantha, of becoming one of my bridesmaids?"

"Yes!" Samantha squealed, throwing herself at Lilly. "Will you come for a walk with me and Emily now, while Eden tends the sick person?"

"If you wish for me to accompany you, then yes, I should love to go walking with you both."

"We shall meet you in the entranceway in five minutes."

Samantha then left as quickly as she had arrived, so Lilly drank her tea, and then found her bonnet and gloves. After slipping them on, she went to find the girls.

"Is anyone down there, Lilly?"

"Pardon?" Lilly looked to the top of the stairs, where Samantha peeked over the banister. Emily stood behind her, carrying a small, white scruffy dog with lopsided ears and a spectacular set of whiskers.

"Is anyone waiting in the entranceway, Lilly?"

"Ah, no, not that I can see." Lilly looked around.

"Quick, Emily, there is no one about!"

"Samantha, we will be caught one day, and I'm not sure we should. Imagine if we fall the other way. It is a very long drop," Emily said, looking anxious.

"Emily, we go through this every time we do it, and after the first attempt it is you who wants to do it again."

Lilly made her way up the stairs, wondering what was going on. When she arrived, Mr. Whiskers's lead was handed to her by an anxious-faced Emily.

"If you could hold him please, Lilly."

She then watched as Emily and Samantha climbed onto the railing.

"Good Lord!" Fascinated, she watched as the very proper and shy Emily flew down the banister behind her sister, both making gleeful noises as they went. Lilly held her breath as they reached the bottom and flew off the end to land nimbly on their feet. Giggling, they both picked up their skirts and ran back up the stairs.

"Just drop his lead, Lilly, and he will follow us down if you wish to try also," Samantha panted as she reached the top.

"Yes, do try, Lilly, it is so much fun," Emily said, her smile transforming her face.

"Oh, I.... No, I don't think—" Before she had finished the sentence they were off again, flying down to the bottom once more. At her feet the dog was watching the progress with his button eyes, trying to work out what was happening.

"I have not done such a thing since my childhood, Mr. Whiskers, and even then I am not entirely sure I did something like this. Do you think I should try?"

Hearing his name, the scruffy dog looked up at Lilly and yipped, which seemed to be confirmation enough.

"Come on, Lilly, this will be our last run or someone will see us," Samantha wheezed as she once again reached the top of the stairs.

"You have to lift your skirts and straddle it," Emily directed.

"Emily was scared the first time, weren't you, Em?"

"Indeed I was."

"I am not scared, precisely," Lilly said, eying the gleaming banister. "It is just not something I have contemplated doing."

"Buttles has it polished with his special mixture, which makes you fly down."

Samantha gave her a wide smile once again, and Lilly felt herself weakening. She would have to be very careful around this child; she obviously had the ability to manipulate a person into doing any number of things.

"It's fun, Lilly, and Em and I didn't have much fun until James came into our lives."

"I didn't have much fun in my household either," Lilly surprised herself by saying.

"Well then," Emily said, gently taking her hand. "Let's have some fun."

Nodding, Lilly followed the directions they gave her and swung her leg over the shiny wood. Her stomach did a small flip as she straddled the railing, and then she let go. Nearing the bottom, she heard an outraged shout. She flew through the air, then landed in a pair of strong arms.

"Oomph!"

She heard Devon grunt as he staggered backward several steps.

"What the bloody hell are you doing, woman!"

"Devon, don't swear in front of Samantha," Lilly scolded him as she slapped down her skirts and righted her bonnet. "Put me down, please."

He did, but kept an arm around her waist.

"You could have hurt yourself. What were you thinking, to behave in such a reckless manner?"

He was growling at her now. Brows lowered, he was attempting to intimidate her; however, she was onto him. He was all bluster around those he cared for.

"Don't be cross, Dev," a little voice said below him. "Emily and I were teaching Lilly how to have fun."

"I fear my heart will never recover," he muttered before releasing Lilly to look down at the little girl.

"We never hurt ourselves, Dev."

"You do this often, Samantha?"

She nodded.

"Well, well, well, Miss Emily, it seems you have been hiding your mischievous streak under that prim exterior. Who would have thought—"

"I will thank you to keep the rest of your comments firmly in your mouth, Cambridge Sinclair."

"Are you telling me that you have never slid down a shiny banister, Lord Sinclair?" Lilly said, ignoring Emily and Cam as they continued bickering.

"Of course I have. I was not, however, an adult."

"Not entirely true, brother. You and the children slid down our uncle's banister when we first arrived in London."

"Shut up, Cam," Dev snapped.

"You're not going to tell James, are you, Dev?"

Samantha was now tugging on Devon's jacket.

"Of course not, Samantha. I was just concerned for you, darling. You know what we older brothers are like."

Dev followed his words by kissing the little girl on the top of her head.

"You however, madam," he then said, lifting Lilly's chin, "should know better." Closing the distance between them, he kissed her softly.

"I enjoyed sliding down James's banister. In fact, I think we should do it again soon, Samantha," Lilly added, giving him a cheeky smile.

"Why is there a gathering in my entranceway?"

"The lord and master has returned," Cam drawled as James walked in through his front door.

"We were just going to take Mr. Whiskers for a walk, James," Samantha said, shooting Dev a pleading look that suggested her brother had no idea what she got up to when he was not there.

"And who is walking with you?"

244

"Two footmen and a maid, and Lilly!" Samantha said loudly.

"Make that four footmen, and I may allow it," Devon said before James could speak.

"We would look ridiculous with four footmen trailing after us, Devon. Be reasonable," Lilly said. "Furthermore, it is not up to you to allow me to do anything. I am an adult and have been making my own decisions for years—"

"And I'm your future husband who recently rescued you from someone intent on harming you."

"With a protective streak two ax handles wide," Cam added.

"Much as I hate agreeing with Sinclair, cousin, I'm afraid in this he is correct. You will not leave this house without an assurance people are watching over you and my sisters."

"Why is everyone standing in the entranceway?" Nicholas questioned, walking through the still-open door.

Lilly seized him by the arm—much to his surprise, as they were still wary around each other.

"Nicholas shall accompany us if that is all right with you, Lord Sinclair?"

Devon's eyes narrowed at her use of his title. Lilly was deliberately baiting him.

"You shall not leave her side, Braithwaite, until you return to this house," he said, glaring from one sibling to the other.

"I shall let nothing happen to my sister, Sinclair, and I will thank you to remember that before you start issuing orders."

"It seems both you and your sister have a dislike for taking orders," he added, which made Lilly smile.

"I can't imagine it is something you respond to either, Sinclair," Nicholas said.

Devon nodded, his smile rueful, and at that moment, if possible, her love for him increased. He was angry with Nicholas and had told her it would take time to forgive him for his treatment of her, but he would not show that grudge outwardly.

"In that you are correct, Braithwaite."

"Obey your brother, minx."

Lilly lifted her face for another kiss, then they left the house.

It was crisp and clear as the small party walked to the park. Emily and Samantha chatted, and Mr. Whiskers went from side to side on his long lead, sniffing everything he could get his nose near. Lilly thought about Cam, imagining him doing the same.

"Danderfield visited me again last night. He blustered and threatened, but there is nothing he can do, as I signed no documents. It was merely my word that I gave, and we both know that was worth nothing then."

"I'm sorry, Nicholas, and yet very glad I am not to wed such a man."

He patted her hand where it rested on his sleeve. "It was to be expected. He is not a man who likes being thwarted, but there is little he can do. I have come to realize after doing a bit of investigating that he has a smoky past and is linked to several underhand dealings, and once again I must beg your forgiveness for wanting to see you married to him."

Lilly waved his words away. "No more apologies, that is in the past. However, I would like to know why are you investigating him?"

He threw her a look, and she could read nothing in his expression.

"Because I cannot rule out that he will create further trouble for you. Plus, I am looking into many people after what happened to you. I want to help Sinclair and Raven, to find out what is going on. Also, there is the matter of those missing children that needs to be sorted."

"I don't know what to say." Lilly looked to where Samantha skipped before them, swinging Emily's hand.

"Did you think I would simply sit back and let James and Sinclair deal with this? You are my sister, Lilliana. I love you, and I may not have always shown you that, but now I want to protect you and support you in what you care for. Those children mean a great deal to you, therefore we need to find out what is happening."

She felt ridiculously close to tears. She had received too many shocks to this point, but this one seemed to have tipped her over the edge, as she started to sniff.

"I have also told James that when the time comes I too shall acknowledge Emily as my family," Nicholas said, his eyes on the straight back of their cousin.

Now that, Lilly hadn't expected. Looking up at her brother, she wondered how it was possible that a man could change so much in such a short space of time.

"Emily is not keen on stepping into society, yet James is eager to see that she does. Of course he has already acknowledged she is his sister openly, but as yet she has not met anyone who would challenge her."

"It won't be easy for her, that much is true. However, with our support and that of the Sinclairs and Lord and Lady Wynburg, I think in time she will be accepted."

"We go to the quieter part of the park, where Emily feels comfortable," Samantha said, looking at Nicholas.

"Lead the way then, Samantha, and your cousins shall follow," Nicholas said, producing a gentle smile for the girl.

"You really have changed, haven't you, Nicholas?" Lilly's words were quiet, but he heard them.

"Yes."

Nothing further was said, but it was enough for now that she had acknowledged what he was trying to do.

They found a pond with ducks that Mr. Whiskers wanted

to jump in and play with. Nicholas took his lead, as the little dog was quite insistent.

"Buttles has given us some bread and James told me that as I cannot yet swim, I am not to follow the bread into the water," Samantha said, taking a small bundle from one of the footmen.

"That child could murder someone and that smile would get her off," Nicholas muttered as he watched the footman blush as the little girl beamed up at him.

"Yes, she is a delight." Lilly laughed.

"It's strange how we have inherited two cousins. Yet I like it, and also this closeness we have with James, even though he is usually lecturing me."

"Yes," Lilly agreed. "Strange and yet comfortable."

They went to the water's edge and proceeded to throw the bread for the ducks, who swam around in circles quacking loudly in gratitude. Nicholas and Samantha soon found a small island which they were convinced they could reach with their pieces of stale bread, and a competition immediately arose.

"Excellent shot, Nicholas!" Samantha squealed as a plume of water indicated the force with which he had hurled his piece of stale bread, even though it fell short of its mark.

"Are you patronizing me, Samantha Raven?"

"I am too young to understand that word!" Samantha cried, hurling her piece with enough force that she had to lunge to the side to stop herself following it into the water.

Nicholas's laugh made Lilly smile. It was unrestrained and a thing of joy, and she could not remember a time when she had heard it before.

"Good shot, Samantha!"

Sending his sister a ferocious scowl, which she ignored, Nicholas picked up another piece of bread.

"Well, well, well, what a lovely scene. Miss Braithwaite, Lord Braithwaite."

Lilly shot Emily a look as the Duchess of Abernathy walked toward them. The woman was a notorious gossip, and Emily was not yet ready to face society and most especially not this venomous harpy.

"Duchess," Nicholas said, dropping his bread and stepping forward to take her hand. "May I say how beautiful you look this morning."

Swallowing a snort, Lilly watched the Duchess preen under Nicholas's compliments.

"La, Miss Braithwaite, I see quite a change in you. No longer wearing glasses, and finding a modiste who makes clothes that actually fit you, in colors more befitting your age."

Lilly gritted her teeth. Of course she had known that changing her appearance would draw attention, but she had no wish to be the topic of discussion for this woman. She said nothing, simply nodded, as she had no wish for the Duchess to linger. The sooner she left, the sooner Emily would feel comfortable once again.

"And now, my lord, you must tell me who this beautiful child is? Her governess I obviously have no need of meeting," the Duchess said, dismissing Emily.

"This is Lady Samantha and Miss Tolly," Nicholas acknowledged Emily. "They are the Duke of Raven's sisters, Duchess," Nicholas said.

"Ah yes, the little bastard daughter."

Bitch, Lilly thought looking at Emily. She was now standing beside Samantha, her face composed. No one looking at her would realize the turmoil she was no doubt experiencing from the Duchess's cutting words.

Samantha opened her mouth to protest, but one look from Lilly stopped her. Intelligent child that she was, she knew not to create a scene that would embarrass her sister any further. Executing the perfect curtsey, the child then took Mr. Whiskers from the groom who now held him, and with a sweet smile on her face, she dropped his lead. Excited to be introduced to someone he did not already know, the dog immediately jumped up and put both his dirty paws on the Duchess's skirts.

"Oh, you beastly animal!"

"It's because he likes you," Samantha said, her features schooled into an innocent look.

"Well, I don't like him! And I will thank you not to laugh," she added, glaring at Lilly. "You would do well to study your brother's manners, Miss Braithwaite. It seems yours are sadly lacking!"

"I would thank you not to speak to my sister that way ever again, Duchess."

Nicholas said the words quietly, and Lilly felt ridiculously happy that he had championed her.

"I am a Duchess, I can speak as I like," the woman snapped.

"Not to my sister, you cannot. Nor to either of these two," he added acknowledging James's sisters.

"Well!" Giving them a final glare, she stalked away.

"Shrew!" Lilly hissed. "Thank you for acknowledging Emily and for what you said, Nicholas. I hate that woman more every time I see her."

"Yes, she is a loathsome witch."

"I heard a rumor once, that you and she…." Lilly waved her hand about.

"I beg your pardon!"

"You and that woman," Lilly said, poking her brother hard in the chest.

"I hardly think this is something we should be discussing

in such a public setting, if at all," Nicholas looked uncomfortable.

"I mean it, Nicholas, I shall do something nasty to you if I hear your name is ever linked with hers." Lilly glared at her brother, who in turn was looking at her like she had sprouted horns.

"Such vehemence, sister. I could almost believe you care for me."

Brother and sister looked at each other for several seconds, and then Lilly said quietly, "I do."

Leaning forward, Nicholas placed a kiss on his sister's forehead.

"Then I shall never so much as dance with that woman again."

"Oh look, Lilly, here comes Toby running toward us!"

Lilly turned to follow Samantha's finger and saw Toby running to where they stood.

"Something is wrong," Lilly said to Nicholas. "He would never willingly seek me out in public."

"This is the boy, Toby, who was hurt? The one from Temple Street?"

Lilly nodded, and then moved to intercept Toby.

"What has happened?" she said as soon as he was close enough to hear her words.

"There has been a fire, Lilly, at Temple Street."

CHAPTER 23

"*G*o back to the house, Nicholas. Take Emily and Samantha with you, and tell Devon I have gone to Temple Street as there is a fire there!" Lilly said, picking up her skirts in preparation to follow Toby.

"You are not running off without protection, Lilly. I forbid it, and your future husband will murder me if I allow it." He grabbed her wrist. "You there," Nicholas addressed the three footmen who were trying to appear inconspicuous. "Take Lady Samantha and Miss Emily back to the residence. Emily, tell Lord Sinclair and your brother what has happened, and I shall take a footman and my sister to Temple Street."

Nicholas grabbed her hand, and they were soon running behind Toby back the way he had just come.

"Hurry and call a hackney, Toby. It will get us there faster," Lilly panted. She watched him sprint ahead of her and out of the park gates.

"I regret, sister, that I get to see your house in Temple Street in such circumstances."

Lilly was panicking. She had visions of Mr. and Mrs.

Davey and any of the children currently there being trapped inside the house.

"I-I am s-so scared, Nicholas."

"I am here with you, Lilliana. We will face it together."

"Quick, Lilly, Nelly says he'll take us there!"

Toby was hanging out the door of a hackney as they reached the road. Nelly, she gathered, was the driver, who gave her a toothless grin. The footman clambered up beside him. Nicholas threw her inside and followed, and the carriage started moving as he slammed the door.

"T-tell me what you know, Toby," Lilly gasped, pressing her fingers to her side to stop the pain.

"Mr. Davey said it was nothing, but Mrs. Davey looks scared so I came to get you. I saw the flames and the smoke was thick."

"But everyone was all right?"

"Sam left for the country yesterday, so no one else was inside."

"Lord I wish you had told me that before I ran to the carriage. Horrid visions were filling my head, Toby."

He shrugged. "I don't know how much damage has been done to the house, but I think everyone is safe."

Lilly didn't know why, but she had a sinking feeling that the fire was to do with her visit to the Watch House and the kidnapping.

"I am slowly starting to piece together things that at the time did not seem right, but I ignored," Nicholas said, giving Lilly a steady look as she battled the panic inside her. "Your shopping trips and visits to friends were, in fact, all to your house in Temple Street, weren't they?"

Lilly nodded.

"God, how could I have been so blind."

Ignoring her brother's muttered words, Lilly was up and out the door as the carriage stopped.

"Looks all right," Toby said, opening the front door.

The smell of smoke still lingered in the air as they made their way through the house. The small front parlor appeared untouched, as did Mr. and Mrs. Davey's bedroom.

Nicholas followed them silently as they checked the lower floor, and then Toby led the way down the stairs to the kitchens, and Lilly heard the murmur of voices. She found Mrs. Davey with her arms in a tub of soapy water and Mr. Davey with several boards in his hand.

"Is everyone all right?"

"Of course we're all right," Mrs. Davey said, quickly drying her hands and reaching for the kettle to heat water. Tea was always called for when anyone arrived at Temple Street.

"Where was the fire?"

"Now then, boy, you should not have disturbed Miss Braithwaite," Mr. Davey said to Toby. "There is no need to worry yourself; it was just a small fire by the back door in a box of old rags we kept outside. The problem was it got hold of the wood I had piled outside and the flames were high enough to cause a few murmurings in the street. If we'd not been here, the damage would have been substantial, to be sure, but we were, so no harm done. If I'd known the boy was running for you, I would have stopped him."

"I thought she should know," Toby said, shrugging as he leaped onto the bench and took the large piece of jam and bread Mrs. Davey handed him.

"Where are your manners, Miss Braithwaite?" Mrs. Davey said, looking over Lilly's shoulder to where Nicholas stood.

"This is my brother, Lord Braithwaite. Nicholas, this is Mr. and Mrs. Davey. They look after the children and run Temple Street. It is their home."

Lilly watched as Nicholas shook Mr. Davey's hand and bowed to Mrs. Davey. Both looked him up and down, neither looking particularly happy to have him in their home. Lilly had never willingly spoken about her family with them. However she guessed her maid and Wilson had, and none of what they had imparted had been complimentary.

"It seems my reputation has preceded me," Nicholas said, shooting Lilly a look, to which she shrugged. "However, will you believe me when I say I have seen the error of my ways, hence my appearance here before you in the company of my sister?"

There was silence in the small kitchen and then Mr. Davey nodded. "Well then, that's as it should be, I'm thinking."

"I wonder if you would be so kind as to take me on a tour of your lovely home, Mr. Davey?" Nicholas added, surprising Lilly. She was happy for him to do just that now she knew no one was in danger.

"Indeed, I would be honored, my lord."

"Can you show me where the fire started, Mrs. Davey?" Lilly said after they had departed.

"Of course, please follow me."

Her heart had resumed its normal beat as they walked outside. The weather had grown colder on the drive, and a brisk wind had risen.

"I'll fetch you a shawl, miss," Mrs. Davey said.

"I shall be all right for a few minutes until I come back inside," Lilly said, moving to the box Mrs. Davey pointed to.

"That is the box it started in."

Lilly studied the area. It was small, with only a tiny patch of grass, a shed, and several chairs. There was a gate at the rear of the property and it would not be hard for a person to slip down the narrow lane and inside to light the fire. Was she being overly suspicious? Walking around the box, she looked at it from all angles.

"How do you think it started, Mrs. Davey?"

"Don't rightly know. Mr. Davey couldn't work that one out either. Oh, I almost forgot in all the goings-on, Miss Braithwaite, that a message was delivered for you first thing this morning."

"Thank you," Lilly said, taking the note the woman pulled from her apron. "Please go back to whatever you were doing, Mrs. Davey. I'll be along shortly."

"Come in when you're finished, and I'll have a cup of tea ready to take off the chill."

"Thank you."

Lilly took out the note and opened it.

I had planned to send you on a long voyage to a certain Kurdish sheikh who will pay an extremely high price for you, as he has a lust for blonde English noblewomen, Miss Braithwaite. That can still be arranged, as can the fact that I can burn this house to the ground and hurt anyone you care about. Stop meddling in my business, or next time I will make you pay tenfold.

Shivering, Lilly wondered what she should do next. If something happened to Devon, or any of the others in her life now, she would never forgive herself.

"I thought we agreed you were not to rush headlong into danger without first notifying me."

Pushing the note behind her back, she turned to face Devon. Lilly could tell he had left the house in haste. He was hatless, his hair standing on end, and the collar of his overcoat was tucked inside.

"I had to come; Toby said there was a fire. Nicholas and a footman are here," Lilly rushed to say. "Mr. Davey is at present showing him the house."

"And what of the danger to you?" he said, ignoring the fact that her brother was there. Taking off his coat, he moved to where she stood.

"I am quite warm," Lilly said, retreating several steps.

"Your lips are blue, and if you wish to hide what is in

your hand from me, then I will not force you to show it. However, I will search your things when you're not looking."

The woman would see him in Bedlam, Dev thought as his heart settled back into his chest. He had been looking over some maps in James's office, while the Duke took his wife driving around the park, when Emily and Samantha burst into the room to inform them that Temple Street was on fire. He had run out of James's house and jumped into the carriage he'd just called to take him to the docks. He had then urged the driver to race at a reckless speed through London and its bustling traffic.

"You wouldn't be so underhand!" Lilly said in shocked tones, which made him laugh.

Something had frightened her. The fire definitely, but also whatever was in that note she had thrust behind her skirts.

"Of course I would. How do you think I kept track of my siblings, without being underhand," he added, wrapping his coat around her shoulders and hauling her close so he could kiss her. All the starch instantly left her spine as she sank into him. Lord, she had the softest lips, Dev thought, an instantaneous tug of lust surging through his body.

"All right," Lilly whispered against his mouth.

"All right?"

"All right, you can read my note," Lilly said, pulling back and handing it to him. "But you must understand that I have no wish for you to start roaring or being even more protective. I am showing it to you because I want no secrets between us."

"I understand," Dev said, wondering what the hell it said. "When did you receive it?"

"Mrs. Davey gave it to me a few minutes ago," she said, handing it to him.

Lifting an arm, he tucked her under it and opened the paper so they could read it together. He felt his blood run cold as he read the angry, slanted words.

"Inhale and exhale a few times before you say anything," she urged him. It was sound advice. The hand she rubbed up and down his chest also helped... but only a little.

"Christ, Lilly."

"I know, but as you saved me, I am not on a boat about to be delivered to a Kurdish sheikh."

"You never will be." Dev hugged her close. "I want you to leave London with me for a while, Lilly. Just until it is safe and this madman is caught."

Her body stiffened against his. "I cannot leave now, Devon, you must know that."

"To lose you would destroy me, love."

"That's not fighting fair, Devon."

"My feelings for you go beyond fair, Lilly, and I will not have you taken from me because you show a reckless disregard for your welfare. This," he waved the note before her, "is very real, and words of a man who is dangerous and intent on achieving his goal no matter the cost. I cannot allow you to get anywhere near him again. Therefore, you must be protected, and to do that, I want you to leave London."

Dev watched the frustration flicker across Lilly's face. She tried to pull away from him but he wouldn't let her. She had to learn that he was part of her life now, and she could no longer make decisions without forethought.

"You are to become my wife. Therefore your welfare is my main concern, and if I sound unreasonable for wanting to remove you from some madman intent on taking you from me, then so be it."

"Of course I understand why you are speaking this way,

but I cannot leave now. Not when the children need me. But if we stay in London, I will do as you say and will go nowhere without you knowing it. I promise."

Dev looked down at her for the longest time and then smiled. "I almost believe you."

"I would never lie to you!"

"Don't look offended, love. I know you would never deliberately lie to me; however, I think you are used to acting alone, as is evidenced by your actions today."

Lilly huffed, then faced him, placing a hand on his chest. "Please."

He was used to his siblings bribing and manipulating him. This woman had a lot to learn if she was entering their family.

"Please, ah.... Please, Dev."

"That was the most pathetic attempt at begging I have ever heard. My siblings would have laughed themselves sick had they heard. You need to speak to Dorrie; she begs better than anyone I've ever met."

"Are you laughing at me?"

"Yes," he said, unrepentant about the fact. Anger still smoldered inside him, but he could at least breathe easier knowing she was close.

Her expression slowly changed before his eyes. Her eyes softened as she wet her lips with her tongue. Dev braced himself as she lifted to her toes and reached for a handful of his hair, then tugged his head down for a kiss.

Innocent she may be, but Dev was soon on fire.

"Please, Devon," she said in a breathy little voice that a courtesan would be proud of.

"All right," Dev said, his voice harsh as he battled his body's response to Lilly's kiss. "But you have to promise to do as I say and if anything further happens, we leave London.

Furthermore, I will not let you win every argument with such an obvious display, even if I enjoyed it."

"I promise."

"Again, I'm not totally convinced, and yet we will leave that for now." Dev grabbed her hand and tugged her back in the direction of the kitchen door. "We have to tell Mr. and Mrs. Davey the truth, love, about everything so they will be ready if anything further happens."

"They know some of it, but yes, you are right."

Dev was surprised to see Nicholas Braithwaite seated at the small table in the kitchen, sipping tea from one of Mrs. Davey's teacups. He looked quite comfortable. The man was trying, he'd give him that.

"I tried to get Lord Braithwaite up to the front parlor, Miss Braithwaite, yet he would not budge," Mrs. Davey said, looking quite happy with the fact.

"It is warmer in here, Mrs. Davey, and this apple tart is quite possibly the most delicious I have ever tasted."

"Is it, Braithwaite? Well, then you had best leave enough for me," Devon said, putting Lilly into one chair and taking the other.

Soon the small party, including Toby, who was still seated on the bench swinging his legs happily and munching yet another slice of bread, was all busy eating and drinking. Lilly brought Mr. and Mrs. Davey up-to-date with everything that had transpired.

"And I would completely understand if you wish to leave London for a time because of this," Lilly said when she had finished her tale.

"Oh no, miss, we'll be staying put and caring for the children when they need us, and of course there's our Toby," Mrs. Davey said, giving the boy a smile that he acknowledged with a small one of his own.

"If you will allow it, Mr. Davey, I will have someone

watch over the house for a time. He'll be discreet so as not to upset any of the children, but it will ease Miss Braithwaite's mind," Dev said.

They were proud people, the Daveys, and he knew they prided themselves on caring for the boys and themselves without any fuss or help. Because of this, he had made the offer sound like it was to ease Lilly's mind and hoped that would make a difference.

"I should be relieved if you would take up Lord Sinclair's offer," Lilly added her voice to Dev's.

"If it will make Miss Braithwaite happy, then we shall allow it," Mr. Davey said.

"Excellent." Dev gave Lilly a wink.

They left the house a short while later, and Dev tried not to think about the letter he now had tucked in his top pocket. He would have to talk to his family and James about it later. Maybe even Nicholas, but for now he said good-bye to Lilly's brother, watching as he strode off down the street, having decided to walk to the business he said he had to attend to.

CHAPTER 24

"Take us around the park and keep to the quieter areas until I tell you otherwise," Dev said to the driver before he climbed into the carriage and shut the door firmly behind him.

"Why are we driving around the park?" Lilly watched him settle into the seat across from her.

"Because I want a few minutes alone with the woman I love without interruption." Dev took her hand in his and then proceeded to remove her gloves. "I want to drive through the park with you and have no one ask me questions," he added, tugging her onto the seat beside him.

"But what if I want to ask you a question?"

"As long as it is not overly taxing, I shall answer it," he said, taking her other hand and removing that glove too.

"Dev, someone shall see us!" Lilly gasped as he kissed each of the fingers he had exposed.

Standing, he wrenched the curtains closed and then reseated himself. She had kissed him at Temple Street and that brief taste had stayed with him as he drank tea and politely answered questions. He had watched her nibble on a scone and remembered the feel of those lush lips on him. The visions he had tried to push from his head of their love-making had risen, and now he wanted her with a need that overrode everything else. He would have her or go mad.

"What are you doing?"

Ignoring her question, he slid his hands under her skirts, pushing them up her thighs. He then picked her up and lowered her to straddle his lap.

"This is your fault," he said, taking off her bonnet and flinging it across the carriage. "You kissed me, and behaved in a thoroughly inappropriate manner, and now I can't stop thinking about you naked."

"Devon!"

She was shocked silent, which gave him time to start on the buttons of her dress. He managed several before the need to touch her overwhelmed him, and he slipped his hand inside her bodice and cupped the soft, full flesh of one breast through her chemise.

"Oh lord, that is wonderful."

"I'm not stopping," Dev growled, tugging more buttons free. He then had her breasts exposed. "You have beautiful breasts, Lilly. Your nipples are like raspberries, begging for me to bite into them."

"Yes, please." Her head fell back as his mouth closed over her and he began to lave the tight peak with his tongue.

Dev had a reputation for being thorough. He prided himself on missing nothing, so he lavished each and every inch of her breasts with the same attention, until she was whimpering and begging him to take her.

"Had I known these were beneath your evening gowns, I would have made more of an effort two years ago," he said, his hands now replacing his lips to stroke and caress the silken skin once more. "I would have taken you into the nearest room…," Dev rasped as she arched toward him.

"Be quiet and kiss me!" Lilly cried, pushing him back on the seat and pressing her lips to his. She was as desperate as he to taste and touch. Her hands were everywhere. Pushing aside his jacket, she opened his buttons and stroked his chest.

Clamping one hand on her neck, Dev wrapped the other around her waist and hauled her close until nothing separated them. Teeth clashed and noses banged as they ravished each other. They were desperate, no longer aware of where they were, only that the fire inside them needed to be extinguished.

Dev cupped her ankles and then traced the contours of her legs as he moved his hands higher. He ran his fingers around the band at the top of her silk stockings before moving higher until he reached her bottom. Tracing the creamy swells, Dev shuddered as Lilly wriggled against him, the friction almost painful.

She forced her hands between them and tried to undo the buttons of his breeches.

"Help me, damn you!"

"Ask me nicely," Dev whispered against her breasts, his warm breath brushing over the sensitive skin.

"Pleasseee."

Ripping open the buttons, Dev clamped his hands on her hips and lifted her, lowering her onto his aching length. Both moaned as Lilly took him deep inside her.

"Yes, love," Dev whispered. "Ride me."

Lilly braced her hands on his shoulder as she rose and lowered. The friction was exquisite.

"Don't stop; you feel like heaven, Lilly."

She did it again and again, each slide and thrust driving him to the point of madness. Gripping her hips, he drove up as she came down.

"Dev!"

Swallowing her cries, he kissed her hard and took over,

pulling her down harder with each thrust until the only sound in the carriage was ragged breathing. Lowering his head, he took one swollen nipple into his mouth and sucked hard, and Lilly fell apart in his arms. She clenched around him as he drove upward once more. Biting back the hoarse cry that came to his lips, he grunted, pouring himself into her as she slumped forward onto him.

Lilly lay her head on his chest, one hand fisted in his shirt as she struggled to regain her composure. Slowly sounds started to make themselves heard once more. The rumble of carriage wheels, the clip-clop of hooves, and people making their way around the park. She should be horrified; Lilly had never behaved so rashly in her life. To make love with Dev in a carriage with people a few feet away.... She should be shocked and horrified; instead, she was sated and ridiculously happy. One of his hands cupped her head, the gesture protective, while the other swept slow circles over her back.

"When can we marry?"

She felt his smile in her hair.

"If you are agreeable, we shall leave at the completion of the season and marry on Raven Mountain in James's church."

"Yes, I like that idea. I do not want lots of people, just our families."

Dev rubbed one of her curls between his fingers.

"It sounds perfect to me."

Giving the curl a tug, he kissed her hard as she looked up at him.

"I like you naked and at my mercy." Lilly shivered as Devon traced the curve of her breast. Pushing herself off him, she took the handkerchief he handed her and moved to the opposite seat. Her large fiancé remained relaxed; his body sprawled across from her.

"When we are wed, I may tie you to my bed and keep you naked from dawn till dusk, wench."

"You could try," Lilly said, reaching for her chemise.

"You'd probably just chew through the ropes," he said, rousing himself to right his own clothing and then help her do up her buttons.

Between them, they got her clothed and then he opened the curtains. Lifting the hatch above his head, he told the driver to take them back to James's house. Sitting beside her, he took her hand, entwining their fingers, and Lilly felt that little shiver of heat that touching him always produced inside her.

"How will we find who is behind all this, Devon?"

"After reading that note, I am going to hire a Runner and a private detective. If we continue probing it will make whoever is responsible all the more eager to stop us, so we must act secretly."

"I like that idea, and reiterate my promise that I shall not take any unnecessary risks."

Seeing something fierce flit across his face, Lilly lifted a hand and touched his cheek. "I love you so much, Devonshire Sinclair, and promise to do nothing to separate us ever."

"And I you, my love, and I will be ensuring that happens."

They drove in silence for a while, content to be alone together as the city of London moved around them.

"I know you have acquired this new property for your children down at the docks, Lilly, and I was hoping you would ask Nicholas to look after the changes you want made there."

"Do you think he would?" Lilly asked. It would do no good to insist she see to the changes; Devon had not pushed for them to leave London, and for that she was grateful. However, she had no wish to antagonize him now she had what she wanted.

"I don't see why not. He is a changed man, Lilly, and eager to show you the difference in him. Now he knows about your children, he may wish to have some involvement."

Lilly thought about that. It was hard to think of her brother in the terms Devon spoke, even though she had acknowledged those changes herself today.

"I understand that you are struggling to accept that he is different, love. I too struggle with it, yet Cambridge saw two of the men he once gambled with cut Nicholas last night at the Hadleigh musical. He then heard insults and murmurs about him, spoken just loud enough for your brother to hear."

"Cambridge stayed with him?" Lilly said, feeling ill at what Nicholas had gone through, but relieved he had not done so alone.

"My brother may be many things, but he is honorable and stayed with Nicholas until he left."

"Considering what he did to Cam, it was very generous indeed. I am pleased he had someone to look over him."

"As do you, love. A fact that I'm sure, given time, will make you want to run screaming from the house; however, never forget they mean well," Dev said, squeezing her hand.

"I think once I get used to it, having a large family will be a wonderful thing."

"It has its moments." He smiled at her. "The Selkirk ball is in two nights, love."

Lilly looked out the window as a carriage passed close by. She had not entered society since the night of her abduction and was not sure she was ready to yet.

"If it affected just you and me, Lilly, then I would be more than happy to snub society," Devon said, understanding her thoughts even though she had not voiced them. "Yet James and I have siblings who will make their debuts one day, plus Essie, Cam, and your brother still walk among society. We need to make an appearance to halt the wagging tongues."

Lilly's sigh was long and loud. "I suppose we must, when you put it that way."

"Cheer up, love, you will be surrounded by family," Dev said, lifting her hand once more to his lips. "I have only one thing to ask of you, my sweet."

"Anything," she said, because she would do it if it were in her power. She'd reach up and grab the moon for him if she could.

"Will you dress as you have today, and let society really see the woman you are? Will you leave off your glasses and wear something that does not upset my stomach, and leave the wild animals and small woodland creatures from your hair?"

CHAPTER 25

"*M*r. Spriggot and Mr. Brown have arrived, my lord."

"Thank you, Pennyroll," Dev said, ushering Lilly to the stairs. "Are they in my uncle's study?"

"Yes, my lord. The Duke and Mr. Sinclair are at present with him."

"Of course they are," Dev muttered, taking the stairs two at a time and dragging Lilly behind him.

Devon had taken Lilly driving in the park. She suspected this was to keep her busy, so she did not go off on her own, but she did protest. Three days after she had received that letter, she was still looking over her shoulder wherever she went.

"They could not simply have waited until I arrived."

Lilly had noticed that only his siblings could make Devonshire Sinclair surly. For the most he was a pleasant, affable man—to those who did not know him well. To the rest, his family and her, he was demanding, officious, and she loved every inch of him, because his behavior stemmed from the need to keep his people safe. She had no doubt if he could

get away with it, he would take them all to an island somewhere and set the boat adrift.

They heard the rumble of voices as they reached the
room. Dev flung the door open and towed Lilly inside. James
and Cam were seated beside each other, and two other men
sat opposite.

"Good afternoon, Lord Sinclair."

"Mr. Spriggot," Dev said, pushing Lilly into a chair. "This
is my fiancée, Miss Braithwaite."

"Miss Braithwaite," the detective said, gaining his feet and
bowing, which caused a few strands of hair on his head to
slip their moorings and dangle down the side of his face
momentarily, until he swept them back into place with a
gesture Lilly was sure he had made many times.

"Mr. Spriggot." Lilly nodded to the innocuous-looking
man. Small and thin, he was dwarfed by the men around him.

"And this is Mr. Brown," Dev said, shaking hands with the
other man.

"Mr. Brown," Lilly said, nodding to him. He had hands
bigger than ham hocks and a large bald head and blunt
features. "Hello, James and Cam," she added. Dev acknowledged them with a curt nod and then prowled to the
fireplace.

"Did you enjoy your drive, Lilly?"

"Yes, thank you, Cam."

"Perhaps you could begin at the beginning, Miss Braithwaite. His Grace and Mr. Sinclair have told me some of what
has transpired, but perhaps you could fill in the gaps, as it is
you who are the intended target."

Lilly watched Dev's shoulders stiffen. His eyes had
narrowed and were focused intently on the man. He had not
liked being reminded of her abduction. Gone was her
amiable fiancé, and in his place was the ruthless lord she
knew he could be.

"It began when I was told the children were being taken." Lilly told the two men everything she knew, and then answered each and every question they politely asked of her.

"Tea, Lord Sinclair."

"Thank you, Pennyroll, and please bring the brandy also," Cam said. It seemed he had also noted the tension in his brother.

"You have been very clear with your details, Miss Braithwaite, and Mr. Brown and I thank you for that," Mr. Spriggot said, waving away the brandy Cam tried to hand him and instead nodding to the teapot. Lilly picked it up and poured him a cup.

"I shall start on my enquiries at once, and I believe Mr. Brown has an associate that he will station at Temple Street. Is that not so, Mr. Brown?"

"Indeed it is. He's a good man and I shall take him there immediately after I leave here, if that is all right with you, Lord Sinclair?"

Devon looked to Lilly. "Will that suit you?"

"Yes, that will be excellent, thank you," she said, giving Dev a small smile to acknowledge he had asked her advice instead of just confirming Mr. Brown's words.

"If I may add to what we have already discussed," Devon said, "this note was waiting for Lilly when she reached Temple Street three days ago, when she went to see the fire."

Silence settled heavily in the room as each man read the words.

James growled, Cam hissed. Mr. Spriggot and Mr. Brown regained their feet.

"Well then, this note would suggest we must move with some expediency. We shall say good day to you all," Mr. Spriggot said, bowing.

Pennyroll appeared to escort the two men out.

"It's a smoky business, this abducting children and then

you, Lilly," Cam said, busy placing two small triangle sand-
wiches on top of each other before jamming the lot in his
mouth.

"Must you continually cram food into that great
cavernous hole, Cambridge?" Dev growled.

Rehashing the entire incident had unsettled him, Lilly
thought, watching Dev glare at his brother.

"I'm a growing lad," Cam said around the food, then,
swallowing, he offered his brother a smile. "And as it is our
uncle's food, it need not concern you how much of it I eat."

Lilly smiled into her teacup as James joined the Sinclair
brothers in their arguing. It seemed they all needed to release
some tension. She wondered if her cousin realized that it was
now second nature to him to get involved, when before he
would have watched in bemused wonder as she did.

"Oh lord, look at the time."

"What's the problem, Raven? It is only two in the afternoon. Did you miss your nap perhaps?" Devon taunted him.

James gave him a foul look before speaking. "No, I forgot
that we," he said, sweeping his hand around the room, "are
meant to be taking the children to Mr. Rolland's Circus of
Strange and Ridiculous Curiosities in precisely forty
minutes."

"I say, are we?" Cam said, leaping to his feet. "I saw the
advertisement for that in the paper. It looks exciting."

"You're twenty-eight years old, man. How can you
possibly be excited about a show that features a bearded lady
and a mermaid?" James looked disgusted.

"I live life to the full and embrace every new opportunity,
James, so I can remain unjaded, unlike you and my brother
here."

James merely raised an eyebrow and then looked at Dev.
"I would rather be classed as jaded, wouldn't you, Sinclair,
than imbecilic."

"Amen to that," Dev vowed.

"That's very harsh criticism of Cam," Lilly said, climbing to her feet and slipping her arm through her soon-to-be brother-in-law's. "I think your enthusiasm is wonderful."

"Wonderful? Well, in that case, you can accompany us and be enthusiastic when the children run their sticky fingers all over you," Dev said, pushing off the mantle to come toward her. "They will be taking some homemade sweets with them that my aunt's cook has made especially for the occasion."

"I don't think—"

"Escape is impossible, I'm afraid," Dev said, planting a kiss on her lips as he passed.

"But I need—"

"To gather your things, as we leave in precisely in twenty minutes," James said, patting her head as he also headed for the door.

"Wrap up warm, Lilly, there is definitely a nip in the air," Cam said, giving her arm a squeeze before he too left the room. She stood there for several seconds just enjoying the feeling of being wanted and loved, of having family, and then with a silly giggle she hurried from the room to find Essex. As she had nothing to wrap up warm in she would need to borrow something from her soon-to-be sister-in-law. She also would need to send her Aunt Vi and Nicholas word of where she was going.

How had she lived for so long without these people to fill her life?

CHAPTER 26

"We have sweets, Lilly."

Dev smiled down into the eager face of his sister as she talked to the woman at his side.

"Yes, your brother told me about them, and I'm hoping you will see your way to letting me sample one as I have not eaten a lot of sweets before."

They were standing outside the small wooden building that housed the revolving cinema, along with the rest of the people wanting to get inside out of the cold. It was a new experience for Lilly, coming here with the entire Raven/Sinclair family, but she appeared to be handling the situation well.

Wrapped up in a long emerald coat of Essie's, she looked young and beautiful, and she was his.

"They are so sweet they make your tongue curl, Mrs. Maricold says."

"Marigold, darling," Eden said, pulling Warwick's woolen hat down to cover his ears.

"And she says that Pennyroll has the record of eating more than ten pieces in one night."

"Pennyroll is obviously a man of hidden talents," Lilly said.

"Right, the doors now appear to be opening," Dev said. "We shall proceed in an orderly manner to the front door. All children are to take the hand of an adult, please."

"Forever hopeful, brother," Cam said, loping up behind Dev.

Taking Lilly's hand, Dev then took a twin and they made their way toward the entrance.

The weather in London had turned the last week. A brisk wind whipped around their ankles, and he was glad they would all soon be inside the theater, as it looked as if the skies were about to open and they would be wet through in minutes.

"It's exciting, isn't it, Dev?"

"It certainly is, darling."

Dorrie skipped and hopped beside him while Lilly walked as she did everything, now she was no longer hampered with yards of ill-fitting material: with a natural grace. Warwick, he noted, had taken her hand, which was interesting. At eight years of age, his youngest sibling was fiercely independent and did not willingly cuddle or hold hands with anyone who was not close to him. Lilly, it seemed, had found a place in his affections.

They filed through the doors and moved into the theater. It was softly lit inside, and they could see the stage, which appeared to be illuminated from beneath. There were plenty of patrons already in their places. The children whispered loudly about whatever they saw, their chatter increasing in volume with every word.

"Please come this way, your Grace."

A man appeared and bowed deeply before James. Dev raised a brow as his nose touched his knee.

"What can I say, people want to impress me," his brother-

275

in-law drawled softly. "Such a shame a few of you fail to understand that with my title should come respect."

These words produced snorts from Dev and Eden, the only ones to hear.

"My name is Mr. Rolland, and I am the proprietor of this amazing performance you are about to see."

He wore a battered top hat and bright red jacket. His mustache was waxed to curl up on the ends and covered the upper half of his mouth.

"How does the mermaid move around London if she has no legs?"

Samantha, who was hanging on to Eden's hand, gave Mr. Rolland a searching look to accompany these words.

"She goes straight back to the sea when the show is over, my dear," Mr. Rolland answered.

"But how does she know when to come back for the next show?"

"Someone must be able to speak mermaid," Dorrie added, a frown creasing her forehead as she tried to work through the weighty problem of mermaid communication.

"And so it begins." Dev sighed.

"What begins?" Lilly said, fighting her laughter.

"The questions," Essex whispered. "It will be endless throughout the performance, and for about a week after. They are insatiable when something interests them."

"They will dissect everything, from the mermaid's tail to how the revolving floor moves," Cam whispered in her ear. "Supposedly we were the same, or so our mother told us."

"But if she has no legs then she can't walk, and I've tried getting about on my belly and it is not easy. It would surely take a day to travel here from the water," Warwick said.

"She is collected from the sea each day," Mr. Rolland said in a voice that was beginning to sound strained.

Dev knew the look in his eyes, like game trapped in a

hunter's sights, because he'd been there a time or two himself.

"But what if her tail dries up, surely that would be dangerous," Dorrie added. "I've heard that when a fish is left out of water it dies. Why doesn't that happen to the mermaid?"

"Can I urge you to take your places along with the other spectators, as the show is about to begin!" Mr. Rolland sounded desperate now.

"I've thought about hiring them out to the Foreign Office to interrogate enemy spies."

Lilly laughed as Dev had intended her to.

"I think they are sweet and show an intelligence that seems to be lacking in their elder siblings."

"You will pay for that comment later, my love. However, now we must gird our loins for the delights of Mr. Rolland's Circus of Strange and Ridiculous Curiosities."

They walked down several steps and onto the floor along with the other patrons. Divided into two parts, the audience was to stand on the outer rim, which formed a circle around a raised platform that Dev guessed the actors would perform on.

"Move for the Duke of Raven and his party, if you please!"

James groaned as several other patrons were shuffled back to allow them to the front of a row.

"No, really, there is no need—"

"Only royalty is higher than you, your Grace. I will not have anyone saying Mr. Rolland's Circus of Strange and Ridiculous Curiosities does not look after its distinguished guests."

"One word, Sinclair."

Dev raised his hands as James glared at him. They shuffled to the front, adults at the back and children placed securely before them.

"No one moves or touches anything, is that understood?"

"Yes, Dev," his siblings said.

"That goes for you too, Samantha," James added.

"Oooh, it's starting!" Somer squealed as Mr. Rolland appeared suddenly above them on a raised platform.

"Please brace yourselves, as the platform you are currently standing upon is about to start moving!"

"Dev, we're moving!"

"I can feel that, Warwick."

"Prepare to be dazzled by the delights of Mr. Rolland's performers!" Mr. Rolland said as slowly the lights went out around them, with only the raised platform still lit. Dev watched as Mr. Rolland was lowered and then a large woman slowly appeared above them, rising out of the mists that now floated around her.

"I am the bearded woman from Venezuela!"

"More like Putney," Dev muttered.

Lilly saw the show for what it was, a group of people that were very clever at the art of disguise, and she loved every ridiculous minute of it. She loved watching the children laugh and squeal with delight, and she loved that she wasn't afraid of the dark because Dev had his hand on her waist, reassuring her that he was close. But most of all she loved being there with all of them, part of these wonderful families.

"I believe you're enjoying yourself, Miss Braithwaite."

"I admit I am. It is a novelty for me, and seeing it through the eyes of the children makes it all the more fun." Turning her head slightly, she brushed his lips with her own. "But most of all I'm so happy to be here with you and the families." His green eyes seemed to glow at her. He didn't speak, just smiled and returned the kiss.

"I will not spoil it for you then, and tell you what I can see."

"Is that hard? Seeing everything that others cannot?"

"Sometimes, but I'm used to it now. Besides, I get to see those dimples of yours when you smile, no matter how far away from me you are."

"I must remember you see everything," Lilly muttered. "I will be able to hide nothing from you."

She saw the flash of his white teeth and then felt his hand stroke her bottom.

"It's the mermaid, Lilly!"

"I can see that, Dorrie, and she is very beautiful, don't you think, especially her blue tail."

"It sparkles," Samantha gasped, clutching her hands to her chest as the mermaid reached the top of the platform, where she proceeded to splash around in a small pool of water.

"She is a very talented mermaid. In fact, I think I may have heard her sing one night while I swam off the cliffs of my home," James said.

"Was that her, do you think?" Cam said, appearing to ponder James's words. "I have heard the singing, but was unsure of its source."

The children were nodding in agreement, stating they too had heard the singing and vowed that it was indeed this mermaid and her family.

"Ooh, do you think she lives near Oak's Knoll, Dev?"

"Mermaids are a bit like migratory birds, I believe, Dorrie. They move around to the warmest climates as the seasons change."

Warwick nodded. "That makes sense. I wouldn't want to freeze my—"

"Thank you, Warwick," Devon said quickly. "I believe we understand your meaning."

"You have tears running down your cheeks, Lilly. Is it because the mermaid is so beautiful?"

Nodding at Dorrie, Lilly bit her lip. She had never laughed so much in her life.

"I hear fire," Eden said softly.

"I smell smoke." Cam spoke at the same time as his sister.

"How far away?" Devon asked.

"Just starting, but we need to move now," Eden replied.

James ducked under the barrier and then climbed up on the stage beside the mermaid as quickly as he could.

"There is a fire, we all need to leave the building. Please move calmly to the entrance at once."

Lilly looked at the entrance. It was some distance away, but she could as yet not see the fire or smell smoke. The building was made of wood, and would ignite in minutes, but with Eden and Cam's warning, they would surely get out before the fire took hold.

"James, look up!"

Eden's scream made them glance skyward, in time to see a lit torch come hurtling toward the Duke.

"Jump!" Dev roared.

Lilly watched the Duke fly through the air to land at his wife's feet. Devon and Cam grabbed an arm each and steadied him.

"Now run!" Devon roared, picking up both twins. "Cam, take Warwick," he added as James picked up Samantha. "Eden, Essie, and Lilly, take hold of a jacket and don't let go. We form a chain and it will not be broken till we get outside. The smoke will soon make it hard to see!"

"I have your shirt, Dev!"

Acknowledging Lilly's words with a nod, he wrapped his arms around his sisters and started for the doors with the other patrons. Around them people were running and screaming. Children had begun to cry.

"I have you safe, darlings, just hold on a little longer."

Lilly listened as he talked to the twins and focused on his voice. Terror built inside her with each step they took. A hand gripped her coat from behind, and she hoped the others were close, and prayed everyone made it out safe.

"Talk to me, Lilly. Reassure me you are there!"

He followed those words with a cough, and she knew he would take in more lungfuls than them, because he was talking.

"I'm here, Devon. Don't talk, just move!" She patted his back, and whatever leg, arm, or shoulder she could reach of the twins.

"Left, Sinclair!" That was James's voice, and Lilly felt a rush of relief at the sound.

The smoke was making it hard to see. The fire had sprung to life as yet another torch was thrown. Placing a hand over her mouth, she let go of Devon briefly.

"Lilly!"

"I'm here, just covering my nose and mouth."

"Get in front of me!"

"You go first and I shall be right behind you," Lilly shouted to be heard above the noise.

"Don't let me go, Lilly!" Devon roared before making another surge for the door.

People tried to push past them and over them, but they kept hold of each other, be it a hand or a piece of clothing. No one broke the link. The smoke was thick now, but Lilly did not look behind her.

"We are at the door, love, just a few minutes more and we will be outside!"

She heard Devon's words and felt the surge of people propel them forward, but she lost her footing and her hold on Devon's jacket.

"Lilly!"

She heard his cry, but could do nothing to stop herself from falling.

Rushing through the door, Dev placed the twins on the floor. "Wait over there for everyone," he told his little sisters as he pointed to a spot nearby, yet far enough to keep them safe from the fire.

"Yes, Dev," they said, eyes wide with fear. He watched them run and then he turned to head back inside to get the others and Lilly.

Nudging people aside, he noted James, Eden, and Essie two feet from the door. Samantha was coughing in her brother's arms. Grabbing his sisters, he pulled them through and James followed in their wake. "I have Lilly!" Cam said, coming through seconds later with Warwick hanging around his neck like a monkey and Lilly clutching one hand, while Emily held the other.

Lilly lunged at him, and he lifted her off her feet and into his arms, and ran down the stairs, following the rest of his family.

"I was so scared for the children!" Eden cried.

"I know, love, but everyone is safe now," James panted, bracing his hands on his knees.

Dev lowered Lilly to the ground as Cam put Warwick on his feet. The little boy was crying, and Lilly quickly gathered him close. Dev hugged his sisters and slapped James on the back before he went to get the twins. But they were not where he had left them.

CHAPTER 27

"I told them to wait there." Lilly watched Devon point to a spot not far from where they all stood.

"Something is wrong," he said, running to the place with the rest of them on his heels.

"Eden, Warwick, take out your earplugs and listen for them!" Dev said as he switched his vision. "Lilly, take off your gloves and step into the circle."

She did not hesitate. Throwing her gloves at Emily, she took Dev's hand, and Eden held the other. Then the other Sinclairs all linked hands and the circle was formed.

Lilly felt the jolt of awareness travel through her as they concentrated on the twins.

"I hear them!" Eden cried, breaking free. She pointed to the back of a fast-moving carriage hurtling down the road some distance away.

"I see them!"

Lilly watched as Devon and the other Sinclair siblings started running down the road. She did not hesitate and started in pursuit.

"Emily, take Samantha and Warwick back to the house in the Sinclair carriage!"

"Of course, James, and God speed to you all," Emily cried, hugging the two now tearful children close.

Realizing she had no hope of catching the Sinclairs, or the carriage that held the twins, she changed direction to where a man stood holding horses.

"M-my sisters have been kidnapped," she lied, as a full explanation would take too long. "Th-they are in that carriage." Lilly waved a hand down the street. "P-please, lend us your horses!"

"I'm being paid to hold them, the men would kill me," the man said, gripping the reins tight, his eyes suspicious.

"I'm the Duke of Raven, here is my card!" James rasped, arriving on her heels. "I will pay for their hackney home and then personally deliver the horses to them later!"

Lilly watched the man waver. Fishing out her reticule, she took out a handful of notes and thrust them at him. "Take these to soothe your worries!" she said, ripping the reins from his fingers.

James threw Lilly onto the back of one of the horses. Vaulting onto another, he then took the reins of the third.

They reached Eden, Essie, and Cam first.

"Cam, take the horse, and pull Essie up behind you!" James called to him.

Lilly galloped on as James pulled Eden up behind him.

Lilly hiked her skirts high and rode low over the horse's neck. She heard the others give chase behind her. Ignoring the shouts and waved fists as they flew down the street, weaving between the carriages and forcing pedestrians crossing the road to run to get out of their way, she searched for Devon and found him up ahead, still running. Surely the carriage that held the twins could not be that far ahead with so much traffic on the streets. Urging her mount closer, she drew alongside Devon.

"Hold out your hand!"

He did, and she gripped it hard, hoping they weren't being incredibly foolhardy to attempt this while the horse was moving. She watched him take one large leap and then he swung up behind her. His arms came around her waist and he held her tight. Lilly could feel the deep heaving breaths he took as he struggled to suck air into his lungs.

"Dear God, Lilly, the twins!" She heard the desperation in his voice, the terror that his two precious sisters had been taken from him.

"I know, my love, but we will get them back!"

She felt him shudder and then briefly rest his forehead on her back.

"Where is the carriage?" Cam said, drawing even with them, a ferocious expression on his face.

Dev pointed. Lilly looked and found it up ahead in the distance. She winced as it veered left, nearly overturning.

"Ease back but keep them in sight. We cannot afford to have them take risks and hurt the twins!" James shouted.

"We can't lose them!" Eden cried, tears streaming down her cheeks.

"Never!" James replied, his handsome face mirroring Cam's.

They rode in single file once the carriage had slowed; presumably the kidnappers believed it was not being followed. Lilly and Dev took the lead, and kept the carriage in their sights as it traveled through the streets.

She felt sick inside, fear eating away at her as she imagined the terror those sweet little girls were going through. They had been so excited not one hour before, and now their entire world had been tossed upon its head. And the elder Sinclairs were suffering too. Lilly had heard the pain in Dev's words and seen the stark terror on the faces of the others. They must get the twins back safe; there was simply no other option.

"They are taking the road out of London!" Lilly shouted. Where the hell were they taking the twins?

"Should we attempt to take the carriage and force it to stop?"

"No, Lilly, it's too dangerous. We will follow and then when they stop we will take back what is ours."

She shivered at the threat in Dev's voice. He would show no mercy. Someone had dared to harm what he protected and loved, and there would be retaliation. Lilly would be there to help mete it out.

They rode in silence, all determined. Lilly fidgeted, trying to get comfortable as her skirts rode up. Hands lifted her, and then she was resettled across Devon's lap. An hour passed, and then thirty more minutes, and finally the carriage pulled off the main road and started down a long driveway. Lilly eased the horse to a halt and the others followed suit.

"Danderfield lives here."

Lilly looked at James wide-eyed. "Dear God, are you sure?"

"Yes, I once visited here to view a horse he was selling. The place is etched in my memory."

Lilly knew by the dark look he threw her that James's memories were not happy ones.

"None of this makes sense," Cam growled. "Why the twins? What reason could force Danderfield to take them?"

"Tether the horses and we will walk up the drive. Keep to the trees," Dev said, jumping down and lifting Lilly to stand beside him.

"Do you think Danderfield could somehow be involved in kidnapping the children?" Lilly said as she started to work through things in her head. "I mean, he tried to marry me and I could never quite work out why, and yet perhaps it was to shut me up, as he is behind this thieving ring?"

"It sounds far-fetched, but it could be possible," James said.

"It matters not why he has taken them, only that he has, and will now pay. After we have them back we will discuss the why."

"Of course," Lilly said, touching Devon's arm to let him know she understood. His muscles felt as though they had been forged in iron, each one clenched and rigid.

They walked through the gates and then made for the trees. Running between, they crept to the front of the house, where they could see the carriage.

"They are no longer inside."

"I hear them, Dev!" Eden whispered. "They just told someone that they would be very sorry they had taken them when their family arrived."

"Thank God they are all right."

Lilly moved in front of Devon as he briefly lowered his head.

"It will be all right, my love." She touched a hand to his chest, and he gripped it hard, pulling her into his body. "I promised her I would keep them all safe, yet I have failed so many times."

"You are not God, brother." Cambridge's words were cold and clipped, and a long way from those of the happy man he usually was. "No one could have raised or cared for us better than you, so I will thank you to stop talking in that ridiculous manner."

No one spoke again as they moved to the next cluster of trees.

"Christ, I'm scared, Lilly. They are so small," Devon whispered into her ear.

"And strong, Devon. You have taught them well, and they will be safe until we reach them."

He squeezed her hand but said nothing further.

They got as close as they could without detection. The shadows were beginning to settle, yet if anyone looked they would still notice any movement in the trees. The house was made of dark gray stone. To Lilly, it looked bleak and empty. The windows on all levels were shut, curtains drawn, and not one speck of light could be seen.

"What do you see, Dev?" Essie asked.

"No one is inside."

"The twins' voices have faded, almost as if they have moved beyond the house," Eden said, frowning. "Outbuildings," she then added softly. "There must be outbuildings, and if Lilly is correct, maybe the other children are being held there also."

"What reason could Danderfield have to be kidnapping children, sister," Devon said.

"Then why kidnap the twins?"

"True," Cam agreed. "We know this is his property, but not that he is involved."

"James, you take Cam and circle the house from the far side while we take this way," Devon said, pointing to his right.

Lilly watched James brush Eden's fingers as he and Cam left. Lilly, Eden, and Essex held hands as they followed Devon. He motioned them to hunch over as he did, and keeping parallel with the house, they made their way to the rear. If Devon lifted his hand, they stopped, and restarted only when he lowered it.

Dev wanted to kill someone; he wasn't picky who, just someone who was responsible for the pain that had taken up residence in his chest. It had been bad when Lilly had been taken; he had felt a furious burning rage that someone had dared to harm her, his woman. And now his little sisters had suffered the same fate. Dorrie and Somer, who looked on the world as a vast and entertaining treat, filled with wonderful, exciting experiences. They were not supposed to feel pain or terror. He and his siblings had done their best to ensure this didn't happen to the youngest Sinclairs. Yet now it had, and he would see whomever had done this deed in hell.

Moving to the shelter of a bush, he looked at the long low building still some distance away. They would have very little cover to reach it and to do so with so many of them would be folly.

"We saw nothing on our way," Cam said, arriving at Dev's side with James on his heels. "In fact, this place looks deserted."

"There is what we are after." Dev pointed to where the building lay. "And there are four armed men patrolling the outside. I can see colors inside, multiple colors, all children, therefore your guess, Lilly, appears to be accurate. The twins are now in there too."

"There is no cover, just that bloody lane in."

Everyone grew silent as they studied the landscape.

"They won't shoot at women."

"Definitely not!" James whispered to his wife. "I will not allow you to go up to that—"

"No!" Dev snapped at the same time.

"And yet we have no other choice," Essie said, removing her bonnet. "This is our only chance. If we can distract them long enough for you, James, and Cam to approach, then well and good. If not, you will have to rush them."

"Exactly," Lilly said, removing her bonnet also. She then took Dev's necktie and tied it around her head in a band. Eden quickly did the same.

"This is ridiculous," Dev hissed, gripping Lilly's wrist. He could not allow something to happen to her.

"Trust us, Dev, and know we will be safe until you reach us."

He held her eyes, saw the determination, and knew he had to let her do it because he had no other way to get to his sisters.

"I don't want to let you do this, but I can see no other way—"

"We are wasting time," Lilly said.

"You are to take no chances," he said, scowling at her. "Any of you," he added, turning the look on his sisters.

"Take my knife," Cam said, handing it to Essie who slipped it into her bodice.

"Can you shoot?" Dev said, removing his pistol and handing it to Lilly, who in turn lifted her skirts and put it in her stocking.

"I walk the streets of London at night, Sinclair; of course I can shoot."

He could lose himself in those eyes, and planned to do so, along with her body, when they were home safe. "Be safe," he said, running a finger down her nose.

Checking Essie over to make sure she looked more like a village woman and less like a noblewoman, he nodded. "Remember you are just to lure them away from the front of the building so we can get there undetected. Attempt nothing further," he cautioned.

"Any sign of trouble, you run, but not in a straight line," James added in a harsh voice. Dev saw the fear he felt in his eyes.

"What do you plan to do?" Cam said, looking worried.

"Flirt." Eden looked scared but determined.

"I've changed my mind—" But it was too late, they'd left

Dev's side and walked out onto the rutted lane that led to the outbuildings.

"Watch carefully, Sinclair, and if you see anything, no matter how small, we run," James whispered. "Simply put, that is my life walking down that lane, and without her I am nothing."

Nodding, Dev stayed silent, because he knew he felt something similar for Lilly. His love, his life.

"Dear Christ, are they singing?" Cam hissed.

They were putting on quite a performance, laughing and swinging their skirts. Linking arms, they skipped along, apparently without a care in the world, singing at the tops of their voices.

"I feel as though my lunch is going to make a reappearance," James whispered. "It should be us out there, not them."

"And yet we would have been shot and be no help to my sisters or whoever else is in those sheds."

Dev remained silent, letting James and Cam talk. They were close now, and looking at the guards he could see their attention was firmly caught. Lilly rolled her hips in an enticing way, and he watched one of the guards lick his lips and run his eyes over her body.

"I'm killing him first," Dev snarled.

"What? Tell me what you see?"

"It's best you don't know," Dev replied. As if he hadn't been angry enough, he felt his spleen begin to boil at the lecherous looks the men were giving his fiancée and sisters.

"Those bastards are comparing the size of our breasts!" Eden hissed, forcing a smile on her face. "So we are going to flirt and then take them around the back so they believe we are going to lift our skirts—"

"Eden!" Essie gasped.

"I'm practicing being bawdy."

Lilly's snort held little humor.

"Remember, try to speak a little coarser," Essie whispered.

"Don't come any closer, ladies!"

Lilly sauntered forward, ignoring the gun waving in her face. "We heard in the village that there was some gents here need a bit of fun." Pushing the barrel of the shotgun aside, she ran one hand up the man's chest and fought a shudder of revulsion as he leered down at her. "Me and my friends is bored," she added, running one finger down the barrel of his gun, now lowered to his side.

"How much?" one of the other men said, crooking his finger at Essie, who moved slowly forward. Lilly blinked at the sultry look on her face.

"How much you got?" Eden said, moving to the last man.

"Enough for you lovelies," the man boasted, wrapping an arm around her waist and hauling her close.

"Got anywhere a bit quieter?" Lilly said, placing her arms around the man's neck. Lord, he smelled foul. She could almost feel the heat of Devon's eyes as they watched her.

"We can't leave here; the boss might see."

"The boss is busy and will be for hours. Come on."

Essie pressed closer to her man as he appeared to waver. Lilly watched his eyes glaze with lust, and then he tossed aside his gun and followed the man who led Eden.

"Got anything to drink?" Lilly asked as they walked away to a smaller shed.

"I got everything a lady could need," he said, then laughed, showing yellow teeth. She prayed Dev arrived soon, because she felt ill at the prospect of this man touching her.

They walked into the building and he let her go to light several candles. It was a small, cramped space and obviously used as sleeping quarters, judging by the belongings spread everywhere. Wrinkling her nose as the foul odor reached her, she looked at Eden and Essie. Both had smiles on their faces; their eyes, however, were like their brothers': cold with rage.

"We'll have an all in," one of the men said, eyeing Eden's breasts. "I like the look of your one's titties."

"Charming," Eden muttered as her man all but fell into her cleavage.

"Perhaps you gentlemen should make yourselves comfortable while we put on a little show for you," Lilly said, pushing her man in the chest and sending him sprawling backward. She toyed with her bodice as he tried to rise.

"Get down here, boys!" he said, licking his lips as she ran one finger down her chest.

Lifting her skirts slowly, Lilly slipped her hands beneath and pretended to fiddle with her stockings, and then pulled the pistol free.

"Hands in the air, please, gentlemen," Lilly said. "And I use the term loosely, I assure you."

"Don't speak if you want to live," Essie said, drawing her knife and waving it before the now wide-eyed men.

"Lie on your stomachs and put your hands on your lower back!" Eden demanded. Once this was done, she and Essie began to bind their hands with the neckties and scarves. Lilly stood over them, pistol at the ready.

"And here comes the cavalry," she muttered as the door burst open.

CHAPTER 28

"Thank God!" Dev found Lilly and his sisters standing over the men. He took the pistol from her as he reached her side. "Did they harm you?"

"No."

Kneeling beside one of the men, Dev pushed the gun into his side. "Are there more men inside that building you were guarding?"

"No, just Finnegan, the man who is training them."

"If you've lied to me I'll come back and put a hole in you."

"I'm not lying!" the man squealed.

"Let's go," Cam said from the doorway. "We need to find the twins."

They shut and locked the building and then ran back to the front. Lifting the heavy wooden bar, they pulled the door open and slipped inside.

Dev raised a hand as he heard voices.

"My brothers are going to make you very sorry you ever took us."

"I'm already sorry," a male voice muttered.

A partition half obscured what was going on in the rest of the building, yet Dev had heard Somer's voice clearly and knew she was close.

"Yes, and our sister Essex knows how to make you sick with herbs, and Eden, our other sister, will probably shoot you with her gun."

This time Dorrie was speaking and he couldn't help but smile. They were, it seemed, in one piece and tormenting someone.

"Be quiet and get down here so I can put you to work!"

"We already know how to pick a lock!"

"I ain't teaching you 'ow to pick locks. I'm teaching you to go into houses and steal fine things."

Rounding the partition, Dev saw the twins sitting on a tall cabinet, swinging their legs while a man stood below them wringing his hands.

"Look."

Following Lilly's finger, Dev noted a group of children standing at the rear of the room bending over a table. They were shackled together by metal cuffs and long chains. They had found the missing children, it seemed, but before he dealt with them, he would deal with the man before him.

"My brothers are big and mean with no front teeth and hands as big as a cow pat."

"Dev!"

Holding up his hands as the twins saw him, he stalled them as they stood up and prepared to launch themselves off the cabinet. He waited for the man to turn, and then planted his fist in his face. "Now you can jump," he said, holding out his arms.

He heard Lilly's sweet laughter as they flew through the air at him, their faces alight with excitement.

"We've had an adventure!"

"Weren't you afraid?" Dev's words were muffled as he kissed and cuddled them.

"At first, and then we knew you'd come for us so we turned it into an adventure!"

Cam took Dorrie and tossed her into the air, then gave her a hug. Dev watched his eyes close briefly as the little girl wrapped her arms around his neck, and knew that like he, the tension inside him had finally eased.

He turned to find Lilly, but she had left his side to go to the other children. He followed after he had found the key to their chains on the man, who was just coming out of the stupor Dev had put him.

"'Ello, Lilly."

He watched the children smile at her, and she back at them.

"I'm very pleased to see you, Timmy," she said, patting the head of a little boy. "Is everyone well?"

"Fink so. Finnegan ain't a bad man, just got caught up with him."

"Who's him?"

Lilly kept the children talking while Dev released the chains around their ankles.

"Dominus. Heard tell he's nasty piece, so I heard Finnegan say, but we ain't never seen him."

"Go and question the man now, Devon. We need to learn all we can about who is behind this business. If it is Danderfield, then he must be stopped."

He ran a finger down her cheek and then went to do as she asked.

"What's your name?" Cam was pulling the man to his feet when he arrived.

"Finnegan."

His chin was starting to swell from the knock Dev had given him.

"You took something that was very dear to us, Mr. Finnegan. To realize that your little sisters were kidnapped by God knows who and taken to God knows where was a torture that I assure you I have no wish to ever repeat!"

Dev felt the bite of anger return as he said the words out loud.

"I-I… They were not meant to belong to anyone."

"Pardon?" Dev lifted one eyebrow at the stuttered words.

"He said—"

"Yes, Dorrie, I heard thank you, love. Perhaps you and Somer could now go and help the others to release the children." Dev gave Essie a look, and she quickly took her little sisters in hand.

"Let me get this straight, Mr. Finnegan," Dev said, his eyes once again steady on the man quivering on the seat before him. He knew Cam's expression was equally as fierce as his, because Finnegan's eyes were darting between them. "You were taking only children with no family ties for your endeavors. Whatever those endeavors are."

"Y-yes." He nodded rapidly, looking like he was bobbing for apples.

"Then why were our sisters taken!" Cam snapped.

"Th-the men who took them found them alone, and as we needed only two more, he took your sisters."

"For what purpose?" Dev questioned.

Finnegan looked from him to Cam, then dropped his eyes to his hands, which were twisted together so tight that his knuckles were white.

"Dominus wants to start a thieving gang and take out any opposition, so that he runs all the children on the streets of London. But these children were for more specialized work. Breaking into the houses of the gentry and stealing things."

"Dominus?"

"That's the name he calls himself."

"Master," Dev said softly. "Dominus means master."

"Danderfield would be just the sort of man to do something like this to my mind."

"He's a nobleman, this man who calls himself Dominus. But I don't know his real name, only followed the instructions he gave me."

Dev did not even want to contemplate Lilly in the hands of a man capable of what Danderfield had done.

"I will leave at once and ride for London. Once there, I will organize transportation for the children," James said, coming to stand beside Dev. "And I have heard what this rodent has to say, and I think we need to work out a plan on how we are going to get that bastard Danderfield, because surely it is he we want."

"Agreed," Dev said.

James kissed Eden, and then left, while Dev and Cam returned to questioning Finnegan.

"Dominus never comes here; the house is locked up tight with only a few servants going in to clean it once a week," Finnegan said, eager to help now he had been caught.

"Tie him to the chair, Cam, while we search the area and make sure those other men are secured."

"With pleasure, brother."

Once a search had been completed and no paperwork or evidence found, everyone made their way back down the lane to the Danderfield house, where one of the children broke in with disturbing ease.

"You will not lift anything," Dev heard Lilly say to the boy as he trailed behind them through the house.

"It's just a little thing," he said, taking a small silver box from his pocket and handing it to her. "He did kidnap me after all, Lilly."

"No, Joe, I will not have you thieving in my presence."

In a drawer in Lord Danderfield's desk, they found what they were looking for.

"There's three of them involved, but Danderfield is the leader," Cam said, reading a letter. "Lord Richard and Mr. Appleton. There is correspondence here that states everything, right down to Lilly's involvement in stopping that boy being taken the night you found her, Dev."

"And to think my brother wished to wed me to such a man." Lilly shuddered beside Dev. He wrapped an arm around her and hugged her close.

Essie and Eden raided the kitchen and found a few supplies that they could throw together for everyone to eat, and then the carriages started to arrive. Children were divided and seated inside, with Mr. Finnegan put up beside one of James's burliest drivers.

Dev mounted the horse they had ridden on and lifted Lilly onto his lap once more. "I want to hold you" was all he said as he and the others fell in beside the slow-moving carriages. She yawned and settled back into his arms with a tired smile upon her face.

"I can think of nowhere else I would rather be."

"Danderfield is about to flee, my lord."

"Are you certain, Mr. Brown?" Dev said, looking at the Bow Street Runner five days later as he entered James's office.

"Yes. My man has been watching his place for any sign of him. This morning, just before the sun rose, he slipped inside. My man then slipped a few coins to a footman who left the house a short time later, and he said Danderfield is fleeing for France tonight."

Dev walked around James's study as he thought about what Mr. Brown had said.

"He has heard about the arrests of Lord Richard and Mr. Appleton," Dev said, "and is making haste to flee before we grab him."

James nodded from behind his desk. "We shall have to move quickly."

They had gathered as much information as they could about Lord Danderfield and what he had been doing. Lord Richard and Mr. Appleton had been more than willing to throw their partner in crime to the wolves when questioned; now all they needed to do was arrest the man so once again everyone would be safe, Dev thought.

"We shall go to the magistrate at once and tell him what we have, and then he can come with us to Danderfield's," James said.

"We want to come also."

Dev turned to find Eden, Essie, and Lilly had slipped into the room.

"I suppose you told them word for word what we were discussing?"

Eden merely smiled sweetly back at Dev.

"She has more right than any to be there when you arrest Danderfield, Dev."

"However, we insist you three stay in the carriage when the arrest is being made, as I do not want to risk one of you getting in the way."

"Thank you, James," Lilly said solemnly.

"Thank you, James," Dev mimicked, scowling at his fiancée, who in turn poked out her tongue.

"Shrew!"

"And Essie and I will keep her company," Eden said. "You will need another set of ears," she added.

James wasn't happy about that, yet could do little about it as he had said Lilly could go. "Fine, however, you will do exactly as I say."

"Of course," both Essie and Eden, said convincing no one.

Lilly and Devon's sisters watched from the safety of the carriage as Cam, Dev, and James, followed by the magistrate and Mr. Brown, went to Lord Danderfield's front door. It was early evening and the sun was sinking fast. They had thought this the best time as the streets would not be too busy.

Holding her breath, Lilly watched the magistrate's hand as it lifted the brass knocker and banged it hard three times. Looking up at the white façade, she noted a second-story window behind which was a faint light. The curtain twitched and then stilled. Lowering the carriage window quietly, she listened.

"Open the door at once. This is the magistrate!"

Still the door remained closed.

"What are they saying, Eden?"

"Two men stay here, the rest will go to the rear and try to get in that way."

Lilly watched as they moved. Dev shot her a warning glance that she guessed meant they were to stay in the carriage, and then he was gone.

"It is intolerable sitting in the carriage not knowing what is going on."

"Ssssh, I can hear everything," Eden said, listening at the window. "They are trying to break down the back door. Cam is howling in pain because he hurt his leg." Eden snorted. "They are in!"

Lilly gripped Eden's and Essie's hands but remained silent, her eyes intent on the front door. Suddenly it opened and James's face appeared, and then the two men who were waiting there entered the house.

"They are moving from room to room, trying to find Danderfield." Eden's eyes were alert as she listened.

"Someone is inside. I thought I saw a curtain twitch upstairs."

"Dev will know where he is, Lilly. He will have seen his colors. Yes, he is directing them upstairs as we speak."

A desperate tension began to build inside Lilly; something bad was about to happen, she could feel it.

"I heard gunfire. Dear Lord, someone has been shot!"

"Devon!" Lilly screamed. Flinging open the carriage door, she leaped from it and ran for the house. She raced through the front door and up the stairs.

"Devon!" Screaming his name, Lilly ran down the hallway, giving each room a fleeting glance until she found all the men huddled in a small parlor. Looking to the floor, she found Danderfield lying in a pool of blood, his eyes staring unseeing at the ceiling.

"Lilly!"

Cam called to her from the right. He was crouched beside Dev, both hands on his brother's chest as he tried to stop the blood flowing from a bullet he had obviously taken.

"Dear God, no," Cam cried, lowering his head over his brother.

"Dev!" Eden was next to scream as she and Essie dropped down beside their brother. "Tell me he's all right, Cam!"

Lilly stumbled forward, falling to her knees beside the man she loved.

No, no, no. This can't be happening, not to him, not Devon.

"Everyone out," Lilly heard James roar, and then the door slammed shut.

"He's not breathing." Cam's words were desperate. "Danderfield caught us by surprise, he said he was surrendering, and then—"

"No!" Lilly cried. "He's not leaving me, he promised."

Biting the end of her finger, she wrenched off her gloves. "I won't let him leave me."

"Lilly." James moved to her side as he reached out to haul his wife close. "He has stopped breathing, Lilly. There is nothing we can do."

"No, I don't believe that." Lilly tore open his shirt, sending buttons in every direction. She felt a fierce surge of strength pulse through her. "He wouldn't leave me, he promised."

She could hear the siblings crying, sobbing for their brother, but Lilly shut them out. Her focus was the man lying still before her. He would not leave her, she vowed silently.

"I need you all to touch me. I want your hands on my hands."

"Lilly, please, he is gone."

"No, he is not!" she roared. "James, I need you to kneel behind me, and do not let me stop until he is healed. I mean it, you must promise me this."

She felt her cousin move behind her, wrapping his arms around her waist, bracing her between his knees.

"Cam, Eden, and Essie, I need your strength. I need you to focus on your brother. He needs you now." From somewhere she found calm, the pain inside her pushed aside to focus on what she must do.

"Come before me and place your hands over mine."

They did as she asked, and she fought not to let the desperate sorrow in their eyes weaken her. Placing her hands over the wound, she focused.

"You will not leave me," she vowed. "Hold me tight, James."

"I promise," he said softly.

"Concentrate now," she whispered, closing her eyes and willing the panic to recede. "Focus on our hands." Slowly, her fingers began to tingle as heat sparked up her arms. Beneath her fingers, Dev began to twitch.

"Dear God, Lilly, something is happening. I felt his body move," Cam said.

She couldn't speak just gritted her teeth and kept her hands over the wound. Her body began to shake and the pain struck at her, swift and strong. She felt James use all his strength to hold her there when her body shook and shuddered for release.

"It's hurting her!" he roared.

The pain was almost too much to bear, yet she held still until she felt the bullet beneath her palm.

"He's breathing," Eden sobbed. "Lilly, you saved him."

Turning over her bloodied palm, Lilly held out the bullet. Seconds later she slumped forward onto Devon's chest, unconscious.

Lilly could hear voices as she drifted slowly to the surface. She had no wish to open her eyes, as this blissful state was wonderful.

"Open your bloody eyes, woman!"

"Dev, stop that. She will wake when she is ready."

"She has been sleeping for two days, Essie. It's enough. She should wake up now!"

"She needs the sleep, brother. Her body needs to heal itself. Saving you took everything she had and more."

"Christ." Lilly heard the breath hiss from Devon's mouth. "Just wake up, my love, please."

She felt his fingers on her cheek, so soft she wanted to purr at the feeling. Instead, she forced herself to open her eyes.

"Lilly." His arms slipped beneath her and she was pulled to his chest. "God, you scared me."

"I'm all right." Her voice sounded raspy and unused. "Just so tired." Lilly wrapped her arms around his neck and held on. He kissed her hair, stroked her back and anywhere else he could reach.

"A-are you well, Devon?"

"Completely, thanks to you." He lay her back on the bed then sat beside her hip, and she had her first look at him.

Unshaven, his face was lined with fatigue, green eyes shadowed, but to her he was the most handsome man she had ever seen.

"You are tired." Lilly ran a finger beneath his eyes. "Are you telling me the truth? You are well?"

"I have no scars or marks. My heart is sound, love. Feel it." He pulled his shirt free, then took her hand and slipped it beneath.

Lilly felt the heat from his body tingle through her palm.

"You saved me, Lilly, and for that I will be forever grateful. Yet I will not allow it again. Never again will I see you drained of life as you were when I regained consciousness. You have slept in this room for two days, unmoving in that bed until I thought you would never again wake."

"Had I been run over by a carriage, the pain would have been less," she whispered. "I felt as if someone had drained the blood from my veins and air from my lungs, and then suddenly there was darkness."

"You were so pale. We had to get James to carry you from Danderfield's house, saying you had fainted in distress over my condition. Then we had to fabricate another lie that the bullet had, in fact, hit a flask in my pocket and the blood was merely from a flesh wound."

"I would do it again to save you, Devon, and you cannot ask different of me."

"We do not know what price you pay for this healing, Lilly. What harm this does to your body." He braced his hands on either side of her head. "I have been scared before, but seeing you like that will be etched in my memory for some time."

"I didn't want to live without you. Promise you will never leave me again, Devonshire Sinclair. I have no wish to dwell in the darkness with no light in my soul and no love in my heart, as I did before you entered my life."

"I promise," he whispered. "I love you."

CHAPTER 29

"*A*re you sure about this? Because I can turn the carriage around and we can make a run for it."

"Very amusing, Nicholas," Lilly said from her position beside him.

They were traveling up Raven mountain and would shortly arrive at the church where she was finally to wed Devon.

"There is something off about that family, though."

"Off how?" Lilly looked at her handsome brother.

They had come so far since her abduction, and still had a lot to learn about each other, but she knew now he was a changed man.

Dressed in a charcoal coat and matching waistcoat, he seemed whole and healthy now. The cynical smile had gone, and he was often found with a genuine one in its place.

"I spoke with the magistrate after Dev's shooting. He said he was sure the man was dead, but then he appeared in the doorway, walking, although he was supported by his brother."

"You know what happened, Nicholas." Lilly looked out

the window. She had never been a good liar and had no wish for her brother to see that.

A month had passed since that day when she had healed Devon, and every minute spent in his company, her love for the handsome, infuriating man grew.

"Yes, but there are other things too. Take Eden, for example. She's always hearing things others do not, and Cam seems to sniff the air a lot. Don't tell me you haven't noticed?"

"Actually, I haven't."

"Oh well, perhaps I'm making more of it than need be. I like them, by the way; they just appear a little odd at times."

"They are wonderful, as is James and his family."

"Yes, it's nice to have them all in our lives." He smiled at her. "You look stunning, sister."

"Thank you, brother."

Her dress was cream-embroidered muslin with a small train, and it was simple yet beautiful. Bee had styled her hair in soft ringlets and she wore a small circlet of flowers.

"We are here."

"Oh, I wasn't nervous before, but now I am," Lilly said, pressing a hand to her stomach, where butterflies seemed to have taken up residence.

"I love you, you know. Never forget that, sister."

"Oh, Nicholas." Lilly started to cry. "I love you too."

"For pity's sake, don't weep, woman. Sinclair will thrash me if I upset you today of all days."

Lilly sniffed and then allowed Nicholas to help her down. Eden and Essie awaited her, along with Dorrie, Somer, and Samantha, who were hopping from foot to foot in their pink dresses. Warwick was looking bored.

This was it, she thought, this was the moment he became hers, and she and Nicholas officially became part of their family. She could hardly wait.

. . .

Dev was sick of waiting. He wanted his future wife, and he wanted her now.

"Not long now, Sinclair."

"Why must the bride always be late, Raven?"

James and Cam stood beside him, both appearing calm when he was a seething mass of nerves.

"It's tradition, I believe."

"Made up by the bride to torment the groom," Cam added.

Dev looked to the door again, but this time, it was not empty. His little brother and sisters and Samantha were there.

"I do believe the guests just sighed," James whispered.

"They are sweet to be fair," Cam added.

Dev said nothing as he watched Eden and Essie appear, both looking beautiful in blue. But it was the woman behind them that caught and held his attention. On the arm of her brother was his Lilly.

"Brides always look extraordinarily beautiful, don't you think, James?"

He heard Cam whisper the words but Dev could not draw his eyes from the woman who was soon to be his wife. She was beautiful, but it wasn't just that, it was what lay between them. They shared a bond that he knew could never be broken. She was his life, and he knew he was hers.

"Inhale, Sinclair. It would not do for you to faint here, in front of so many distinguished guests."

Dev did as James suggested, filling his lungs before exhaling slowly as Lilly started the walk to him.

She would be his soon. He would wake with her in his arms and go to sleep the same way. He would see her at the breakfast table, travel with her in his carriage. He could kiss her sweet mouth if he wanted, right there in the middle of the day. Lord, he could not wait.

"Sinclair." Nicholas nodded to Dev when they arrived.

"Braithwaite."

"Hello, Devon," Lilly whispered.

He smiled, and then leaned in to kiss her cheek, much to the enjoyment of the guests.

"Hello, my love."

The service began, the children fidgeted, and their vows were made, and when it was done, Dev drew in another deep, steadying breath and turned to kiss his wife.

"You can't escape me now, Lady Sinclair."

"I'm sure it's not the thing to be this happy." She laughed, the smile lighting her beautiful eyes. "But I don't care."

"Neither," he lowered his head, "do I."

The kiss was interrupted by Warwick, who declared that Lilly must travel with him to the castle. The twins and Samantha decided they had no wish to be left out, so Dev found himself in the carriage with his wife pressed to his side while three little girls and one boy chatted incessantly.

And there was quite honestly no place he would rather be.

THE END

TOUCHED BY DANGER

The Sinclair and Raven series continues...

Betrayed by the man she thought loved her, she will not give her heart again

Healer, Essex Sinclair understands her family's heightened senses are a result of a long-ago pact between the Sinclairs and the powerful Raven family, but has always struggled to feel worthy of bearing the legendary Sinclair name. Unlucky in love, Essie has resolved to live a quiet, solitary life as a healer and leave passion to the young and foolish. When Max Huntington falls into her herb garden, a bullet hole in his side, her only intention is to heal him quickly and send him on his way. Then she touches him, and from that moment on, fate steps in with dangerous consequences for them both.

Someone wants Max dead. It was only the actions of his beautiful healer, that saved him. Miss Sinclair is sweet, deter-mined and makes him yearn for things he'd long left in the past. His deliberate fabrication has her believing him a penniless nobody, his caress has her yielding, but Max must lie, and leave, for Essie's own good. When broken-hearted Essie returns to London, she once again encounters Max, and discovers his true identity. Horrified and angry that yet another man has played her for a fool, she vows to have nothing more to do with him, but destiny won't be denied and soon they are embroiled in a desperate chase to find his would-be killer before he finds them first.

SEDUCED BY A DEVIL

Tasked with protecting the King, the Deville brothers are part of a secret alliance forged centuries ago, but when it comes to affairs of the heart they are yet to be tamed.

Desperate for his help

Gabriel Deville, Earl of Raine, has never met a woman like Dimity Brown. Mysterious, alluring and utterly infuriating, she has no respect for him. In fact, the piano teacher treats him like he is the underling, not her. His beloved sister, however, calls her friend, and when Dimity disappears, he cannot refuse his sibling's urgent plea to find her.

Gabe's first shock is finding Dimity in a seedy tavern, dancing on the bar. The second is seeing the feisty young woman vulnerable and scared. He soon realizes that what he feels for her is a great deal deeper than anger and he will stop at nothing to keep her safe. Earning her trust and uncovering her secrets will be a challenge, but securing a place in her heart will be the biggest challenge of his lifetime.

Powerless to resist

Dimity had believed her life would never be anything more or less than it currently was, but then her father dies, and everything changes. She is thrown out of the only home she has ever known, and finds a letter in her father's things that turns her life completely on its head. Penniless, confused and desperate, she has nowhere to turn until Gabriel Deville steps back into her life.

Lord Raine is arrogant, ridiculously wealthy, and far too dangerously handsome. Despite the sparks that had always flown between them, their interactions had been coldly civil. When he insists she accept his help, Dimity takes it, certain she can resist him, and what is growing between them long enough to unravel the secrets of her past.

Can they overcome their differences and society dictates to forge a life together?

ABOUT THE AUTHOR

Wendy Vella is a Kindle Unlimited all star and USA Today
bestselling author of historical romances that have sold more
than a million copies worldwide.
Known for compelling and uplifting stories laced with witty
humor, sensuality and intrigue, Wendy has hit the bestseller
ranks many times with reader favorites, the Sinclair & Raven
series, the Deville Brothers and Langley Sisters series.
She lives with her husband and spends time with her
children, their partners, and four delightful grandchildren.

Wendy also writes contemporary romances under the name
Lani Blake.

51426701R00191